Viva Jacquelina!

L. A. MEYER

Viva Jacquelina!

Being an Account of the
Further Adventures of Jacky Faber,
Over the Hills and Far Away

HARCOURT
Houghton Mifflin Harcourt

Boston   New York   2012

Harcourt is an imprint of Houghton Mifflin Harcourt Publishing Company.

www.hmhbooks.com

Text set in Minion Pro

Library of Congress Cataloging-in-Publication Data
Meyer, L. A. (Louis A.), 1942–
Viva Jacquelina!: being an account of the further adventures of Jacky Faber, over the hills and far away / written by L. A. Meyer.
p. cm.
ISBN 978-0-547-76350-7
[1. Sex role — Fiction. 2. Adventure and adventurers — Fiction. 3. Spies — Fiction. 4. Seafaring life — Fiction. 5. Europe — History — 1789–1815 — Fiction. 6. Great Britain — History — George III, 1760–1820 — Fiction.] I. Title.
PZ7.M57172Viv 2012
[Fic] — dc23
2011041931

Manufactured in the United States of America
DOC 10 9 8 7 6 5 4 3 2 1
4500372384

As always, for Annetje . . .

. . . and for Medca, too.

Prologue

'Tis Forty Shillings on the Drum
For those who Volunteer to come
To enlist and fight the Foe today,
Over the Hills and Far Away.

Over the hills and over the Main
To Flanders, Portugal, and Spain.
King George commands and we must obey,
Over the Hills and Far Away . . .

Part 1

PART I

Chapter 1

"It is time to cut it off, Higgins," I announce firmly, seating myself in front of my mirror. "If you would be so good. I do not think it would serve me well here in Portugal."

"I believe you are right, Miss," agrees my good Higgins. He takes comb and scissors from his kit and surveys my head appraisingly. The Faber head now sports a long pigtail in back, with a short, peach-colored fuzz over the rest of it. I had stopped having my skull shaved several weeks ago, so the hair that resides thereon is presently about three-quarters of an inch long.

My head, hair, and all the rest of me is now contained in a small cabin on the troop ship HMS *Tortoise,* which lies at a wharf in Lisbon. Its men, supplies, and horses are being offloaded, as are the other ships of our recent convoy that had accompanied us across the Channel and down the coast to the Iberian Peninsula — a total of six thousand men and all of their gear.

So goodbye to London and to all of her lovely charms — and hello to a gritty, dangerous, and dirty life on the path to war. Oh, well, I have been there before and am certainly no stranger to dirt, nor to war, for that matter. Because of what my poor self has been through in the way of abandonment, street fights, naval battles, storms, shipwrecks, maroonings, fires, kidnappings, tar-and-featherings, near-hangings and near-beheadings, imprisonments, enslavement, and other personal disasters, I have long since given up the notion that I am mistress of my own fate. I am but a thistle blown about by the breeze. *Lord, in your wisdom, send me where you wouldst have me go, and to that place I will go. Amen.*

Higgins gently lifts the doomed pigtail and I feel the cool of his scissors against the back of my neck. There is the *snick, snick* of hair being cut and presently the shorn pigtail dangles before my eyes.

"What shall we do with it, Miss?" asks Higgins, making it wiggle as if it were a snake. I know that Higgins has never been particularly fond of my Chinese hairstyle, but he was even less fond of the collection of rather garish wigs that I had acquired over the past few years to cover up several instances of severe and sudden hair loss that I have experienced in my somewhat turbulent life. Consequently, before we left London, he purchased for me a nice sandy-blond wig that closely approximates the color of my own locks and is, I believe, quite presentable.

"Oh, just put it in my seabag, Higgins. It might come in handy sometime," I reply. "Perhaps someday I shall have to fashion a false mustache or beard out of it."

"Considering your past history, Miss, I do not consider that statement to be at all outlandish," he murmurs, laying the braid aside for later storage. "Now, let me even this up."

·

He once again applies the scissors to the back of my neck. *Snip, snip* . . .

"There. That should blend quite nicely with the rest as it grows back," he says, plainly satisfied with the result. "However, it does lay quite bare that mythological beast you wear on your nape."

He is, of course, referring to the fire-breathing golden dragon tattoo that Cheng Shih had emblazoned on the back of my neck when I was on her ship last year, and she had me under her rather fierce . . . *ahem* . . . love and protection. It was she who had my head and hair fashioned into its current state, as it pleased her to see me that way — and woe be to anyone who displeases the pirate queen Cheng Shih, admiral of seven hundred ships and twenty thousand men. Since I cannot see the mark without twisting around in front of several mirrors held just so, I do not think about it much. Not that I dislike it, for it has come in handy at times in the past when I needed to go all exotic. But that was then, and this is now. *So back to being a proper English maiden with you, girl.* Yes, well, sort of proper . . . and, yes, well, sort of a maiden.

"The new hairpiece should sufficiently hide that lovely little piece of Oriental art from prying eyes." Higgins sniffs. "Into the tub with you now."

I rise, let the light robe I have been wearing slide from my shoulders, and I slip into the hot and lovely tub my good Higgins has procured for me. *Ahhhhh* . . . I know it took some doing, but Higgins does have his ways, as I have mine. 'Course we couldn't have this when underway, because of the rolling and pitching and yawing, but here, with the well-named *Tortoise* tied securely to the dock, all the sloshing of the water in the tub is due solely to my writhing about in it in absolutely sinful, sensual pleasure. *Ahhhhhh . . .*

Higgins turns to lay out my clothes, and when out of his sight, I take the opportunity to trim my toenails with my teeth, soap up and wash various Parts, and then lie back to let the steaming water soak out some of the care and worry of the recent past . . .

Ah, Jaimy, where are you now? Oh, I know your dear body is on its way to Rangoon in the care of some very good Oriental friends of mine, but where are you in the way of your mind, your poor tortured soul? Have you cast out your demons and returned to some semblance of sanity? Have Charlie Chen's doctors, with their mysterious potions and herbs, and Sidrah's gentle words and touch brought you back from the edge of complete madness? Oh, how I wish I knew! Heavy sigh . . . *But, I realize I shall not know, nor can I come to join you till this mission is over. "King George calls and we must obey," as the song goes. Right . . . Obey, or else . . .*

"Your lieutenant's jacket, Miss?" asks Higgins.

"Yes, and the matching blue skirt, if you would, John, and my boots," I add. I sink down a bit, such that my lips are below the surface, and blow bubbles in the now soapy water. Soon I've created a fine froth in front of my face. Now, if I were bathing in my lovely little copper-bound tub back on the *Nancy B. Alsop* — my beloved little sixty-five-foot Gloucester schooner — I'd be thinking of tossing one Joannie Nichols into this tub after I'd gotten out of it, but, alas, both she and the *Nancy B.* have been sent back to Boston.

But, Jacky, I don't wanna go back to school!

6

You must, Joannie. It is for your own good that you become educated and refined.

Joannie Nichols was a fellow street urchin back in the days when I ran with the Rooster Charlie Gang in the Cheapside section of London, before I went off to sea. There's still a lot of the street in both of us.

Refined, my Cockney ass! I wanna go with you!

You can't, Joannie. I'm being sent on a tour of duty, and only Mr. Higgins can go with me. And furthermore, I don't see that it's gonna be all that much fun, anyway. So come on, don't you want to see your gallant young Daniel Prescott again — the same lad whose face you covered with kisses before you ran off from the Lawson Peabody to stow away on the Nancy B.?

I suppose. But Mistress is gonna beat the hell out of me for taking off without permission.

Even though Mistress Pimm, headmistress of the Lawson Peabody School for Young Girls, no longer uses the rod that had been so often applied to my own poor backside when I attended that institution, her hairbrush does remain a formidable weapon.

Now, now, you shall suffer a bit, yes, but think of the joy you will have in regaling your sisters with tales of your recent adventures. Hmmm . . . ?

Yeah, I guess . . .

Good. Now give me a last hug and go below and change into your seagoing gear. They are about to throw off the lines. Study hard and be a good girl, and I will come back and we will go a-rovin' again. I promise.

Yes, the *Nancy B. Alsop* did cast off, and with tears in my eyes, I watched her disappear over the horizon, taking with her some of my dearest and most faithful friends.

Goodbye, Tink, give my love and regards to everyone. Davy, my best to our dear Annie and I pray that all goes well with her. Fare thee well, Brother. And John Thomas and Finn McGee, my bold and strong sailor lads, be as good as you can be and stay out of trouble and teach the young ones what you know about the seafarin' life . . .

Then, standing before me, my own sea dad, Liam Delaney, he who had crossed the world to save my poor wayward self. Goodbye, Father, may God go with you. My love to Mairead, and do not be too hard on Ian McConnaughey, for my sake, please. Here, let me wrap my arms about you and lay my head upon your broad chest one last time and . . . Oh, Liam, do be careful!

I pushed a bundle of letters into his hands, planted a kiss upon his cheek, and turned to . . .

Ravi. Goodbye, my beautiful little brown-eyed boy.

I had crouched down and put my hands on his shoulders.

When you get to Boston, Davy will take you to Mr. Pickering, and he will see that you will be set up in a good school and given warm lodging. Here is a letter for you to give to my good friend Ezra.

He took the letter and put it inside his jacket. We had bought for him several suits of European-style clothes, which should serve him well in his new home. Ravi was wearing one of those suits with a certain amount of pride, but those big brown eyes still welled up with tears.

This poor boy does not want to go away from Missy Memsahib.

I know, Ravi, I know, and I don't want you to go away. But where I'm going, you can't follow. Do you understand?

Great blinking of eyes . . . both his . . . and mine. Then he nodded and put his thin arms about my neck.

Goodbye, Mommy.

Steam lingers about my stateroom as Higgins begins to deck me out in my finest — first, the drawers with flounces about the knees and calves, then chemise and white shirt with lace at the throat and cuffs. I had wrung every bit of sensual enjoyment out of that tub, knowing full well it might prove to be the last real soaking the Faber frame shall have for a good long while, in that we are debarking today to join up with the British army somewhere in the interior of this war-torn country, and bathtubs are a rare commodity when on bivouac. I have been assigned by British Intelligence to the staff of General Arthur Welles-ley, Commander of British Forces on the Iberian Penin-sula, as translator of Spanish, French, and Portuguese. This was part of the deal that kept the tender necks of both Jaimy Fletcher and myself from being wrapped in their assigned nooses — me for General Larceny and High Crimes Against the Crown and Jaimy for roaring crazily around Blackheath robbing travelers on the broad highway south of London as the dread Black Highwayman. It is true that he was a bit off his nut when he did all that, but still, it took a bit of doing for me to gain him a pardon, which I did by convincing a rich Chinese merchant to bring valuable and mostly looted antiquities to donate to the British Museum, and then — oh, it's all too much to think about. I'll just let my biographer and very dear friend, Amy Trevelyne, sort it all out when she goes to put it down on paper, just as she has already done with my other adventures. For now, suffice to say that Jaimy is being taken on Chopstick Charlie's ship to Rangoon to recover his senses.

Do not worry, Ju kau-jing yi. We will take care of him. We have potions . . . herbs . . . soothing medicines . . . He shall be fine when next you see him.

But, Charlie—

But nothing, my Little Round-Eyed Barbarian, just stop crying and go. We must leave now . . . The authorities are a bit agitated, you know . . .

. . . and I am being sent to the war zone to do my duty to Crown and Country. *Hmmm* . . . Perhaps Jaimy is getting the better deal. I well remember the charms of Charlie Chen's palace in Burma—that turquoise pool, Mai Ling and Mai Ji . . . and Sidrah . . . Oh, well, enjoy, Jaimy, but maybe not too much . . .

I shake my head and I'm back in my stateroom on the *Tortoise* and Higgins is finishing up. He places the rump roll on the small of my back and attaches it with clips, and the blue skirt goes over that, cinched at my waist, and flowing down in pleats to the tops of my boot-clad feet. That roll thing has replaced the rather cumbersome bustle in female fashion and I rather like it—it adds a bit of jauntiness to my tail without getting in the way. And hey, if the lads find it pleasing to gaze upon a well-rounded female rump, well, then, I could use a little help in that regard, since I am still rather skinny, in spite of all the food I have put down my neck over the past few years.

"I wonder if the General has commandeered a house for his headquarters. Or is he working out of a tent?" I ask as Higgins adjusts my gear. Trust Jacky Faber to wonder what her future accommodations will be. She much prefers a cozy room to a drafty and often-damp tent. Oh, well, it is my nature to take what comes in the way of shelter, be it made of sturdy stone and plaster or sodden canvas.

"You shall not have to wonder for long, Miss. I have been informed that General Wellesley had a great victory at Rolica last week but does not want to push his luck, so he has sent his main force here to guard this landing. Six thousand men, after all, would be quite a loss, should the troops be surprised and taken. We should soon have good information as to our immediate future."

There is a knock on the door.

"Yes?"

"An army officer is asking for you, Miss. On the outer deck."

"Thank you, Johnny. I'll be right out."

Higgins holds up my lieutenant's jacket — all deep blue, with high collar and gold trim — and I thrust my arms through it and button up the front. There. All tight and trim, just the way I like it.

The blond wig goes on and is adjusted.

"Your hat, Miss?"

"I think my midshipman's cap will serve. I look ridiculous in that lieutenant's hat."

"It does tend to overwhelm your rather small features, Miss," agrees Higgins. "Your medals?"

"Just the Trafalgar. I don't want to alarm the poor general."

"Very well, Miss," he says, taking the medal out of its box and looping the ribbon about my neck such that the silver medallion with the image of Lord Nelson struck on its gleaming surface rests upon my chest.

"Thank you, Higgins. Shall we go up?"

"You go, Miss," says Higgins, opening the door for me. "I have some final packing to do."

Cap on head, I go out into the corridor to find Midshipman Harrington standing at attention.

I place my hand upon his arm and say, "Lead me on, Johnny, my fine young sailor lad, lead me on."

When we gain the deck and step out into the sunshine, I am very gratified to see Cavalry Captain Lord Richard Allen waiting for me, looking absolutely splendid in his scarlet regimentals — blazing red jacket with white turnouts and gold buttons, white trousers, black boots with spurs, and gold-braided shako on head. *Ah, yes, every inch my bold dragoon!*

"Good day, my lord," I say, with a small curtsy. "It is so good to see you. I hope you passed a pleasant night?"

"Pleasant enough, Miss Faber," says Richard Allen, looking pointedly at my hand, which still rests on the arm of my young escort. "Considering you were not by my side."

I feel the midshipman's arm tighten at that.

Richard gives Johnny a look that plainly says, *She's way out of your league, puppy, so forget any hot thoughts you might have in that regard. Back to your lonely hammock, boy, and suffer!*

"Carry on with your duties, Midshipman," growls Lord Allen to the poor middie. "I have custody of the lady."

I give Midshipman Jonathan Harrington a smile, a wink, and a final squeeze of his arm as he flushes, salutes, casts a look upon me, does an about-face, and strides off, full, I am sure, of young male resentment.

"Could it be that you have made another conquest, Princess? Another Pale and Loitering Knight in Thrall to La Belle Jeune Fille Sans Merci?" asks Allen, watching the lad retreat, with some contempt writ on his face. "Seems to me there would be scant sport in bringing one such as him to heel."

I laugh. "Oh, come on, Richard, he and I are of the same age and he is a nice young man. He was good company to me while you were off supervising the daily disposal of several tons of horse manure, or whatever other manly things of great importance that you do when you are not trying to toss my fallible self into a handy bed."

Allen gives a lordly snort. "The beasts do produce a lot of that rather smelly commodity, and they are difficult to care for at sea, poor devils, being afraid of the constant movement," he says with a smile. "But enough of horsy lore." He bows slightly, taking my hand and kissing the back of it. "May I say, you look lovely, my dear little woodland sprite?"

"Thank you, sir. And may I say in return that you look absolutely smashing?"

"You may," replies the rogue, running his tongue over his lips. "But, I must say, the dear little hand tastes of soap . . . and as for that bed—"

"I have just come from my bath." I sniff, all prim and proper, and withdraw that same hand. "And never mind about my bed."

"Hmm . . . An interesting image comes to mind — young Princess Pretty-Bottom, late of the Shawnee Tribe, the *Belle of the Golden West*, various backwaters of the Mississippi

River, the *Lorelei Lee,* and other similar environs, lolling about in luxurious suds. Ummm, yes. However, I must banish it from my mind, lest I go mad with lust."

I give him a poke. "Be good, you."

"Mind you, soap is fine, in its place, but I much prefer your natural flavor — or flavors — Princess."

Time to change the subject.

"Never mind me and my meager charms, milord," I say. "Tell me about our situation here."

Lord Allen turns and guides me to the rail of the ship, such that we might observe the goings-on at the dock.

"Our gallant forces, under General Wellesley, have just won a great victory at Rolica. Of course, we outnumbered the Frogs four to one, but no matter. It is still the first British victory over Napoleon and we will take it, however one-sided things were. The French, under the command of General Delaborde, were retreating in disorder and our army could have overwhelmed and slaughtered them, but Wellesley, hearing that this force of six thousand was arriving at Lisbon, instead sent the army here to cover our debarkation."

"So he is a careful man?"

"Yes, though Old Nosey is a bold fighter, he is never one to take foolish chances, and the loss of the six thousand of us would be quite a blow to his cause."

"Old Nosey?"

"Yes. He has a rather prominent nose. I would advise you not to stare at it when you first meet the great man."

"Um, I shall take that to heart," I say, nodding. "What sort of leader is he?"

Allen considers, then says, "His men respect and admire him and are glad to have him as their general, for their safety depends on his sound judgment, but they do not love him."

"And why not?"

"He has a rather harsh personality. It is said that he does not suffer fools gladly."

"Hmm. I wonder if he suffers jumped-up young female twits gladly," I say with some trepidation. "Where is he headquartered?"

"He has taken over a building in a place called Vimeiro, where I believe there is to be a battle. We are to catch up with him there."

"I hope you will be able to go with me, Richard?"

"Yes, I have been assigned to convey you to the great man and watch over your precious tail till we arrive. And, yes, I shall be allowed to introduce you to him, as it were. Lordship does have its privileges."

"And after that, my good and most protective lord?" I purr, lifting his arm to place it around my shoulders and snuggling a bit into his side.

"After that, Cavalry Captain Allen, and the unruly pack of scoundrels he calls his men, will report to the Twentieth Light Dragoons, Seventh Brigade, to assist in bringing Napoleon's minions to bay."

Looking out, I see Bailey, Captain Allen's trusted top sergeant, trying to bring some order to the chaos on the dock below. He has his hand wrapped around the reins of a particularly recalcitrant beast.

"Ahoy, Sergeant!" I call out, giving him a merry wave. "And there's Private MacDuff, too! Hello, Archie!"

The two soldiers look up and knuckle their brows by

way of salute. A bit ruefully, I suspect—my having peppered the whole of Richard's troop of dragoons with rock salt shot from my cannons on the *Belle of the Golden West,* back there on the Mississippi, but I believe they have largely forgiven me for that.

"I will hate to see you go, Richard," I say, giving him the big eyes. "And I want you to be very careful. I have a feeling things are going to get very messy around here."

"Thank you for your concern, Princess, but we must go where Fortune sends us, must we not, as it is the poor soldier's lot. Ah, there's your coach. Are you ready to go?"

"As soon as Higgins comes up with our stuff. Ah. Here he is now."

"Then let us be off, Princess," says Lord Allen, offering his arm to lead me down the gangway. "And into the Peninsular War."

Chapter 2

How many of my poor teeth are still left firmly in my jaw after that bone-shaking journey from Lisbon to here, I do not know. Suffice to say, the Portuguese have a lot to learn in the way of road building. God, I so much wanted to be outside that cramped coach and on a good horse, riding and singing next to Richard Allen — or maybe just riding up behind him, double like, with my arms wrapped around his middle. But such was not to be, oh, no. Frail female had to be delivered in sturdy coach, military regulations and all, don'cha know; never mind her poor aching backbone.

We rattle through miles and miles of dry, rocky, and scrubby land before we finally pull up before the big white stone building General Arthur Wellesley has taken for his headquarters here in Vimeiro, and we emerge from that wretched coach to stand in the sunlight and stretch. I put the knuckles of my right fist into the small of my back and grind it till things feel a little bit better back there. Give me a rolling, pitching, yawing ship thrashing about in gale-force winds and heavy seas any day of the week, I say.

Anyway, we are here. Two red-coated soldiers stand guard outside the entrance of the building, together with a junior officer. They do not look at all welcoming.

"I shall stand by, Miss, until given instructions as to where we will be quartered," says Higgins, seeing to the removal of our baggage from the coach.

"Very good, John. We shall soon find that out. Captain Allen?"

Allen, having dismounted and given his horse off to Private MacDuff, strides to the door and announces, his hand on the hilt of his sword, "Captain Richard Allen to see General Wellesley."

The officer who stands by the door asks, "For what purpose, Sir?"

"None of your goddamn business, Sir. Announce us," answers Lord Allen, frosting the man down to his boots with his patrician gaze, a gaze honed by centuries of ancestors using the same in putting underlings in their place. "That's *Lord* Richard Allen."

The composure of the very junior officer crumples under that gaze and he retreats into the interior of the building.

Presently, he comes back out and, with a bow, ushers us in.

It is a large room, and at the far end is a long table at which are seated a number of men. In the center of them is a man who, given the deference shown him by the others, must be Sir Arthur Wellesley.

We advance to the table. General Wellesley, not waiting for explanation, asks with a certain amount of irritation in his voice, "And what is this, then?"

Richard Allen steps forward, bows, and says, "General Wellesley, I am Captain Lord Allen, Twentieth Light Dragoons, at your service, Sir. May I present Miss J. M. Faber? She has been sent from Naval Intelligence to aid you in the way of Spanish, French, and Portuguese language translations. Miss Faber, General Sir Arthur Wellesley."

I curtsy, but he does not bow — nor does he rise from his chair.

Wellesley's cold gray eyes travel over the both of us. Then he looks down what does prove to be a very long, thin nose and speaks.

"From Intelligence, eh? Sent to spy upon me, no doubt. How jolly."

Richard was right. This man does not mince words, and he does not seem very jolly when he says that. In fact, I suspect the man is seldom jolly.

"I am very pleased to meet you, Sir," I say, all respectful. "But spying on my fellow countrymen is not my field of endeavor, Sir, nor is it part of my orders." It is, of course, *exactly* why I was sent here. To be a fly on the wall, as it were. "My orders are to come here and to assist you in any way I can, mainly as a translator of the local tongues."

That gets me a short snort through that very long nose.

"I already know how to speak French, girl. There are many with me who can help me with the Spanish and Portuguese." He gestures to the men who sit by him, two on each side. "I do not think I need you hanging about."

"Very good, Sir. I am glad to hear that you are so very well served. If you have no need of my services, then perhaps I might be allowed to return to England?"

Hooray! If I am able to get back, I'll be able to book pas-

19

sage to Rangoon and find out what's up with Jaimy! Oh, please, let me go!

"By all means, go. Get out of my sight."

Fuming at being treated such, but relieved by the turn of events, I go to turn on my heel and head for the exit. *Hooray! Come on, Richard, let's get out of here!*

But I don't turn on my heel, nor do we get to the exit.

The man to the right of the general says, "Wait, Miss. Please, Sir. Take a look at this." And he hands him a paper.

Uh-oh . . .

The Wellesley eyes scan the paper and then he looks up at me.

"Napoleon himself?"

"By that do you mean, 'Have I met him?' Then, yes, Sir, I have."

"Where?"

"At the Battle of Jena. I stood by his side as the fog lifted."

"And just what were you doing there?"

"He and I were having breakfast."

"Don't be cute. I repeat: What were you doing there?"

"While under the orders of British Intelligence, I had gained a commission as a second lieutenant in the Grand Army of the Republic. I was assigned as a messenger to *l'Empereur's* staff."

"Hmmm . . ." Another paper is passed and read. He looks up at me again.

"I see you wear that medal," he says. "Where did you get it? In a pawnshop?"

I ignore his sneer and reply, "I was at Trafalgar, Sir."

"Oh, you were? And what was your rating? Trollop?

Ship's Pump? Gunner's Wife?" There are snickers from the toadies at the great man's table.

"Sir, I must protest!" says Richard Allen, close by my side.

"Be quiet, Captain, else I will have you removed and demoted, Lord or not. Go on, girl. Exactly what were you doing there?"

"During the battle, I was doing my duty as a lieutenant in charge of a gun crew."

"As a lieutenant? Is that why you are dressed in that outrageous fashion? A naval officer's jacket on a girl's back? Come, come. You must know that many here would call that a sacrilege of the first order."

"If it please you, Sir," I say, hitting a brace, "I was made midshipman by Captain Locke of HMS *Dolphin*, having been in several engagements with pirates, and promoted to lieutenant by Captain Scroggs of HMS *Wolverine*, after an encounter with a French gunboat. To my knowledge, Sir, my commission has not been revoked, nor have I resigned it. I was briefly in command of the *Wolverine*, and in that capacity, I took many prizes that greatly enriched the King's treasury. Furthermore, I was present on my own ship at the action between HMS *Dolphin* and the Spanish First-Rate *San Cristobal*, which resulted in the taking of that eighty-eight-gun man-of-war," I say, puffing up into a state of high indignation. "So, I ask you, my good sir, who else is more qualified to wear this jacket?"

"General, I can attest to the truth of what she is saying, as I was there," says Richard, refusing to be silenced.

Wellesley's eyes shift to my gallant light horseman.

"Lord Allen, I perceive that you wear a cavalry uniform

on your person and it bears the insignia of a captain in that service. Am I right in that perception?"

"Yes, General, you are," replies Richard, through clenched jaws.

"Then you must have a unit to which you are obliged to report?"

"Yes, Sir. The Seventh Brigade, Twentieth Light Dragoons."

"Good. Then go report there. You may leave her here. Good day to you, Sir."

I feel Richard bristle at the brusque manners, the implied insult, but I put my hand on his arm to restrain him from any rash action on either my behalf or his.

"Go, Richard. I will be all right. Thank you for your kind protection" is what I say with my voice, but my eyes fix on his and they plead, *Oh, Richard, please be careful! Do not worry about me. No silly heroics now, please.*

Lord Allen gives a *very* short bow to General Wellesley, and a very deep bow to me. He then turns and leaves me to once again stand alone in front of a table with disapproving males seated behind it, shuffling papers and glowering at my poor self. My back is straight, my arms held stiffly down at my sides, my eyes cased, and my knees locked. I wait for what is to come, with not a great amount of hope.

The questions come quick and fast.

"Not much to you, is there?"

"I believe there is enough of me to get by."

"You look to be about twelve."

"I was starved as a child. I was a beggar on the streets of London. Perhaps it stunted my growth."

"How old are you?"

"Seventeen."

"You don't look it."

"I am sorry that I do not meet your expectations."

"You do not seem very sorry."

"I am not, Sir. I am what I am."

Another sheaf of papers is passed to General Wellesley. I get to cool my heels as he reads all about me.

Presently he looks up and says, "Remarkable . . . Even more remarkable is that you have not yet swung from a gallows."

I risk a shrug. "The Crown and I have not always seen eye to eye on some things."

"Indeed," he says, musing as he reads further. "And why have you not yet been hanged?"

"Perhaps it is my winning personality."

"It is certainly not your beauty."

"Thank you, Sir. I shall treasure that compliment for the rest of my life, however short that life may be. But, should I displease you in the way of appearance or otherwise, I do beg to be excused, as I do not wish to give offense."

"Not yet." He peruses another sheet of paper. "You say you were assigned as a messenger to Napoleon's staff. It seems preposterous."

"I was a messenger in the Grand Army. I volunteered as an American and gained the rank of *sous* Lieutenant. As such, I delivered many messages for *l'Empereur*. Both to . . . and from him."

"Hmmm. It says here that you delivered one particular message that could have turned the tide of that particular battle — a message from Bonaparte to Murat ordering him to charge the Prussian line in order to save Marshal Ney's foolhardy ass. This is beyond belief. A mere girl . . . Why should we believe all this twaddle?"

"Believe what you will, Sir," I say, reaching inside my jacket and pulling out a scrap of paper. I fling it on the desk. "But have any of you ever seen one of *these?*"

There is a gasp as they see what the paper has on it — a seal in bright blue wax showing the large "N" surrounded by acanthus leaves impressed thereon. Below it is written the word "Charge."

"Yes, gentlemen," I say. "It is, indeed, Napoleon's imperial seal. He gave it to me as surety when he sent me off to deliver that message to Murat — the message that I did, indeed, deliver."

Wellesley fumes, his hands crumpling the papers.

"Could you possibly know" — he pauses — "how much easier this war would be to win if Napoleon had fewer battalions? Which he might have been bereft of had you *not* delivered that accursed message?"

"I am not a military tactician. I am only a poor girl who seeks to do her duty for her country."

There are snorts of derision all around.

"Why do I not simply pull out a pistol, right now, and shoot you down as a traitor?" He brings those flinty gray eyes to bear upon mine. "I believe none would blame me."

"Many, I am sure, would applaud and sing your praises." At that, I reach up and unbutton the top of my jacket, exposing the frilly white shirt beneath. "Here is my chest, Sir. Underneath it lies my heart. I am sure you have a pistol close at hand. I trust that, as a soldier, your aim will be true and I will not suffer much. I also hope I will not mess up your bloody floor too very much with my unworthy blood."

Several of the subalterns are trying to stifle laughter. Wellesley reddens and casts warning looks all around.

"Why do you still have the seal in your possession?" he demands.

"Marshal Murat handed it back to me, there on the Plain of Jena, saying he had plenty of them and I should keep it to show my grandchildren," I say. "And I shall, should I live long enough to have any such issue."

General Wellesley ponders this, and then says, "Very well. Quarters will be found for you. Go there and refresh yourself and report back here at two o'clock. You will then tell me every single little thing you know of Napoleon Bonaparte — what he said to you, the orders he gave at Jena, how he was dressed, everything, down to the buckles on his shoes . . . Do you understand?"

I nod, give a medium Lawson Peabody curtsy, spin on my heel, and exit the room.

Another battle fought . . . and, I believe, won.

Chapter 3

Yes, Higgins, it was quite intense," I say. "General Sir Arthur Wellesley is definitely a tough piece of work. I am due back in his office at two o'clock to report on my dealings with Napoleon. Will you accompany me?"

"Of course, Miss. Will you change?"

"Yes. I'll wear my Hussar's uniform — *with* the trousers. And the Legion of Honor, too."

"Might that not be a bit extreme?" he asks, with raised eyebrow.

"Don't care. I didn't like the way I was treated this morning. If the great General doesn't like it, he can shove it up his nose — his very large, extremely long, and very thin nose, I might add. Should fit."

"Very well, Miss," says Higgins. He opens my bag and takes out the dark blue uniform and drapes it over a chair.

"And have you gotten a horse for me? From what I hear, I might be needing one soon."

The word is that there is a battle shaping up, a big one, and if I'm to be a part of it, I know I'll feel better on the back of a good horse.

"Yes, Miss, a quite nice little gray mare. She is tethered in the stable around the corner. But here, stand up, and we shall get you changed."

Higgins is billeted next door, which I find rather comforting. In general, even though these quarters are somewhat Spartan, on the whole, they're not too bad. After all, we could be quartered in a tent, and then I would be sleeping on the ground. From what I have seen of it, the ground of Portugal looks to be no softer than that of Germany, when last I had the pleasure of slumbering on that unyielding earth . . . harder, even. The layout of this building gives me the feeling that it must have been a hotel of some sort before General Wellesley requisitioned it as his own.

"Changed? You say that like I am still in nappies, Higgins," I say, bouncing to my feet and stripping off my outer clothing. I retain my short underdrawers and chemise. "I am wounded."

"I am sorry, Miss. Please don't take offense, but you do require quite a bit of . . . maintenance."

"Aw, 'Iggins, luv," I tease. "Ye know it's coz I weren't raised up proper."

"Ummm . . . Here, first the trousers. Step in, please." He holds out the pants.

I rest my hands on his shoulders to steady myself and step in. He pulls up the pants, tucks in the undershirt, and fastens the belt. The trousers match the jacket, both in color and fabric, with the addition of a strip of polished leather that runs up the inner side of each thigh, joining at the crotch. It is there to prevent chafing when one is in the saddle for a long time. My leather strips are quite well polished, owing to the time I wore them riding with the French army in Germany last year.

Higgins then adjusts the garment guards, the leather devices that rest under each of my armpits, put there because, while undergarments can be washed with strong soap and made fresh smelling and new again, fine broadcloth jackets cannot. When in a tight spot, I sweat like any other little piggy, and I expect to be in just that kind of spot this afternoon. Knowing that, Higgins has dosed the shields with an extra bit of wheat powder, so I should be set for a while in the way of armpit dryness. This is good, for I would not like to mess up the fine jacket that Higgins now holds up for me.

It is dark blue, a gray-blue rather than a navy hue, with much gold braid frogging across the front, and three rows of vertical buttons. I climb in and Higgins fastens all the frogs and buttons. It has a high collar, so we don't go with the spilling-out lace with this one. It feels good as it tightens around me.

The boots are back on, my pants are tucked inside, my sword harness is strapped about my hips, and *Esprit* hangs, once again, by my side.

Higgins has taken out my Legion of Honor medal, and I turn to receive it on the left side of my chest—just where *l'Empereur* wears his.

"There," he says, giving my shoulders a bit of a dust-off. "I believe you are presentable."

"Thank you, Higgins. Have we anything to eat?" asks the ever-hungry me.

"Alas, no, Miss. But I did manage to bring along several bottles of quite good Madeira. Shall I crack one?"

"Please do, Higgins. Dealing with General Wellesley is sure to be hot work, and I'm certainly not looking forward to this afternoon's session."

Higgins brings forth a bottle, places two glasses on the small table in the room, expertly draws the cork, and pours out two glasses of the ruby liquid. Ah, yes, that Higgins, he's always prepared.

He hands me a glass and takes one himself. I hold mine up to him. *"A sua saude, Joao,"* I say, and take a good long pull on the very fine, very sweet wine. *Mmmmm.* Ah, yes, this is really soothing to a very dry throat.

"And to your health, also, Miss," answers Higgins, lifting his own glass to me. *"Saude."*

Before we had left England, both Higgins and I had been given some quick instruction on the major differences between the Spanish language, in which we are both fairly conversant, and Portuguese, a closely related Romance language, so we have practiced speaking it during the voyage here. The languages are similar but not exactly the same.

We both plunk our empty glasses back down on the table and Higgins hands me my bearskin shako, with its polished leather brim, gold braid, and beaten-silver shield. After donning it, I turn to regard myself in the mirror that hangs on the wall.

"There. That ought'a nail 'em," I say with some satisfaction. "Let's go."

We enter the hallowed chamber to find a great number of what I perceive to be high-ranking officers, some of whom are bending over a large map spread across several long tables lashed together. Others confer at a single table. Sir Arthur Wellesley is one of these, I see. I also notice a sideboard laden with food and beverage.

Higgins and I advance across the floor to stand in front of General Wellesley. Heads jerk up and a hush falls across the place as I bring my hand to my shako brim in salute, announcing in a curt tone, "Lieutenant Faber, reporting as ordered, Sir. May I present Mr. John Higgins, also of our naval service? Mr. Higgins, General Arthur Wellesley."

I whip off my shako, stick it under my arm, stand at attention, and wait.

Wellesley, calmly aware of the stir I have caused with my entrance, looks us over and disposes of Higgins first.

"Mr. Higgins, welcome," he says, plainly not meaning it. "Since you are allied with this . . . creature, I assume you are also sent as a spy upon my operations?"

"My good sir," says Higgins with a bow. "While it is true I am a member of Naval Intelligence, I am most often put to use as an analyzer of raw data rather than as a field agent. I do hope to be of some service to you in that capacity."

"Ummm . . ." says Wellesley doubtfully. "But, whatever. This is my spymaster and cryptographer, Mr. Scovell." He gestures to his right to a well-dressed civilian, who wears an expression of avid interest.

"Mr. Higgins!" fairly shouts this man. "I am delighted to make your acquaintance! You come highly recommended by our mutual friend, Mr. Peel! Oh, please do come around, my dear man; there is much to discuss!"

Hmmm . . . How come I don't come highly recommended anywhere? Why am I never received as such? Grrr . . .

Higgins, with a slight nod to me, does, indeed, go

around the table to confer with Mr. Scovell. They are immediately head to head over some papers and soon I hear expressions of *You must look at this, Sir,* and *My word! Fascinating! How did you ever . . . ?*

And so I realize that Higgins is lost to me for the time being and I am on my own, as General Wellesley now casts his gimlet eye upon me.

"You will now explain why you are again dressed in an outrageous costume."

"This is not a costume, Sir," I say with narrowed eyes. "This is the very uniform I wore when I was in *l'Empereur*'s service. I had thought, General, that you might want to see me in it."

I sense, gathering about me, several large males whom I had formerly seen ranged around the map table.

What is this, then? I hear muttered from those looming over me, and *Who the hell is she?*

"My good sir," I say, as if we have been passing conversation of the most pleasant sort, "do you realize that if I had received you on any of my ships — and I do own two, you know; four hundred and fifty tons' displacement, combined, by the way — that I would have given you refreshment and bade you to sit down and make yourself comfortable, rather than make you stand trembling like a disobedient schoolgirl, as you now force me to do?"

Again, the frosty piercing look.

"Very well," he says. "Steward! Prepare for her a plate."

"And a glass of wine, Sir?" I ask.

"Yes, and that, too!" he blusters. "And you may sit yourself right there!"

He points at a chair across from him, where I go to

place the Faber bottom firmly upon it, taking great care not to trip over my sword as I do so. The steward comes over and places a plate of various meats, cheeses, and bread in front of me. A glass of wine appears, and I take it up and hold it before me, the brim at level with the General's eyes.

"Rule, Britannia," I say, then knock back a good mouthful, daring him to not return the toast.

Wellesley picks up his own glass in acknowledgment of the offhand toast, as well he must, lest he be seen as less than patriotic in this exchange.

"Long may Britannia rule," he growls. The liquid in his glass is pale, and the bowl in front of him holds what seems to be a rather thin gruel. It is plain that the man does not take much pleasure in the more sensual delights of this world.

I lay in to some of the food put before me and I find it very good, and I wait for his next thrust. It does not take long.

"That medal. What is it?"

"It is the Legion of Honor, Sir."

"How came you by it?"

"Napoleon gave it to me."

"Where and for what reason?"

"In his coach, after the Battle of Jena. He thought I had given good service. Perhaps, when this is all over, you will award such a medal to me, too."

"I sincerely doubt that. Why were you in his coach?"

"He offered me a lift, and then gave me a letter to deliver to Empress Josephine. Which I later did."

The circle of other officers crowds in around us.

Unbelievable! It is not possible!

Wellesley ignores the skeptical throng and says, "Very well, girl. Tell your story."

And I do it. I lay out the thing as clearly as I can, from the overland march of the Grand Army — *Yes, I saw Napoleon himself, holding a lantern such that his men could drag a gun carriage out of a ditch in the middle of the night* — to the morning of the great battle, when a stiff breeze swept away the fog that had covered the field. *Ah, that is much better, he had said, as he'd surveyed his battalions* — *they were one-hundred-and-sixty-thousand-strong, five Corps, under Lannes, Ney, Davout, Bernadotte, and Augereau, and Marshal Murat's Reserve Cavalry. And, yes, I carried many messages back and forth between them all, including the last one to Murat, ordering him to charge the Prussian line. Right, that's where I got that Imperial Seal . . . and, apparently, earned the enmity of many of my countrymen.*

"Enmity, indeed," grumbles the General. He stands. "Let us go to the map."

I rise, knock off the rest of my glass, and follow him to the table and gaze down at the display laid thereon. It is a map of the environs around the town of Vimeiro.

Wellesley points to an area east of a river. "General Junot has massed his troops there. Thirteen thousand men under Generals Delaborde, Loison, Montmorand, Thomieres, and Margaron. What is your opinion on how they will attack, for surely they will, the day after tomorrow, by our best estimate?"

I consider, thinking back to the instructions in the art of war given to me by my great and good friend Captain Pierre Bardot . . .

You see, Bouvier, this formation, being essentially a square, gives l'Empereur the ability to attack in any direction, merely by ordering simple flanking maneuvers. And, since the length and the depth of the army is only a two-day march, l'Empereur *will be able to bring down the full force of his attack on any point in only forty-eight hours. Brilliant,* n'est-ce pas? *It is not for nothing that he has been called the God of War.*

"I know, General, that *l'Empereur* prefers to fight in columns of men, rather than lines. His generals mostly follow his example. So, Junot will bring his main force through here." I point my finger at a space between two low ridges.

"I agree with your assessment," says the General. "They will attack in columns, and we will fight in lines, and we will win the day."

"And, eventually, the war, Sir?" I ask with a bit of mockery in my tone. Perhaps that dollop of wine that is warming my belly has given me a bit of Dutch courage.

"Eventually."

"You feel you are the one to bring down Napoleon Bonaparte?"

"I do."

"Good luck with that, Sir."

He looks at me and says, "You know, Miss, there are several things about you that really irritate me — "

"I am sorry, Sir, if I give offense."

" — the chief of which is the reverence in your voice when you say '*l'Empereur*.'"

I puff up a bit and say, "He was kind to me."

He considers this for a moment and then says, "Oh, he was? Then how kind do you find this? He has ordered his

34

generals in Portugal and Spain to be utterly ruthless in putting down the popular uprisings that are springing up all over the peninsula."

"So? War is hell. We both know that."

"Yes. But do you know that his General Louis-Henri Loison, when laying siege to the town of Evora last month, demanded surrender of the city, and when the inhabitants refused, he ordered a charge, overwhelmed the defenders, and then had every surviving man, woman, and child killed?"

"I cannot believe that," I gasp. "Children, too?"

"Yes. A baby skewered on a steel bayonet and held high is apparently the new Napoleonic standard."

I am staggered — sickened — and my face must show it, for Wellesley smiles a grim smile and says, "I believe I have cracked your reserve, Miss Faber."

"In-indeed you have, Sir. May I be excused? I do not feel well."

"Yes? Well, get out."

I turn and plunge out the door.

I need some air . . .

Gasping, I run to the stables and order up my horse. As soon as she is saddled — *and no, I don't want a goddamn side-saddle!* — I am up on her back and away I ride.

I want to keep riding west till I leave this poor country, with all its grief and horror and misery, to what's sure to be its unhappy future. I want to get to the coast and book passage back to Boston and pick up the *Nancy B.* and sail off to Rangoon to be with Jaimy in his hour of need. I want . . . I want . . .

It doesn't matter what you want, girl . . .

I see a troop of light cavalry up ahead and rein in next to them.

"Lieutenant!" I call out to the officer in charge. "Can you tell me where the Seventh Brigade, Twentieth Light Dragoons is quartered?"

The young man looks me over, salutes, and says, "About three miles up ahead, on the right, by a low ridge."

"Thank you, Suh!" I shout, returning his salute. Then, digging my heels into the mare's flanks, I fly off down the road to seek solace in the sweet company of Captain Lord Richard Allen.

Chapter 4

James Emerson Fletcher
Seeker of Wisdom and Enlightenment
The House of Chen
Rangoon

Jacky Faber
Location unknown, at least to me

My dearest Jacky,
 I am, at this moment, kneeling in a Buddhist temple, clad in a saffron robe, with my head bowed. The Lady Sidrah kneels by my side.

I am trying to bring my mind to some sort of eventual understanding and acceptance of your death and resurrection, and the actual death of sweet Bess, she who stood by my side in my hours of madness, she who paid the ultimate price of friendship to me and died in her own heart's blood back there in the dark on Blackheath Moor.

Yes, Jacky, memories of that trying time are slowly coming back to me — how in my despair at your loss, I turned in a maddened state to robbing the broad highway, with revenge uppermost in my shattered mind, revenge against those who had condemned you and caused, I had thought, your ultimate destruction: Bliffil, whom I now remember that I killed in cold blood there in the moonlight on that dark road, and the detestable Flashby, whom I fear still lives and, and . . .

Sidrah's hand is placed on my shaking arm. Even in this quiet sanctuary, even with all the Oriental medicines that have been doled out to me, even with my brother monks' gentle instruction in the Way of the Buddha, even with all that, still, sometimes, I begin to shake, uncontrollably, with rage.

Yes, Sir Harry Flashby, that unspeakable bastard, continues to draw breath and, I suspect, free air at that. My kind host, Lee Chen, head of the House of Chen, whom you know as Chopstick Charlie, chortled as he recounted your rather elaborate plan to substitute Flashby for me in the ultimate capture of the Black Highwayman: *Confucius be praised, you should have seen his face, Mr. Fletcher, eyes bugging out like a squeezed toad as he was hauled off to prison! Ha!* But we both know, Jacky, that the slippery snake will manage to wriggle out of Newgate and will soon be back in a position to do damage. And, I am sure, he has his nemesis, Jacky Faber, full in his sights.

Yes, my arm does shake, and the good Sidrah does put her calming hand upon it, saying, *Please, Jai-mee-san, calmness . . . calmness . . . Empty your mind. Surrender yourself to the peace of Buddha.*

We both gaze up at the benign countenance looming

above us in the dim interior of the temple. Incense smoke swirls about the smiling face of Gautama Buddha and I strive to accept it all . . .

Yours,

Jaimy

Chapter 5

"Princess!" says Lord Allen as I arrive in his encampment. "Come join us! Welcome!"

There is a table set up outside a large tent and at it sit four men, one of whom is Richard Allen. He rises, grinning broadly, and comes over to take the reins of my horse as I dismount. My boots have scarcely hit the ground when he encircles my waist with his strong right arm, bends me back, and plants a quick one on my mouth. I reflect that this is probably the first time I have taken a kiss while still wearing my shako. Rather awkward, actually, but still, I enjoy it.

"I must say, Pretty-Bottom," murmurs Lord Allen in my ear, then releases me, takes my hand, and leads the way to the table, "you look absolutely smashing in that rig. A French Hussar are you now?"

"At one time I was, Richard, but now, once again, Jacky Faber is just a humble servant of King George."

Two of the men still seated there are dressed in Cavalry scarlet, the other one in mostly black. They all look up in some surprise at my appearance and the welcome I had just received from Cavalry Captain Allen.

"Colonel Robbe, may I present Miss Jacky Faber, Lieutenant, Royal Navy. Lieutenant Faber, Colonel Kenneth Robbe, commander of the Twentieth Light Dragoons."

I give a slight bow and, hand to brim of shako, snap off a salute, saying, "Honored, Sir!"

"And Major Gavin MacLean."

Again, a nod and salute. All three men are now standing, it having finally dawned on them that I am female and manners demand that they get to their feet to greet one such as me.

"And this is Senhor Montoya, leader of a squadron of partisans that will be joining us in this little skirmish."

The two rather stunned British officers mumble something that passes for salutation — *Ah, yes, charmed, I'm sure*, and *Good afternoon, uh . . . Mum* — but Senhor Montoya is much more eloquent.

"*Boa tarde, Senhorita*," he says, smiling widely and looking me directly in the eye. He reaches out his hand to take mine, then bows low, putting a kiss on the back of the Faber paw, making me glad I had washed that very same paw earlier and scrubbed out its fingernails. "I rejoice to see such a beautiful lady in the midst of the English army. I hope you know you have brightened my day."

"*Muito obrigado, Senhor. Você e' muito amável*," I reply with a slight dip. "You do not seem too surprised to see me here."

"Ah, no, I am not. You see, fair one, we have many brave women in the ranks of our fighters. Many brave and beautiful women."

Montoya is a darkish fellow, swarthy of complexion, medium height, compact and sturdy-looking, with black hair pulled back from a high brow and tied with a red ribbon. He wears a thick mustache, also black, and a short goatee, all of which frame a very toothy smile. His breast is crisscrossed with thick brown leather belts, each adorned with white musket cartridges. He is quite good-looking in a rough sort of way and does not seem to be the kind of man who is abashed by stiff British officers, or by me.

Richard Allen leads me to a chair and I sit down, pulling off my shako and placing it top down on the table. He calls for wine and it is brought — *ah, this is good; it was a dusty four miles from there to here* — and then we get down to business.

"How did it go with our noble leader?" asks Allen, lifting his glass and holding it up to me.

"About what you'd expect. He as much as threw me out," I say, lifting my glass to him and to the others around the table. "*After* he gleaned all the information about Boney he could drag out of me."

"The man is very methodical, for sure," says Colonel Robbe. "But I think that is a good thing for us. He is not a man to sacrifice troops needlessly."

There are nods of agreement all around.

"Nor does he mince words, Colonel," I pipe up. "While it was plain that he had very little regard for me, he also had some harsh things to say about cavalry in general. If I may quote, 'Vainglorious idiots waving swords and charging at anything that moves, no plans, no foresight . . .'"

"Hmm . . ." Robbe glowers. "Be that as it may, he could possibly find us 'vainglorious idiots' quite handy in the next few days."

"He also said something I found quite unsettling. He said that when French General Loison took the town of Evora, he ordered every man, woman, and child in that city put to the sword. Is that true?"

The man Montoya answers for him. "It is true, Senhorita. Every bit of it." He is no longer smiling.

"My God . . . What could Loison hope to gain from that? He already had the city at his feet."

Montoya leans over the table. "He hoped to scare our people into submission. What he has gained is the exact opposite. As the story of the atrocity spreads across Portugal and Spain, the people are rising up even now against the invader Napoleon and all his generals. When before they saw Bonaparte as a liberator, delivering them from a backward, inbred, corrupt, and stupid aristocracy, they now see him as the cruel despot he really is. He has made a big mistake, Senhorita, count on it. People do not forget . . ."

Indeed, they do not, yet so many would-be conquerors believe that they will . . .

" . . . and if you will excuse me, Tenente Faber, I must go see to *meus companheiros. Bom dia.* Meeting you was a great pleasure."

He rises, bows, flashes another wide grin at me, spins on his heel, and strides to the side of a horse that is tethered nearby. He leaps upon it and is gone in a cloud of dust.

"Quite the dashing one, that," I observe, having checked out the broadness of his shoulders, the narrowness of his hips, and the length of his straight legs as he walked away.

"Yes," says Richard. "A veritable cock-of-the-walk, as it were. Still, he and his guerrillas have proved most useful in keeping track of the French advance."

Colonel Robbe also rises, as do all of us. "I, too, must be off to see to the disposition of my forces. Good day, all."

He leaves, and we plop back down in our chairs. I believe I notice a general lightening of the atmosphere at the table, now that both the superior officer and the foreigner have gone.

The steward comes back and refills our glasses. It is quite hot, here in the late afternoon sun of Portugal, and I say, "Do you mind, Major, if I remove this, as it is rather warm?" and with that I doff my wig and stuff it into my shako. "Ah, that feels much better." I sigh, as the slight breeze ruffles my natural stubble.

Major Gavin MacLean is a bit stunned at the sight, but he recovers. "Not at all, my dear," he says, then turns to Richard Allen. "Richard, just how do you do it, continually coming up with such delightful things?"

"This one just sort of popped up one day, in the wilds of America, if you can believe it, Gavin. I have been forever grateful for that chance meeting."

"Suppose I had taken off my hairpiece earlier," I ask, playing the coquette with fluttering eyelashes.

"If you had" — MacLean laughs — "I'm sure our Senhor Montoya would have scooped you up and borne you away right then, my dear. He seemed quite taken with you."

"She does not scoop up all *that* easily, Gavin," says Allen, a bit testily, I note with some satisfaction. "And as to who's dear she is — "

"So they will come through there?" I ask, pointing down the valley to a place between two low hills.

"Yes," says MacLean. "Montoya reports about thirteen

thousand, arranged in three divisions, with artillery to each side."

"Umm," I say. "Sure to be bloody."

"It always is, Miss," he says. "But we hope for the best."

"Indeed we do, but the best is what we seldom get," I say, with some foreboding.

A tinkling of female laughter is heard from a nearby wagon, and I look in that direction.

"Some of the lads have brought their wives with them," explains Allen, seeing my ear cocked to the sound. "They are quite the spirited crew."

"It seems they are quite merry," says I, having yet another sip of the very good wine.

"You know, Jacky, if you would marry me, you could join their merry band. 'Course, things do look a bit crowded in there, but you could hop right in the wagon with the bunch of them. After, of course, we enjoy a lamentably brief but surely lusty honeymoon in my poor tent. Hmm? What do you think?"

I think, my good Lord Allen, that you are putting on a bit of a show for the benefit of your friend Gavin, here. Do you want me to blush and look all demure? Men, I swear . . . But I will play along.

"I am sure I would find their company most congenial, and your tent seems right cozy, milord, but I must demur, for I am sure you would not be able to find an ordained minister in this crowd of military men to perform the service, and as I am a good Christian girl, I would require the proper words to be said before I would go into your tent with you."

45

"True, alas, Old Nosey does not travel with a chaplain," says Allen.

"More's the pity," I say, rising. "Major MacLean, a true pleasure meeting you. I hope you will be safe in the coming days. I must get back to headquarters. Richard, will you walk with me a bit before I go?"

We walk, my blue-clad arm wrapped around his red one, along a cow path, then over a low hill, and look down upon a small river curling about below. This land of Portugal appears lush where land meets river and stream. When no water is around, the land goes scrubby and arid. I suspect Spain shall be the same. Fine for growing oranges and tangerines, so that's all to the good, I suppose.

"It is the Maceiro River, Higgins has informed me. Is this not a beautiful view, Richard?" I sigh, leaning my head against his shoulder.

"Indeed it is, Jacky. 'Every aspect doth please,' as the poets would have it," he says as we pause to take in the scene. "But I'd rather look upon thee, my sweet little river sprite, as I find that aspect much more interesting. Perhaps we should ride down and have a bit of a dip in that bend in the river there. Looks like it might have a rather inviting pool. What say, Princess? For old times' sake?"

I blush at the thought of that and give the rogue a poke in the ribs for his cheek. I know, of course, he is referring to that delightful but ultimately disastrous watery romp we shared back there on the Mississippi River.

"That little river is not the Big Muddy, Richard," I say sadly, thinking on those rather carefree days. "And that was then and this is now."

I take a deep breath and snuggle into his side. "Oh, why could we not have come here on some Grand Tour, just the two of us, to sample the joys of this beautiful land and its lovely people? A nice drink in some charming country café, a stroll with our arms about each other down some pleasant street, a picnic on the green banks of that river down there, your head in my lap as I curl your beautiful hair about my forefinger and breathe some poetry into your ear. Why not that? Yes, just the two of us, each enjoying the sweet company of the other. Some music, some laughter, some dancing, a gentle kiss and caress here and there. Why not that, Richard, instead of this?"

I look over to the left to see rank upon rank of soldiers, legions of men lining up, muskets primed and at the ready, artillery caissons rattling down rough roads, all getting ready to do their brutal work.

"Thousands of men getting ready to kill each other, and me and you in the middle of it. Why this and not the other?"

He follows my gaze and says, "I do not know the 'why' of many things, Princess, but I do know one thing — war is my business and I must attend to it."

"I know, Richard, I know, but please hold me and give me a kiss and make me feel better, if only for this moment, this fleeting moment."

I bury my face in the front of his chest and feel his arms go about me.

"I've got a bad feeling about this one, Richard, I do. Be careful. You must not — "

He smiles down on me. "Now, Princess. You must stop with that nonsense. Every soldier judges the odds before a battle and weighs his chances, wondering if this is the one where the bullet with his name on it finally finds its way to his heart. Ah, come on, Prettytail, it's silly stuff. Questioning Fate is — "

I twist around and grab him by the upper arms and gaze intently into his eyes. "No, Richard, I will not have it. You talk oh-so-flip and carefree, but I know you have your brave and careless and foolhardy ways. And I will not have it, no, I won't! You hear me?" I give him a shake, my eyes starting to fill with worried tears.

"Yes, Jacky, I will be careful, I promise."

"No charging windmills, my sweet lord?"

"Ah, not me, my pretty little miss. My duty and nothing more," he says, putting a light kiss on my brow and chuckling deep in his throat. "But as for charging windmills, I well recall the eight-gun *Nancy B. Alsop* charging into battle against the eighty-four-gun behemoth *San Cristobal* back there on the Caribbean Sea. Do you recall that as well, Captain Miss Faber? Hmmm?"

"That was different, Captain Lord Allen, that was — "

"No, it wasn't. It was foolhardy and crazy and you damn well know it. But you did it, anyway. Now, alas, we must get back. My men have probably all deserted by now. Here, let's get you squared away."

I had shoved my wig back on my head and it sat there all askew, its locks falling about my streaming eyes.

"There," he says, straightening my hairpiece and placing my shako upon it. "All Shipshape and Bristol Fashion. And let's kiss those tears away."

"I know I'm a bit of a mess," I say, beginning to blubber. "Why do you bother with me, Richard?"

He laughs. "Because I love you, Jacky. You are the light

of my life. Now, you stay at headquarters and out of trouble, you hear me? You're in this, too, and given your past behavior, well . . ."

I put my arms around him and my tears are kissed away.

I love you, too, Richard. One last kiss, Richard, one last one, oh please . . .

And then we turn and head back to our duty.

As I mount up and return to headquarters, all disconsolate and full of grim foreboding, an old Irish song taught to me by Mairead McConnaughey comes unbidden into my head.

> *I know where I'm going,*
> *And I know who's going with me*
> *I know who I love,*
> *But the Lord knows who I'll marry . . .*

Chapter 6

Deep in the dark of the night I hear a distant rumble of artillery. I cringe and burrow further down into the covers and pull the pillow over my head. It does not shut out the sound.

In the military there is a term called "four o'clock courage." It means that, while it is easy to feel brave and hopeful on the eve of battle, when you are eating and drinking with your friends in the glow of a warm fire and good fellowship, things tend to look a lot different in the cold light of the predawn when, alone and fearful, you must climb out of a warm and safe bed to confront what is sure to come. The soldier who can do that and not quiver and shake is said to possess "four o'clock courage."

That is all very well. However, I, Jacky Faber, do not have that kind of courage, and never have. In fact, I have very little of any kind of courage at all.

I burrow deeper, but — heavy sigh — I throw off the covers and get up to dress and face the coming day, the butterflies in my cowardly belly in full flight.

Shivering, I climb into my Royal Navy gear, which Higgins had laid out for me the night before. If grim Death does find me today, I prefer to go off with him in Navy blue. I do not bother with the wig. What good would it do me today? My own hair will have to serve whether I end up at the Pearly Gates or at the Gates of Hell.

At least I won't be buried at sea, I think as I pull on my boots. *That's some consolation.*

With sword rattling at side, shako somewhat askew on head, I go next door to tap on Higgins's door. He is, of course, already up and has procured from somewhere some good hot coffee and small sweet cakes, which do much to restore my spirits. In the soft light of a lantern, we share a battlefield breakfast.

"You will go to be with Mr. Scovell?"

"Yes, I think that would be the best place for me. The man is absolutely amazing in his ability to crack enemy codes. He has given me a relatively simple message to try to break, and I believe I just about have it."

He reaches into his jacket and pulls out a small leather-bound notebook and shows me some meaningless figures written thereupon. Under them are some words in French, undoubtedly parts of the deciphered message.

"Dear Higgins," I say, with a fond smile on my face and a hand on his shoulder. "Verily, it is just the place for you and your fine mind."

"And you, Miss?" he asks, returning the notebook to his vest pocket. "I advise caution, and I hope this time that advice will not be in vain."

"Don't worry, Higgins. Remember, you are talking to Jacky Faber, Committed Coward. I shall be all right. I will go to headquarters with you and stand by Wellesley's side, whether he wants me there or not. It is, after all, where my orders directed me to be, and where I should be safe. Generals seldom die in battle, and neither do their aides-de-camp."

"Well, that is to be hoped," says Higgins, a bit doubtfully. "Shall we go, Miss?"

"Yes, Higgins, lead on."

We exit our wing of what I have come to call the Hotel Vimeiro, and I go to the stable to collect my mount, whom I have named Isabella, she being a pretty little thing, while Higgins goes off to join Mr. Scovell.

I lead my little mare around to the front of the building and find that Wellesley has moved his campaign outdoors. There is a slight rise of ground that gives a fine view of the battleground.

I tie Isabella to a rail that is already lined with horses and walk over to the center of activity, in the middle of which is, of course, General Sir Arthur Wellesley.

Dawn is beginning to pink up the eastern horizon, and that is the direction from which the French will come. There is a road leading between two low ridges to here.

And there they are, all in red, white, and blue . . .

The sun is even higher now, and we can see the advancing French columns surging right up the road leading to the town. There's certainly nothing very subtle about the direction of their march over the plain. They are heading directly for us and mean to overpower our poor lads with their overwhelming might.

Oh, Lord . . .

"I see you are being English today, Miss Faber," growls the General upon seeing me. "What are you doing here?"

I bring heels together, put hand to brim, and snap off a salute. "I was messenger to Bonaparte, and I shall be messenger to you, Sir, as well."

"*Harrumph*. Well, stay out of the way, girl."

I give a slight bow, more of a nod, really, and step back to stand with a group of red-coated junior officers — plainly messengers, I surmise, and I find out I am right when one of them is called to the big table, given a paper, and sent off to the north. Undoubtedly to Anstruther's Seventh Brigade, which lies over the hills in that direction.

My fellow messengers eye me curiously, but I am certainly used to that. Excitement is high, but one of them who steps from the throng manages to ask, "Are you really Jacky Faber? It's said around camp that you are, indeed, she."

I give him the Lawson Peabody Look — eyelids at half mast beneath the brim of my shako, lips together, teeth apart — and say, "That's *Lieutenant* Jacky Faber, Ensign, and yes, I suppose I am."

"My word," he says, visibly impressed. "Jacky Faber standing right here. Imagine that."

There are none of the regular brigade commanders here, all eight of them — Crawfurd, Anstruther, Acland, Fane, Ferguson, Nightingall, Bowes, and Hill — are off with their troops. There are, however, two generals in our midst whom I had not seen before. Curious, that . . . arriving on the scene so close to the start of the battle.

"Imagine what you will, lad, but who are those two?" I ask of my new admirer, nodding in the direction of the two brass hats.

"Generals Burrard and Dalrymple, newly arrived from

home." He leans into me and whispers, "From what I hear, I don't think Old Nosey is at all pleased."

"Hmmm . . . 'Many cooks spoil the stew' comes to mind."

"Indeed, that is the supposition. Ahem . . . Would you mind, Lieutenant, if I were to touch your arm?"

"Wot?"

"It would mean a lot to me, Miss," he stammers, "if I could tell all and sundry that I touched the arm of the one who rubbed shoulders with Napoleon himself."

I cut him a sharp look. "Where did you hear about that?"

"That new book, *My Bonny Light Horseman*, came out just before we left England. It was in all the bookshops. I enjoyed it hugely," he says, blushing prettily. "Especially the part where you — "

"Never mind that," I say, working up a bit of a blush myself, as I can well imagine to what part — or parts — he is referring. *Geez, Amy, did you leave nothing out?*

I give him a quick look-over. He is a very pleasant-looking lad, seventeen if he's a day, and probably anticipating his first real shave.

"You know my name, soldier," I say. "What's yours?"

"Connell, Miss. T-T-Timothy Connell," he says, stuttering.

"Well, Ensign Timothy Connell, you may tell all and sundry about *this . . .*" And I lean over and plant a kiss on his downy cheek.

The blush triples in intensity.

"Oh, Miss!" he exults, the upcoming battle apparently

forgotten in the magic of the moment. He puts hand to recently kissed cheek and dons a faraway look. "That will be a story to tell!"

Boys, I swear . . .

Just then the very irregular Commander Montoya rides up, followed by several of his similarly irregular troops — all of them dressed in ragged dark clothing with bandoleers crossed over their chests, black broad-brimmed hats on their heads. He dismounts, tosses the reins to an orderly, and strides over to the big table. He hands a packet of papers to Wellesley's spymaster Scovell. He and Higgins snatch them up avidly and begin referring to code sheets and scribbling.

Must be nice to be able to read the enemy's dispatches at a time like this, I'm thinking. I'm also reflecting on the former bearers of those messages, French couriers who are now probably lying dead in dusty ditches along lonely roads not far from here. My sympathies extend to those fallen messengers, for I myself was very recently a French courier and had many friends in that close-knit corps of riders. *C'est la guerre, mes amis.*

I turn again to watch the French advance up the road. Their artillery continues to pound, and puffs of shot and shell hit near our village. I look to the south and see the steeple of the local church, thinking it is probably making a fine target for the French gunners.

Sure enough, there is a high whistling sound and then a thud as a ball hits a building next to us, crumbling a wall. My traitorous knees start in to quivering. I hope no one notices.

As fine dust from the collapse of that building rains down upon us, the French columns come relentlessly on, and then the fog of war sets in for real . . .

"He's trying to turn our left flank!" shouts Wellesley, squinting through the dust. "Signal to Acland and Bowes! Stop them!"

From what I can see, Anstruther's brigade has just come out of hiding and is attacking the French columns in long lines of two rifles deep. Men, in all their military finery, are beginning to fall on both sides, lying like little tin soldiers on the ground. But they are not toys, no, they are not. They are poor boys who were once living and breathing young men, and now, in a flash, in a single horrible instant, they are not — they neither live nor breathe but rather lie still on the ground that they will soon be part of.

Good God, the slaughter is on!

The ranks of my fellow messengers are thinning, as each is called up to fly off with a message to one of the field commanders. As Ensign Connell mounts up, I give him a salute and a pat on his leg.

"Go, Tim, and Godspeed!"

He wheels and is gone.

There are signal men posted on the nearby roof, waving flags in prearranged patterns to transfer orders to those brigades that can see them.

"General Junot is sending brigades along the ridgeline to attack the village! There is a column attempting to enter the village on the left!" shouts an officer on the roof, a long glass to his eye.

"Contact Fane! Tell him of the situation and get men into the houses to defend the town! Goddammit to hell! Do it!" yells Wellesley.

Another messenger rides off and I see that I am the last one left, and will be so till one of the others returns from his mission. None such reappears, not yet, anyway.

Wellesley stands at the table, hands clenched behind him, looking out over the battle, his teeth clenched as well.

"Messenger!" he roars. "Get down to Colonel Robbe and tell him I want his dragoons up here *NOW!*"

He looks up and sees that the messenger is me. I get up on Isabella and reach down for the order.

"Good God, you again? Christ, what a war . . ." He looks about for a more suitable male messenger but finds none. "Well, just go on and do it, for God's sake! And don't fail, girl!"

I take the paper, cast him a level glance, wheel, and I am gone.

"Bernier is attacking the town!" I shout as I see Richard Allen riding toward me at the head of his troops, looking more stern and resolute than I have ever seen him. "Wellesley wants you up there!" He pulls up, as do I, and I hand him the message. He reads it, then stuffs it into the front of his jacket.

"We already know that. All right, lads, let's go," he says, putting spurs to his horse. I see Sergeant Bailey and Private Archie MacDuff behind him, and Tommy Patton, Seamus McMann, too.

"Richard, I—"

"Jacky, you must go back to headquarters. Now!"

"But, Richard—"

"But nothing. Go back where you can do some good. The fighting in the town will be hand-to-hand, as nasty and dirty as it gets! It always is. And you are no good at that sort of thing! Now, go!"

With that, he whips out his sword and slaps Isabella on her rump with the flat of the blade. She starts, then takes off with me and I let her have her head for a bit, then turn her, to watch Richard Allen and his men thunder down a street and into the heart of Vimeiro, swords drawn and ready.

God, please watch over them! I pray, then guide Isabella back to the command post, as ordered.

Things there are in turmoil . . .

Wellesley has his glass to his eye. I suspect it has seldom been away from there.

"Here comes Kellermann with his Grenadiers. Look! They are veering to the east to avoid Anstruther's Ninety-seventh. They're going to the village . . . They've reached the church!"

I look in that direction and see the flash of bayonets and hear the shouts and cries of desperate men in hand-to-hand combat, and I know that Richard is in the middle of it. *Oh, Lord!*

Wellesley whips around and points his long glass north.

"And Solinac is trying to turn our flank again! But there's Ferguson and his six thousand foot soldiers! That's stopping them, by God! Good show!"

That flank secured, the General turns his attention back to the trouble in the village itself . . .

And in case you haven't noticed, General, we are also in

this village! whimpers my cowardly self as a shell explodes behind us, spooking the horses and causing a light dusting of white powder to rain down upon us.

"Messenger!" roars Wellesley. "Get over here!" He begins to write out something as one of the other messengers steps forward. "Take this to Comandante Montoya. Tell him to aid the defenders of the town!"

I think of Richard and his lads pinned down in the village, facing insurmountable odds and in the greatest need of help, and I step in front of the young horseman, snatch the note, and say, "I'll take it, General. I know where he is. Montoya knows me and I will give him the order. He is probably illiterate, so these written words will do no good."

Wellesley glares at me. Another shell explodes behind us. He considers and says, "Go, then, and do not fail."

I leap into the saddle and head off in the direction of where I know Montoya's forces lie hidden behind a ridge. As I go, I see Higgins look up. I give him a wave and I am gone.

I pound down the road and am rounding a curve as another shell goes off to the right of me. My bowels churn, but I've managed to hold my water thus far. Isabella starts but does not slack her speed — *Good girl! Not too much farther! There!*

I see, sheltered in a ravine, Montoya and his force of guerrillas. There are about a hundred of them, and they are mounted and ready to go.

"Comandante Montoya! General Wellesley desires that you ride into Vimeiro to aid the defenders there!"

Montoya grins widely, exposing his strong white teeth. "*Naturalmente,* Tenente. Lead on."

I wheel Isabella about and gallop back the way I came,

with one hundred very irregular but very determined fighters behind me.

Soon, the roofs and spires of the town appear and Montoya comes up to ride by my side.

"You see the church steeple?" I shout, pointing. "That's where the fighting is the fiercest!"

"And that is where we will go, Tenente," says Montoya, waving his band of guerrillas on. "I hope to see you again, *menina!*" He gives me a look I can only describe as lecherous, salutes, and surges on into the town.

I would follow, but the street is too narrow and I am stopped by a wall and must pull back and wait for the main force to enter before I can do anything.

What to do? Follow them in? Pull my puny sword and wave it about? Go back to Wellesley and await further orders? What?

Bombs fall and there are dull thuds and clouds of thrown-up earth when they land. I hear the horrid shrieks of the mindless metal rockets that fly overhead and I hear the screams of anguish torn from human throats when those uncaring missiles fall and do their awful damage.

No! The coward in me says, *No! Go back, Jacky! Do as Richard says! Go back to Headquarters!* But . . . I cannot do it. Allen and the lads are in there and I must go join them.

Deep breath, let it out, and I put my heels to Isabella's flanks and down the narrow street we plunge, terrified girl on terrified horse.

I keep the church steeple in my sights as I gallop down one empty street and up another, and . . .

There they are!

I see our red-coated Dragoons lined up against a low

wall, on the other side of which is a vast plain and on that plain is rank upon rank of French infantry marching relentlessly on toward us. Our men fire their muskets with military precision and the French fire back. Bullets whistle all about like angry bees, but oh-so-much-more-deadly than mere insects. A bee will sting, but a bullet will kill.

Lord Richard Allen is in the middle of his men, firing his Kentucky Long Rifle with deadly accuracy. He pulls the trigger and I look out and see a Frenchman in the first line pitch forward into the dust.

I drop down off Isabella and crouch next to Richard as he is reloading.

"Princess, godammit!" he growls, fixing me with a look of complete exasperation. "You shouldn't be — "

"Too late, Richard!" I cry and duck my head. A rocket has hit the base of the steeple behind us. I turn to see it totter and fall into the street, blocking a quick way out up that road, anyway. A cloud of white dust from the destruction floats down over us all.

Pulling my pistols from my belts, I lean over the wall and point them at the French, aiming low, hoping to wound, rather than kill, but in the heat of battle, who knows where one's deadly bullets fly — into the tough hide of a grizzled old veteran who grunts and pushes on, or into the tender heart of a young boy who lies down and quietly dies. In the fog of war, no one knows anything.

I pull both triggers and feel the pistols buck in my hands. Turning, I slide down, my back to the wall, to reload. Pull the white cartridge from my belt, bite the bullet out of the corner, and pour the powder down the barrel. Then spit the bullet down after it and pull the short ramrod from its bracket under the barrel and cram the leaden slug down all snug against the powder. The tiny percussion cap is pressed down on its nipple, and the pistol is loaded and ready.

As I load my other gun, I look up and down our line — our very thin red line — and see that Montoya has spread his men out on our left flank. *Good man*, I'm thinkin' . . . Then I see one of ours cry out and fall backward onto the cobblestones to writhe in pain . . . and he is not the only one. Three others lie still and unmoving.

Who? Oh, God! No, Archie; not Seamus, not —

"Sergeant!" roars Allen. "Close up the rank!"

I turn again to fire my puny pistols, so small in all this mayhem, and see Sergeant Bailey directing men to fill the spots of the fallen.

The French are much closer now, perhaps only fifty yards away . . . now forty . . . now thirty . . .

Again, I fire, seeking only to wound, to stop that dread advance, but I know full well that those who press forward seek not to wound but to kill, with shot, shell, or bayonet . . . and in a few minutes, it will be hand to hand, and it will be with those cruel blades.

A bullet hits the top of the wall next to my face and ricochets off over my shoulder, throwing a shower of gritty dust into my eye. *Yeouch!*

"Keep your stupid head down, Jacky!" Richard yells over the din, shoving me below the wall. I rub at my eye to free it of the dirt. "Twentieth Dragoons . . . fix bayonets!" he bellows.

There is the rattle of metal on metal as, all along the line, Captain Allen's order is obeyed. Across the field, the sun glints off the French bayonets as well and . . .

Oh, Lord, it's gonna get nasty. Soon those cruel barrel-borne knives will be thrust into soft bodies to grate upon bone and life-blood will flow down the bayonets' blood-gutters to spill upon the ground.

Twenty yards . . . now ten.

"Another volley, men!" shouts Allen, standing and leveling his rifle. "Let's slow the bastards down! Lay on, lads, steady down! Steady now. Give it to 'em . . . Give it —"

I sense, rather than hear, the bullet that thuds into Richard Allen's chest.

"Damn. Deuced bother . . . Sorry, Princess." He gasps and then slumps against me.

Richard! No!

But yes, it is true, a much darker stain of crimson creeps across the front of his scarlet coat. His eyes are closed and he knows no more of this battle.

"Sergeant! Archie! Tommy!" I cry, wrapping my arms about Richard's shoulders. "The Captain is down! Come help, boys, oh, please, come help me!"

But they cannot come, for the battle is too fierce and they must fight on or else all will be lost, all will be wounded, all will be dead.

I stagger to my feet.

We've got to get out of here, Richard, we do. There's Isabella there . . . If I can get you on her we can get to . . .

But we can get to nothing.

Through all my fear, sorrow, and confusion, I hear the high whistling sound of an incoming shell. Then there is a flash and a scream and I hear and see no more.

All is the deep darkness and silence of the tomb . . .

Chapter 7

There is a great ball of fire in the sky and it burns my slowly opening eyes as I climb back into consciousness. *Oh, God, let me be, please, let me alone, I hurt, I hurt . . .*

"Is she alive, Joachim?" I hear someone above me say.

"*Sí*, comandante."

"*Bueno.* Pick her up and take her to the hospital. It is right over there."

I feel myself being lifted and carried. The eyelids finally flutter open and I see Montoya above me, astride his horse, his black sombrero framing his face.

I twist my head and look about, all confused. There is a large jagged hole in the road where that shell hit . . . and, oh, no . . . there lies my poor Isabella on her side, her neck stretched out, and all the rest of her quite still and, I know, quite dead. *Oh, I only knew you for a little while, but you were a good little mare. If there is a heaven for horses, I hope you are there, little one, and I hope the grass is green.*

As all of my shaky senses return, I realize a strong young

man has his right arm under my legs at the knees, and the other arm around my shoulders, while my head lolls about, my shako dangling from my neck on its leather strap.

I start to squirm.

"No . . . no, I am all right," I protest. "I don't have to go to hospital. Just let me down, please, just let me get back. I must find — "

"The battle is over, Miss, and we have won the day, *gracias a Dios,*" says Montoya. He is no longer smiling.

"But then, why?"

"Because I think you will want to go there, Senhorita," says the very rough man, with some kindness in his voice. "The man who kissed you the other day when I sat at his table. I found him *simpático.* He is in there. With many others."

I gasp. *Richard!*

I wriggle out of the man's grasp and discover that I am standing in front of a large warehouse. From the sounds of pain and agony coming from within, I know exactly what it is — a battlefield hospital, little more than a charnel house, a place of butchery and despair and death.

I meet Sergeant Bailey coming out, supporting a wounded Archie MacDuff, who has a bandage around his head, through which blood is seeping. Seeing me, he says, "Over to the left. Fourth bed. Sorry, Miss."

I rush in the door and am once again greeted with the cries and groans of the wounded. I had been in a hospital like this on the battlefield of Jena, where I said my last goodbyes to Captain Bardot. *Please, Lord, don't let it be like that this time, please.*

There he is. He lies on his back on a rude cot. There is a cut to his head and blood covers half his beautiful face, but that worries me less than the bloodstain on his left side just below the rib cage.

"Oh, Richard," I sob. "Can you hear me?"

His eyelids flutter open and fix on me. He smiles.

"Hello, Princess. Good to see you."

"Richard, dear, I am so sorry!"

"Ah. It is but a scratch." He moves a bit and groans, proving it is not just a scratch. "Did we win?"

"Yes, the day is ours."

"My men?"

"I saw Sergeant Bailey and Private MacDuff outside. They are all right. I don't know about the others. I think most came through."

"That's good, I . . . I . . ." his eyelids droop and fall shut.

No, Richard, don't die!

A man stands next to me and, seeing my concern, says, "We have given him something. For the pain."

"Will he live, Doctor? Oh, please say he will!"

"He might. And you should get that scrape patched up."

A cut on my forehead, which I had not yet noticed, persists on bleeding into my eye. Must have happened when I hit the dirt.

I wipe it away and say, "Never mind that. What will happen to him now?"

"HMS *Tortoise* is being made over into a hospital ship. As soon as we fill her up with wounded, she'll be off for Britain. Then we'll fill up HMS *Guardian*, too."

In spite of its distress, my mind clears and turns practical.

"Do you want to make an easy one hundred pounds?" I ask the surgeon.

"I would not mind it."

The man has a notebook and he is writing in it — the names of the recently dead, no doubt.

"Please give me something to write on."

He lifts his eyebrows but passes me the book and pencil, and I write furiously in it. When I pass it back to him, I say, "Make sure this man gets on the first ship and is well cared for. Afterwards, get him to this address, such that he comes under the care of a Dr. Stephen Sebastian. Present this note and you'll receive your one hundred pounds. You will see words to that effect right there."

"How do I know they'll pay?" he asks, skeptical.

I open my jacket, pull up my shirt, and open my money belt. I take out three gold coins.

"Here's twenty pounds as earnest money. If this man dies on the way, you'll still have that. If he lives till you can deliver him, then you shall have the additional hundred. How can you lose?"

The man shrugs. "I reckon I can't. Here! You, there! Get this man on a stretcher. Careful, now!"

The stretcher is brought and Lord Allen is laid upon it. The movement, with its accompanying pain, wakes him up and he speaks to me again.

"Will you marry me, Jacky? I'm not joking this time," he says with a low chuckle. "If I recover from this . . ."

I pat his arm, tears streaming down my face. "*When* you get well, my gallant Dragoon, you may ask me that again. You're going to the *Tortoise* and then to Dr. Sebastian. It's been arranged."

He manages a wan smile. "Thank you, Princess. Hate to fall under the tender care of a navy sawbones."

"No, Richard, we can't have that." Tears run down my face as I grasp his hand in both of mine and hold it to my lips.

The stretcher bearers lift their burden, and as he is borne away, he says, "Oh, Princess, you have made it all worthwhile."

I stumble out of the hospital, intending to follow him as far as I possibly can, but I do not get to do that.

Ensign Connell appears at my side.

"Lieutenant Faber, the General wants to see you. Now."

"What?" I am confused.

"Come quickly, Miss. There's hell to pay. General Wellesley has been relieved of his command."

Chapter 8

"It cannot be true, Tim," I say, as Ensign Connell and I hurry along to headquarters. "Wellesley has just won a great victory."

"It is true, nonetheless, Miss. General Burrard has taken over. And you are bleeding, Miss."

Oh my. Old Nosey's nose must really be in a twist!

"How is he taking it?" I ask. We are coming up on Hotel Vimeiro.

Ensign Connell cuts me a nervous glance. "About as you'd expect."

But this could be good for me, I'm thinking. After all, I was assigned to Wellesley's staff . . . Maybe if he is sent back to England, I would go with him, and then I could look after Richard! Maybe . . .

"In fact, not well at all," says Connell. "Best keep your head down when we go in there."

Hmmm . . .

"What was the Butcher's Bill for this little battle?" I ask, dreading the answer. "Have you heard?"

"It seems we suffered around seven hundred killed or wounded. The French have about twice that."

Damn. Carnage, indeed . . . Many a mother shall weep, many a sweetheart shall moan, be they French, Spanish, or English.

The open door looms before us. We look at each other and hesitate before entering the den of what is sure to be the fiercest and most angry of bears. The sounds from within are not encouraging.

"Goodbye, Ensign Connell," I say, as he prepares to go off to join the coterie of messengers. "It was a pleasure knowing you. I do not think I will be seeing you again." I lean into him and put a kiss upon his cheek. "I wish you well."

"Goodbye, Miss, I cannot tell you, but — "

I don't listen for the rest. A light kiss from La Belle Jeune Fille Sans Merci, as well as a bloody one from Bloody Jack herself, should be enough for any young ensign, I figure. Sucking in my breath, I plunge into the room.

Everything is in turmoil. Junior officers fly about the room. Charts and maps are being rolled and stuffed into tubes. Papers are stacked, wrapped in oilcloth, and tied up with twine, and in the midst of it all stands General Sir Arthur Wellesley, ramrod straight, and in a state of obvious rage.

"Stupidity! Rank stupidity! The braying jackasses of Britain have done it again! Hurrah! Hurrah for rank asininity!" he cries, waving his arms about. "Stand up, ye gods of misrule! Stand up and cheer because Britannia bends her knee to you!"

If I did not know the man was of an abstemious nature,

I would swear he was blind drunk. I duck down through the crowd and find Higgins with Mr. Scovell, collecting their own papers into folders.

"Higgins! What is going on?"

Higgins looks up.

"Good to see you, Miss. You have something of a nasty scratch there. We must see to that."

"Later, Higgins. What's up?"

"General Wellesley has been relieved by General Burrard." Here he lowers his voice. "A man of very little experience in the field. That is bad enough, but . . ."

"But what?"

"Insult to injury, Miss. We have just been informed that General Dalrymple, the other gentleman you might have seen hanging about of late, has just signed the Treaty of Cintra."

"And that would be the surrender of General Junot's French forces?"

"Ah, no, Miss," says Higgins. "The treaty states that the defeated French forces, with all guns and all of their loot, are to be transported back to France in British ships."

"WHAT? Oh, God! And then?"

"And then they'll be let go to do what they will do. They are to be debarked at Toulon."

"But that is absolutely crazy! The French were on the run! They faced either complete surrender or else slaughter! Junot was ready to capitulate!"

"I know, Miss. We all know. Most of all, General Wellesley knows."

Seething with indignation, I say, "I have been ordered to report to him. I must go."

"Careful, Miss," warns Higgins. "I have been ordered to accompany Mr. Scovell back to Britain. As for you — "

That's all I hear as I plunge back through the crowd to worm my way to Wellesley's enraged side.

"Sir!" I say. "You sent for me?"

He looks down and sees me standing there, filthy, dusty, and a bit torn in the face.

"Ah," he says, calming himself a bit. "Here's one who looks like she's been through a battle, rather than lounging about here at headquarters and taking her ease like the rest of you sorry lot."

"I'm sure all here have done their duty, Sir," I reply. "The shells fell all around us, and we know they are not at all selective in whom they hit."

He looks at me curiously. "Well said, girl. I'm beginning to think . . . but never mind." He crosses to a desk and points at a spot on one of the few remaining maps spread out thereon. "Here is the city of Madrid, in Spain, of course. You are to go there . . ."

With sinking heart, I realize I will not be going back to England with Higgins and I will not be any help to Lord Allen, beyond what I have already done.

" . . . and gather information on the forces and the political climate you find there. I must perforce go back to England to clean up this mess, but I shall be back, believe me, and I will need all the good information I can get about Madrid. Information that will be obtained by *you*, Lieutenant Faber. Comandante Montoya has agreed to take you there, under cover of night, and he will be your contact during the time you spend in that city. Do you understand?"

Yes, I'm thinking, *I understand that all my dreams have turned to dust, and now I must do as you say.*

I hit a brace, nod, and bow, for I know there is nothing else. *"Oui, mon générale,"* I say, without thinking.

Uh-oh . . .

But he lets it pass, managing a slight smile and saying only, "Who knows where your loyalties lie, Miss Faber."

"They lie with my country and my friends, Sir. Of that you may be assured."

"Well, good. Be off with you, then. Montoya will want to leave shortly." He turns from me to continue his enraged rant — *Goddamn stupid, ass-kissing, suck-up bureaucrats. God damn them all to hell and back!* — and I nod to Higgins and point outside and leave the room, much less hopeful than when I entered it.

Higgins has a small pack open, and into it he is stuffing clothing and some other things — perfume, caps, underwear, spare dresses, both fine and lowly. No telling what I will need when I get to Madrid.

Montoya leans against the wall, arms crossed, grinning at me as I make my preparations for departure. He could have waited outside, but he did not. The ill-bred brute has not removed his sombrero, either.

"It is best you travel in simple clothing, *muchacha,* so you do not stand out on the way," observes Montoya. "Plenty of time for finery in Madrid. You will see much of that there. The *Majas* and all."

We agree, although I don't pursue the *Maja* thing just yet. There is a dressing screen in the room and I duck behind it to change. I shed my uniform and climb into my good old Lawson Peabody serving-girl rig—black shoes, hose, and skirt; white drawers and blousy shirt; and brown weskit cinched tight around my ribs. I leave my shiv in its sheath on my left forearm and I cover my short blond locks with my dark brunette wig so as to blend in better with the local populace. My pennywhistle is tucked in my vest, and all else I currently own goes into my seabag for Higgins to take back to England with him.

That done, I step out and fluff up my now-black hair. Higgins places my black mantilla on my head and I wrap it around my shoulders and look to Montoya.

He smiles in appreciation.

"Much better, Señorita. You are now the *muchacha campesina perfecta.*"

Higgins straightens up and prepares to take his leave, saying, "I do not wish to offend you, Senhor, but I must point out to you that even though she is entrusted to your care, she remains Crown Property and, as such, must be returned to us in the same condition as when she left."

He is not offended. He sweeps off his hat and bows low. "She shall be treated as the Sanctified and Holy Sister of My Soul in Our Common Struggle Against Tyranny."

Higgins and I exchange glances—as if we believe *that* for even a moment.

"You will like Madrid, Miss. It is quite a lovely place, in spite of its being overrun with those French pigs. I was born and raised there."

"So you are actually Spanish, then?"

"I am many things, *mi querida,* and being actually Spanish is one of them."

"So we can drop the Portuguese, then, Señor, and stick to the Spanish?"

"*Sí, Señorita.*"

"*Bueno.* I am easier in that language."

"It is, indeed, a loving tongue, full of the promise of romance."

Hmmm . . . Just who is this man?

"Well, Señor Montoya, neither love nor romance is in the picture. It is duty that calls and we must go. Are you ready?"

"*Sí, Señorita,*" he says, bowing and gesturing to the door.

I turn to John Higgins and place my hands upon his chest.

"Don't worry about me, John. I have handled randy males before. I have money, clothes, and my shiv. This should be a rather easy assignment. Please give my compliments to Dr. Sebastian and Mr. Peel, and to my grandfather and any of my other friends you might happen to meet. Please write to Ezra and explain the situation. I have told you of my arrangements for Lord Allen. Please do what you can for him. Go now, John. Godspeed."

I push him out the door, sniff back a tear, and hand myself over to Comandante Montoya.

"I am ready, Señor."

"Good. Will you require a coach? A carriage?"

"No, *mi patrón.* Just a good horse and a regular saddle."

"*Bueno.* We shall be off, then."

Indeed we are, and as for what Fate has in store for me, I cannot imagine.

Chapter 9

The light from the campfire flickers on the faces of those of us gathered about. I sit on the ground with my legs pulled up against my chest, my arms around my legs, chin on my knees. We have just eaten a very acceptable mutton stew out of tin containers, washed down with copious quantities of *tinto* — the local red wine — drunk from wineskins held high over open mouths. The moon is high in the sky, sentries are posted, and the gentle strumming of a *guitarra* is heard in the warmth of the Iberian night. It had been decided, mainly by Montoya, that we should travel to Madrid in a small group of his most trusted men, so as not to attract unwarranted attention.

"There are not only bandits out there, Señorita, but also bands of deserters from the French army, who can be even more dangerous than your common outlaw. It is best that we travel light."

And so we did travel.

Montoya is stretched out beside the fire, picking his teeth with a sliver of wood and regaling me with tales of Madrid.

"The beautiful River Tagus runs through the city. Here is a verse from a song that sings of her, little one." He lifts his voice, a voice that is surprisingly soft for such a rough man.

Yes, my hair is turning white,
but the Tagus is always young,
She flows through Madrid as the very blood of life,
Till the end of all time.

"You have something of the poet in you, Comandante," I say. "May I ask what is your first name?"

"If I can have yours, *guapa,* then thou shall have mine."

"I was born with the name Mary."

"Ah, Maria . . . How beautiful . . ."

"But now I go by Jacky."

"I shall call you Maria. It is a name that sits more easily on my tongue," he says, sidling up a little closer to me. "And please, sweet Maria, you must call me Pablo."

Hmmm . . . It seems it is time for a little diversion here.

"Pablo, would you like for me to sing you a song?" I ask.

"By all means, Maria. It would give me great pleasure."

"Then, if I could borrow a guitar?"

"Joachim! Be so good as to lend *nuestra chiquita bonita su guitarra.*"

The instrument is passed to me by the young man I recognize as the very one who had picked me up when I had fallen on the battlefield at Viermo and taken my limp self to hospital. As he hands it to my waiting hands, he smiles and his gaze says to me, *Yes, beautiful English girl, Pablo Montoya is our esteemed leader, the strongest and bravest of us, but I think, pretty one, you would have much more fun with one such as me.* I nestle the guitar into my lap and return the gaze, silently agreeing with him.

"I learned this song in Havana. I hope you will like it." *And I hope you will like it, too, Joachim.* With hooded eyes and a glance to the young man, I strum the first chord and begin:

> *Tú, sólo tú*
> *Has llenado de luto mi vida*
> *Abriendo una herida*
> *En mi corazón.*

"Most beautiful, Maria, perhaps another, to warm a poor man's soul?" Montoya reaches out to pull my mantilla a little bit from my face. "Pardon, *muchacha*, it is only so I can gaze upon your fair countenance in the firelight."

I launch into another of the few Spanish songs I know. *What's going to happen when I run out of them?*

> *Malagueña salerosa*
> *Besar tus labios quisiera*
> *Besar tus labios quisiera*
> *Malagueña salerosa*

He beams in satisfaction and repeats the verse in English:

> *Rose leaves of Málaga*
> *To kiss your wanted lips*
> *To kiss your wanted lips*
> *Rose leaves of Málaga*

And then he adds a bit more:

> *And telling you, beautiful girl*
> *That you are pretty and magical*
> *That you are pretty and magical*
> *As the innocence of a rose*

For a rough country guerrilla, this guy pitches the lines pretty smoothly. *Randall Treveleyne could take a lesson,* I'm thinking.

"Another verse, *mi corazón,* and then perhaps we might lie down together and sleep."

Ummm . . . All right, another verse.

> *Yo no te ofrezco riqueza*
> *Te ofrezco mi corazón*
> *Te ofrezco mi corazón . . .*

CRAACK!

That's as far as I get, as the strings suddenly go limp under my fingers . . .

Wot?

It occurs to my formerly lazy and sleepy mind that a bullet has just shattered the head of the guitar and it is ruined, but worse, now I am in grave danger.

"*DIABLO!*" shouts Montoya, jumping to his feet. "*Asga sus armas, mis hermanos!*"

There are shouts and curses all around.

Banditos! Damn them to hell!

I dive to the ground in a blind panic and scramble away, the rough dirt grinding into my elbows and knees, my mind fixed only on escape. *Please, God, not here, not now!* Bullets whiz all about me as I head toward the scant cover of a low bush.

Allez enfers, Spanish dogs. Go to hell, cochons! Die like the filthy pigs you are!

There are more shots, more screams of agony, more pleas for mercy . . . and from the awful sounds of men gurgling out their last breaths, I know there is very little of that mercy given.

I'm now about twenty yards away from what had been our cozy campfire. I lie still and listen, my breath coming ragged, my heart pounding. The shooting has stopped, but I still hear men running around shouting. I can see shapes darting about in the moonlight, but I cannot tell if they are our men or the attackers.

Best lie low, girl, and wait. When you hear Montoya call out for you, then you will rise and go with him, but not till then.

As I lie there, I reflect that perhaps my singing had lulled the sentries into complacency and for that I am surely sorry. We all should have been more careful. We should have—

Uh-oh! I hear footsteps close by and . . .

"There she is! I told you there was a girl with them!"

Two men loom above me. I try to get to my feet to run, but I am grabbed and thrown back down.

"And you were so right, André, and she looks like a pretty one, too, a proper reward for a poor soldier."

French! Deserters from the Grand Army — surely desperate men! I am lost!

The one named André reaches down and starts tearing

at my clothes. Giving up trying to get into my sturdy vest, he reaches up under my skirt and starts pulling down my drawers. I wriggle and squeal and shout for help, but none comes.

"Oh, this will be so sweet, so sweet, so — "

He stops abruptly. He has found my money belt.

"What is this?" He manages to undo it and opens it up. "Mon Dieu, Henri! It is gold! Much of it!"

There is a high-pitched whistle and a call of *Allons! Allons!*

"Damn! We must go! Damn!"

"Ah, Henri, the gold will make us feel much better. We will be able to buy many women. Hide the pouch from the others. There is no need to share."

In a moment, they are gone and all is silence. Breathless, I wait for signs of Montoya and his men, but nothing comes. No call that all is well, no rescue, no nothing.

Not wanting to silhouette myself against the moonlit sky, I crawl farther away and into a small ravine.

I wait . . . I wait . . . and then curl up into a ball and then . . . sleep.

Chapter 10

When dawn breaks, I poke my head cautiously out of my hiding place and look out over this particularly dry and desolate part of Spain, and try to quell the despair that's about to overwhelm me. There is not a soul to be seen, neither French enemy nor Spanish friend.

Groaning, stiff in every joint, I rise to my feet and look in all directions. I see nothing but low scrubby trees, reddish-yellow dirt, and rocks . . . Lots of rocks. Although I know that England is no younger than Spain, somehow this land gives the impression of having been ground down to its very bare bones, then weathered through the ages. Not a country for those looking for the lush life. Not here, anyway.

I stumble down to our former campsite. I see the dead fire, ringed with now cold stones, and I see blood spattered here and there, but I do not observe any bodies. They probably took their dead with them. Montoya must have been killed, else he would have come back for me. I know that he would have . . . *Requiescat in pacem, Pablo.*

There is the overturned pot of shepherd's stew, now

empty, and discarded cartridges scattered about. Nothing else — nothing that might aid me in . . . *Ah, what's this?* It is a wineskin, and it seems to be about half full. That's something. I shan't die of thirst. Not right off, anyway.

Again I look around, this time a little more carefully, shading my eyes with my hand. I am on a hilly plain, but there — far to what I perceive to be the north — is a low line of mountains. The Sierra de Gredos, Montoya had called them, telling me they lay to the west of Madrid, with the River Tagus running through the foothills of that mountain range.

Bueno. I shall go in that direction, but first I need to take stock of my situation. This is what I possess:

1. Self, relatively whole
2. Black skirt, stockings, shoes, cap; brown vest and dark wig; white shirt, drawers
3. My shiv, secure in its sheath
4. My pennywhistle, no, alas. Somehow it got lost in last night's scuffle. I had looked around for it but could not find it. Maybe some faun will pick it up to entertain the local nymphs. From the dryness around here, I fear the river naiads will be few.
5. Black wig and mantilla

That's it. I look at what I have and decide what to do. First I take off the wig, shed the dress, rip the flounces off my drawers, and strip off the vest and shirt. Then, wearing the vest as an underlayer, I cinch it tight, throw my shirt back on over it, and stuff all the remaining items into a pouch made of the mantilla, which now looks very much like a fisherman's net bag. Some dirt is rubbed over stubble on head and little Maria once again becomes bold young Jacques . . . or Juan . . . or whatever it is in this country.

A young girl alone on the road, very much in danger. A ragged boy alone on the road? Who cares? I reflect once again that sometimes it's easier being a boy.

After I trudge along for a while, I mount a small hill and see, with some relief, a road. A crude road, to be sure — it's no more than two narrow furrows worn in the hard ground by countless wagon wheels — but still a road, nonetheless. *I will take what I can get,* says I, and I hurry down to take advantage of it. Where there is a road, there will be people, and that is what I want and very much need. I am growing hungry . . . very hungry.

I take the wineskin from my shoulder, open the nozzle, lift the skin, and squirt a bit of the juice of the grape into my mouth. It is good, but sometimes water is better, and right now, I wish I had some.

I walk on, humming a tune to keep my spirits up, and I think of friends . . .

Dear Amy, I cannot post a letter to you, dearest Sister, from where I am, but I can think fondly on thee. I hope that thou art — sorry, in speaking Spanish one picks up these idioms — I hope that you are well and in good spirits. Where am I, you might ask? Well, somewhere in Spain, ragged, dirty, and trudging along a dusty road, seeking some relief from thirst and hunger. But, hey, you know that I can deal with that sort of thing.

A friend told me of the River Manzanares, which lies

somewhere up ahead and flows through the city of Madrid, so I know that if I can find that river, it will lead me there.

I play a game of kick the pebbles as I walk along, assigning myself the task of kicking the pebbles as far as they will go while still staying on the roadway. Did pretty well on the last one . . . Let's see if I can beat it . . . there's a likely looking rock, I'll —

Later, Amy. Someone's coming!

I hear a wagon lurching up the road far behind me. As it approaches, I look it over carefully, ready to run if necessary, but it seems to contain only an old man who is vigorously cursing the mule that is reluctantly hauling him along. I go to the side of the road and wait for them to draw abreast.

"*Perdoneme, Señor,*" I say, putting on my best poor-little-waif look as he pulls up next to me. "I am going to Madrid. Can you tell me how far I have to go?"

"Madrid? Ha! You have a ways to travel, boy. I am sure you shall wear out the soles of those shoes well before you get there!"

"Then perhaps, Señor, you might offer me a ride and save my poor feet from destruction? God will bless you for it."

"Perhaps He might, *chico.* But maybe if there is good wine in that sack and if you are of a mind to share it, perhaps Papa Padron will give you that ride."

"*Por supuesto,* Señor Padron," I say, eagerly climbing up into the seat next to him. He clucks at the mule and we begin moving forward while I pull the wineskin from my shoulder and offer it to my host. He uncorks it, holds it to his mouth, and then slowly draws it away, the wine making a fine red arc from its nozzle to his open maw. He corks the skin, swallows, and hands it back to me.

"*Madre de Dios!*" he exults. "That feels good on a poor man's throat!"

I lift the wine and take a draught myself, figuring that the wine will soon be gone and I should make sure to get my share.

"I am pleased you like it, Papa Padron," I say, settling in for the ride. I note with disappointment that the wagon is filled with firewood, not with something that I might eat. Pity, that.

"You speak in a strange way, lad," observes Padron. "Why is that?"

"I come from America, Señor. My name is Juan. I learned to speak Spanish while sailing on the Caribbean Sea."

"Is that so? Then you shall tell me stories of America and I shall take you to where this road crosses the River Manzanares. You follow that river north for some sixty miles and it will lead you to Ciudad Madrid!"

And tell him stories I do, and Papa Padron discovers that I am very good at it. The miles roll by most pleasantly, as the wine goes down and is soon gone. It turns out that Papa does have a bit of cheese and bread, and he shares it with me. I'm finding that, while there is much that is evil and vile in the world, most people are good at heart.

Later, much later, as night is about to fall, we come to a stone bridge crossing a small river.

"Here is where our paths must part, *chico*," says Padron, allowing the poor, long-suffering mule to stop. "It is the

River Manzanares. Madrid is that way." He points upriver. "Good luck to you, Juanito. You were good company."

"Muchas gracias, Señor," I say, climbing down. "Thank you for the ride. May you live long and prosper, Papa Padron."

He clucks at the mule and his wagon clatters over the bridge and is gone.

I leave the road and walk down to the riverbank, where I look at the water flowing past me and think on things . . .

I know, from the maps laid out before me back at General Wellesley's headquarters, that this river flows down to the River Jarama and the Jarama flows into the Tagus and the Tagus flows through Spain and Portugal and out to the Atlantic at Lisbon. I look downriver. *Hmmm . . . I could steal a boat and float on the current till I reached that port and could then book passage back to London . . . or Boston. Naval Intelligence must surely have lost track of me by now. Or I could take a ship to Rangoon and see about Jaimy . . .*

But then again, I have no food, no money, and with my whistle being gone, no way to get any, and it's a long way from here to Lisbon. Besides, once there, what would I use to book passage?

I look upriver. *Madrid is up there. If I go to that city, I will still have no food, no money . . .*

As if adding its voice to the discussion, my belly rumbles. I know I have eaten today, but tomorrow that belly will demand more, and it will be most insistent. I face north and begin walking.

To hell with it. Let's see what Madrid's got. At least it's closer.

PART II

Chapter 11

The sixty miles from Papa Padron and his mule to the city of Madrid are some of the hardest miles I have ever traveled, be they at sea or on land.

I do not lack for water, for there is plenty of that along the River Manzanares as I work my way into Madrid. Remembering how I had gotten mighty thirsty on the way here, I fill up my wineskin for future use. I do, however, lack for food. My empty belly comes up to rest against my backbone yet again.

But the weather is mild, so I resolve to stop whining and make the best of things and push ever on, stopping only at night to sleep under a convenient tree or bridge. Most of the traffic along the river is by canal boats far out in the stream, so there is scant chance of my catching another ride. I know oranges grow in Spain, but I sure don't see any. There is some sort of root vegetable growing in a field that borders the river, but when I go to investigate, I am chased away by an angry farmer waving a very lethal-looking pitchfork.

Oh Lord, it's been three days since I've had anything to eat and your poor girl is so very, very hungry . . .

I see nothing of the edible plants Professor Tilden had told us about back on the *Dolphin*. When first I came to this slow-moving stream, I had gone down the riverbank to see what I could find. There were reeds sticking up out of the water all around me and I choked down a few of their leaves, but they were bitter and my belly rebelled and threw them right back up. When I was with the Shawnee, back there on the Mississippi, Tepeki and the other Shawnee girls showed me the good things to eat that grew along their big river, but there sure ain't no cattails nor wild rice around here, no. I've been gnawing on about everthing I can find, but I ain't found nothin' edible yet. Things are looking grim. My belly is flat and I'm still a long way from Madrid. What I would give for a nice, fat turnip, even though I don't really like turnips . . . or didn't used to.

Ah, dear Amy. Yes, it's me again thinking of you and the dear old Lawson Peabody and in particular those wonderful breakfasts that Peg would serve—eggs fried sunny-side up, the yolks all gleaming golden yellow, crisp bacon browned just right, melted butter oozing off a hot, fluffy biscuit. Oh Lord, please . . . Wait, what's that?

That is a mushroom, a big mushroom, standing right over there. It is a rather pretty mushroom, considering it's growing out of what looks like an old pile of cow flop. I squat down to pluck it up and I gaze at it closely. It's got a shiny orange top and its gills glisten with a purplish irides-cence. It looks uncommonly juicy out here in all this desert dryness. My mouth waters . . .

And yes, I did eat that mushroom. I closed my eyes and ate it. It felt good in my mouth, tingling even on my tongue, but it wasn't very filling, so I just swallowed and pushed on down along the riverbank . . .

I don't get very far when things start to look a little . . . strange . . . weird, like. *Must be the hunger,* I'm thinkin'. The sun is hot and beatin' down on me brain and *what was that?* From the corner of my eye, I thought I saw a mouse skitter away . . . just a little mouse, but in a white suit of clothes and a top hat, of all things. Curious, that. I swear he tipped his hat as he skittered off. *Wot the hell?* I shakes me head to clear it, but that don't help much, no it don't. *There seems to be a slight purple haze around the edges of things . . . geez . . . I blink my eyes and my vision clears, but I dunno . . .*

I go on staggerin' along the river, turnin' over rocks, looking for anything, *anything,* to eat — a nice fat grub don't seem all that disgusting right now. But all I find is slimy centipede-like things and I ain't quite ready for that. Ain't seen no people in a while — the last ones I did see was too poor for me to beg anything off of so I didn't even bother, no, just keep pushin' on.

I'm on my hands and knees in the reeds and suddenly I hear *Mary . . . Little Mary Faber . . . Come to me, my child,* and I look up and, wonder of wonders, there is a white-robed figure, surrounded by a brilliant purple haze, standing on the opposite bank, his face glowing with a heavenly radiance, his arms upraised and beckoning to me. It's . . .

Jesus? Lord? You've finally come for me! Oh, yes, Lord!

I stretch my own arms out to Him, but then I blink my

eyes and Jesus is gone. In His place is the trunk of an old, dead tree, its outstretched limbs withered and sere.

Must be the sun, I'm thinking, and not too clearly at that. I lean forward and duck my face into the cool water. *I wish it had been you, Jesus. I'm sure You would have given me something to eat. I just know You would've 'cause you loves me . . . Manna from heaven, and this water turned into red, red wine, milk and honey, loaves and fishes, even, oh, yes . . .*

It's then that I see him. He's right over there, 'cross a little stretch of water. No, no, not Jesus again, no . . . It's a big, *big* ol' bull, bullfrog. I peer through the reeds and see him right over there, across the shallow water, sitting on a hollow log — yes, he is a mighty bullfrog. A nice *fat* bullfrog. Must be a good two, three, maybe four pounds, if he's an ounce. As I watch him, drool beginnin' to pool in my mouth, he puffs up his big throat till it looks like a big shiny ball and then he lets out with a big . . .

BARRROOOOOOMMMM.

Shedding my pants and shirt, I flip them and my bag over on dry land and slip into the water. I find, as I move forward, the water betwixt the frog and me is about waist deep.

My mind, which is busy doin' some real funny things, goes back to that time in the Caribbean with Joannie and Daniel on the *Nancy B.* with Jemimah Moses tellin' her animal tales, and my crazy brain slips right into it . . .

Hello, Brother Frog. How you been?

The bullfrog brings his big googly eyes to look upon me.

Well, hello, Sister Girl. I been jus' fine. Whatcha got on yo' mind?

94

My mind is to eat you, Brother Bullfrog—legs, belly, croaker, and all, that's what.

Hmmm . . . I might be havin' a bit of a problem wi' dat, Sister Jacky. What makes you tink you can 'complish dat t'ing?

It's 'cause I'm low and cunning and powerful hungry and I'll get it done, you'll see, Brother. You be restin' in my belly soon.

Y'know, Sister, I recalls that Brother Fox and Brother Bear tried alla time to eat Brother Rabbit but it never happened, no. And Brother Heron and Sister Crane alla time tryin' to bag my skinny ass, too. Brother Black Snake give it a try or two, as well, but it ain't happened yet, no Ma'am. Don't 'spect it's gonna happen here, neither.

Yeah, but I'm smarter and quicker and a whole lot hungrier den dose brothers and sisters and I'm afraid it is gonna happen to yo' sweet self.

Ahhhh . . . uuummmm. We see.

Y'know, Brother Bullfrog, I done et up a bunch o' froggy legs when I was in France, all fried up crispy and crackly, and they was right good, you bet. Yer legs'll be good, too, even though I ain't got nothin' to cook 'em on.

I mourns for my poor French brethren, but this here's Spanish land, Sister. You'll find me a whole lot cagier than them other poor frogs. I got some gypsy frog in me.

We'll see, Brother Bullfrog, we'll see 'bout dat. You'll notice I'm creepin' closer and closer to your delicious self, movin' smooth through dis water just like any Mississippi bayou gator.

My big googly eyes do see dat, Sister.

You jes' sit still now, Brother.

Cain't do that, Sister Girl. Been good talkin' to you, but I gotta be off on my bidness.

With that, the frog gathers his strength and launches himself into the air above my head, chucklin' to hisself.

I, however, gather my own strong legs and leap high out of the water and grab his slippery self right behind his big ol' belly and wrap my hands around his nice, plump legs.

Got you now, Brother!

Oh, Lawsy, I think you does, Sister Girl! I'm one gone bullfrog!

That you is, Brother, that you is. Prepare to meet de Lord!

Just then a bunch of little frogs on the bank set up to peeping — *peep peep, peep peep, our Big Daddy's got hisself caught, peep peep!*

Dat's true, chillun, looks like yer Big Daddy's goin' off to heaven. He gon' croak in dat Heavenly Choir! Hallelujah!

Dat's right, Frog, says I, hardenin' my heart and tightenin' my grip. *I hears dey needs a good bass-o pro-fund-o up dere and you be just the ting, I'm t'inkin'.*

Yo' prolly right, Sister Girl, buts now I gots to say goodbye to my fam'ly . . . Ahem! You peepers be good to Big Mama now and help her when Big Daddy done gone off to his reward . . .

We do dat, Big Daddy, but oh, peep peep, we hates to see you go, peep peep!

. . . and you tadpoles swimmin' 'round Sister Girl's toes, you grow up big and strong and make yer Big Daddy proud, y'hear?

Hmmm . . . I do notice somethin' messin' about my feet,

and bubbles, little purple bubbles, rise to the surface by my knees and each one pops with a *peep* when it bursts.

Peep peep, peep peep, the tads go, *peep peep peep, please, Sister Girl, don't take our daddy, don't take our daddy . . . peep peep peep.*

No, t'ain't no use, tads. Sister Jacky has hardened her heart. Big Daddy gotta go, chillum. He bein' called up yonder.

Oh, Big Daddy, please don't go! Peep peep!

Oh, he's a-goin' all right, I says as I lifts him up, open my mouth, and bare the Faber fangs. *He's a-goin' straight down inta my belly! Oh, yes!*

Sister Girl, I gots one last request 'fore I goes off t' join dat heavenly band.

And dat is, Brother? I say, takin' his head outta my mouth and lookin' in his big ol' eyes.

I wants to give one last big croak so's Saint Peter be knowin' I'll be showin' up at the Heavenly Gates.

Awright, you do dat, Brother Bullfrog, but make it quick.

The frog huffs and swells up his throat till it looks like a big shiny ball again and then lets it out . . .

BARRRROOOOOM!

. . . right into my face.

Oh, Gawd, Brother, that is so foul! I say, gasping for breath. *What the HELL have you been eatin'?*

Oh, just the usual, Sister Girl, flies and moths and sluggly bugs. Hey, wait'll you get to gnawing on my belly — lots o' surprises in dere.

I fall to my knees in the shallow water and despair of my fate.

Peep peep, peep peep, the tads go, *peep peep peep!*

I'll let you go, Brother Bullfrog, on one condition, says I, givin' the rascal a good squeeze such that his eyes bug out even more.

And dat is, Sister Girl? he wheezes, unable to draw breath.

THAT YOU TELL THEM TO SHUT THE HELL UP AND GET OUTTA MY HEAD!

Peep peep, peep peep . . .

Awright, quiet down now, chillun, says Brother Bullfrog, and the swamp goes silent.

I gently return Big Daddy to his pond and watch him as he kicks slowly back to his log, not hurrying a bit, oh no, as that is plainly not his style. He then climbs back upon it, in the same spot where I first laid eyes on him.

Looks like you won, Brother, I says, still on my knees in the water with my head down. *And I'll prolly be joinin' the heavenly band 'fore you, as I am feeling mighty weak right now, and I am gettin' ready to slough off dis mortal coil and go be with the angels.*

Now, Sister Jacky, don't despair o' dis world jus' yet, says the Bullfrog, fixing me with his googly eyes and smilin' all 'cross his face. *Y'know, under the flat rock yo see over dere? Yeah, dat big shiny black one . . .*

I looks over and sees the one he means.

Now, under dere you just might find some crawdaddies — yep, the very same smartass crawdaddies what have been pinching at Big Daddy's webbed feet after I told 'em not to, and you know dat ain't right, no. See you later, Sister Girl, you keep well now, y'hear?

• • •

98

Later, as I trudge along, my mind now clear, I spot some more of those mushrooms and I pick them. I don't eat any more of 'em, oh no. What I do is spread them out on rocks to dry when I stop for a rest, and it don't take long for them to shrivel and dry up real small, so's I can stash them in my bag. Specimens for Dr. Sebastian, I tell myself. But who knows?

And, as I push on toward Madrid, I wonder just how much of the last hour was real. I dunno . . . But what I do know is that three nice crawfish tails now rest in my belly, giving me some sustenance, and three well-sucked heads now lie empty on the bank of the river.

Thanks, Big Daddy.

Chapter 12

I enter the city of Madrid on its southeastern side, still following the River Manzanares. The banks of the river change from earth and mud to the stone walls of a canal as it wends its way into the heart of the city. I would find it quite beautiful if I weren't still so damned hungry.

I eventually come to a large, open plaza that lies along the shore, and I see tall cathedrals in all directions, busy streets with many market stalls lining them. There are charcoal braziers smoking in some of the stalls and very good smells come from them. I am about to fall to my knees, ready to beg for something, anything, to eat. It's been three days since the crawfish and they are now but a sweet memory.

No. You have come too far in this life. You will not beg. You have no whistle, you have no guitar, you have no paints, no brushes, you have nothing you can sell . . . nada . . . But no, there is one thing that you can sell, and that is your body, and that is what you shall sell . . . and you will do it now.

I duck into an alley and quickly turn back into a

girl — black skirt and stockings on, vest in proper place over my white shirt, wig on head, with mantilla over that. Done.

When I had first come to the plaza, I had noticed an artist sitting before an easel, painting a picture of the river and the flowering bushes that grow along the banks. He is pretty good, I notice. He is wearing a white smock and a floppy straw hat to keep the sun from his eyes.

I go up to him.

"Your pardon, Señor," I say, hands clasped behind me, all demure and respectful.

He looks up at me, suspicion writ plain on his face.

"What do you want, girl? I am busy."

"My name is Jacquelina. I am a model, and I will pose for you in return for food and lodging."

He looks me over with what I take to be scorn.

"What you are is a peasant girl run off from some dirty little farm," he sneers. "But that does not matter to me. No. I only paint God's green earth."

"I am sorry to have disturbed you, Maestro," I say, backing away.

I think calling him "master" softened him up a bit.

"Wait," he says, as I walk away. He takes his brush and points to a house up a nearby street. "Go there. Go to la Casa del Sordo."

I follow his point. *What is it? A brothel?* I am confused.

"I don't understand, Señor. I don't know what that means."

"It is the house of the deaf man. Go to him. His name is Goya. He hires models to pose for him."

I thank him and head for the doorway of the house he

had indicated. Weak with hunger, I manage to get to the door, lift the knocker, and give it two sharp raps. I put my weary forehead against the heavy oak and wait.

Presently the door is opened a crack and the sharp, inquisitive face of a young woman pokes out.

"*Qué quiere usted?*" it asks.

"I wish to apply for work as an artist's model. I was told to come here."

She gives me the once over, then says, "No. You were told wrong. Go away." The door begins to close.

I'm about to heave a heavy sigh and move on when I hear, "Wait, Carmelita. *Qué pasa?*"

I stick the Faber foot in the door to prevent its closing.

"I am Jacquelina Bouvier. I am a professional model, looking for work. Will I find some here?"

The door opens and a young man looks out at me. He says nothing, but only looks me over in an appraising way.

"Well, does your master hire models or not?" I persist.

"He does, but — "

"Where is he? I will speak to him." I frost the young man with the full Lawson Peabody Look from under my black mantilla, which I suspect does not appear very impressive, given my current condition. Still, I push my way into the foyer. It is not in my nature to be rude and forward, but the gnawing hunger in my belly gives me the will to do this.

"He . . . he is in the studio."

"Good. What is your name, young man?"

"A-Amadeo . . . I am Maestro Goya's student."

Even in my present state of near desperation, I see that

he is quite the good-looking young lad—short-cut glossy black hair, liquid brown eyes, trim body . . . *Hmmm* . . . very handsome, indeed. A bit shy, too . . . all to the good.

"Very well, Amadeo. Introduce me to the great man, *por favor*," I say, laying my hand on his arm and giving him what I can work up in a sultry stare. "You won't regret it, I promise."

Amadeo shrugs and leads me on. The girl, Carmelita, shoots a look of distaste my way, but I ignore it as I follow the student artist down the hall, through some doors, and into a large room illuminated with high windows and filled all around with canvases in various states of completion. There are many of a historical nature, many portraits . . . and some nude studies. *Oh, well, everyone knows I am not shy in that regard, and if I were promised something to eat, I would pose starkers on top of a flagpole in the town square.*

It turns out I don't have to do that. Not right now, anyway.

The painter sits at an easel, apparently touching up the background on a medium-size portrait of a young blond girl, about ten years old, very richly dressed, and very well done.

Maestro, indeed.

Goya is a man of late middle years, broad of build, wearing a blousy white shirt. He seems intensely concentrated on his work. He does not turn around at our approach.

"The Maestro cannot hear. He can speak, but you must write out anything you wish to say to him." Amadeo nods toward several small slates scattered about the studio. There is a large one on an easel, as well. Chalk dangles on a string from that one.

Amadeo motions for me to follow him into the painter's field of vision. When we enter it, the artist glances up from his work, looking not at all pleased.

"What is this, Amadeo?" he asks in a low, growly voice.

I take my cue and go to the large board and pick up the chalk to write.

"My name is Jacquelina. I am a model. Will you give me work?"

He puts down the brush and looks me over. I have been looked over a lot today, I reflect.

"You have worked as such before?"

I nod, and say, "*Sí, Señor.*"

"*Desnuda?*"

"*Sí, Señor*," I say, and apply the chalk once again. "For a sculptor, Maestro Simms, of Boston, *un ciudad en los Estados Unidos de America.*" I do not mention that old Simms was a woodcarver whose main business was in providing ships with figureheads, rather than being a true sculptor. But I did pose for him. And in the altogether, as it were . . . or was.

"You are from there?"

"*Sí, Maestro.*" I write *por favor* in big letters with two exclamation points on the board and put on the full woeful-waif look.

He looks doubtful. I know I am not very large in certain of the usual female attributes. *Voluptuous* is a word seldom associated with the Jacky Faber frame, but I do have an ace in the hole, and I play it.

Reaching up, I pull off both my mantilla and wig, then

hold up my face such that the light falls on the planes of my features. The blind Shantyman, Enoch Lightner, once told me I had good bones as he ran his knowing hands over my face that night in my cabin on the *Lorelei Lee*. I hope he was right.

Goya shows a bit of shock. His eyes play over my hopeful countenance and shorn head. Then he smiles and says, "Yes, you may stay. You shall help around the studio. You'll sweep up and you will grind paints. And you will pose. Amadeo, take her away and acquaint her with her duties—"

"Oh, *gracias, Señor!*"

"And get her something to eat. She looks like she could use it."

Oh, glory!

Chapter 13

"You eat like a pig," snorts this Carmelita, gazing down upon me with complete disapproval, her arms crossed on her chest, her eyebrows drawn down into a frown. She is thin, dark, and, as far as I can tell, about my age. She was assigned to see that the new member of Estudio Goya got something to eat, and she plainly did not like being given that task.

We are in the kitchen of Casa Goya, and I have been given a spoon and a bowl of delicious stew. She stands over me as I eat.

Oh God, thank you! It may not be your manna from your heaven, but it's so awfully good!

I take my nose out of the wonderful bowl of greasy broth swimming with chunks of meat and dumplings long enough to glare at her and say, "I have not eaten anything in three days. You try it sometime, Carmelita. You'll find it does nothing for your manners." I stick the nose back in the stew and commence shoveling it into my mouth and down my neck. *Oh, this is so good!*

"To you, girl, I am Señorita Gomez. You have been

hired as a servant and as a model, nothing more. It would be well for you to remember that."

"Very well, Señorita Gomez, as you will have it."

I reflect that, once again, Jacky Faber is being told her place in this world — well, so be it. I am reminded of my welcome to the Lawson Peabody School for Young Girls by my old enemy, and sometime ally, Clarissa Worthington Howe. She put me in my place, that's for sure.

"You are merely a model," continues Señorita Gomez. "You debase yourself by taking off your clothes in front of men." She draws herself up and looks down her nose at me. The nostrils of that nose, I notice, are dilated and quivering in a high degree of disgust.

But whereas Clarissa had a rod of steel rammed up her backbone, I sense that this one has not. Neither inner strength nor class, and Clarissa had class up the ass, that's for sure, and sometimes class does tell.

"As such, you are nothing but a common slut." She puffs up. "I, however, am a respected student here, like Señor Amadeo Romero and the others. You will stand naked before us and I will draw you, but I will not like it. I have no wish to gaze upon your dirty body and I so wish you were not here."

Ah, Clarissa, my enemy, my friend, my sister-in-arms, where are you now? Causing trouble and breaking hearts, I hope.

I take spoon from mouth to look up at my present tormentor. Somehow I get the feeling that this girl and I will never call each other "sister" with any affection, but I do not care about that. I run my finger around the interior of the bowl of stew, and it encounters a nice small marrowbone. I take it up, bite off the top, and suck on it loudly.

I lean back in my chair, legs spread wide, bone in hand, and grin up at her. "But Amadeo Romero just might, eh?"

She is astounded.

"Puta!" she spits as she turns and rushes out the kitchen door.

"The dirtiness of my body could be resolved by a nice bath!" I call after her retreating form. "Can you arrange that, Señorita Carmelita Gomez, Respected Student?"

She does not answer and I go back to my stew. *Ummmm . . .*

I do not care about any of her opinions, nor am I concerned over what any of them think. My once-slack belly is now full, and for the moment, it is content and so am I. As my hunger abates, I look around the rafters of the kitchen hung with much good food, and I ponder things.

Do you realize, Señorita Carmelita Gomez, that, discounting what I already have put in my belly, there is much here that I could steal if any of you should turn your backs for even a moment? Oh, yes, I am quite an accomplished thief, born and bred to the art. Ah, yes, now, what would I take from here to stuff into my bag? Hmmm, well, maybe some of those fat sausages hanging there, all dark brown and shiny with goodness, or perhaps those thick and heavy braided breads? Why, they could sustain me for weeks as I make my way back to Lisbon. I know the watery route and I'm confident I could get there, many days away from your silly little kingdom, you smug little bitch. Know, too, that given a darkened alcove and a moment's notice, I could whip out my shiv and slit that nasty little throat of yours.

Ah, yes, but let us not speak of that. I will stay to see just how things lie here at Casa Goya. There might possibly be something profitable for both me . . . and my mission. Who knows? There were some pretty fancy people portrayed in those portraits I saw in the studio. One of them looked like she could be a princess. Hmmm . . .

I may stay, and I may not. We shall see.

Soon after Carmelita Gomez had rushed out in a fury, Amadeo Romero entered. Somehow I thought it would be so.

He stands before me.

"Please be seated, Señor Romero, and join me in a glass of *rioja*."

No wine has yet been offered to me, but this does the trick. He signals to someone and a bottle and two glasses are produced. He pulls out a chair and sits across from me. It is he who pours the ruby red wine.

"Muchas gracias, Señor," I say, lifting the glass to him. I pick up the small cloth that has been provided for me, and dab it at my lips, playing things much more demure and ladylike now that my demanding gut has been satisfied for the time being. "Perhaps you will tell me how things are here at La Quinta Goya?"

He gazes at me over the rim of his glass and says, "I will do that, Señorita, but first you must tell me something of yourself. To begin with, how came you by that very interesting thing on your neck?"

With my wig off, my dragon tattoo is now quite visible to them what deigns to look. The wine is now warming the stew in my belly, so I proceed to tell him, sticking pretty much to the truth . . . and I tell him also of the other tattoo, the one on my hip, and how I got it. Why not? He's going to see it soon, anyway.

"You seem to have had many adventures, Señorita. I am amazed."

"True, but there were none of them that I really wanted to have, and they were much more terrifying than amazing," I say. "But now that I have told you something about my poor self, Señor, you must tell me of how things lie here. I need to know."

"Well, the cook, whom you have already met, is Ramona."

Ramona, from her station at the stove, raises a ladle in greeting upon hearing her name uttered.

"You are a very good cook, Ramona," I call over to her, having just tasted the results of her skill. "My compliments."

She nods her head in appreciation but does not turn around.

"And you have been *er . . . welcomed* by Señorita Gomez."

Here I give him a knowing wink, and he smiles in return and continues.

"There are two other students, a young man named Asensio Julia and a lad named Cesar Rivera. You shall meet them later, as there will be a class this afternoon and you will be required to be there . . . in a servant's role, this time."

"Of course, Señor. I expect nothing more."

"And Maestro has a manservant, Manuel Garcia, and there is the chambermaid, Paloma, and that is all. It is a very simple household."

"Does he have a wife? Goya, I mean."

"Yes. Her name is Josefa, but she is quite ill. You will not see much of her. They have had many children over the

110

years but only one, Javier, survived infancy. So sad. Maestro has many very gloomy days."

Ah, the Black Cloud of Despair. I know it well.

"I heard you tell the Maestro that you are from America. Is that true?"

I point to my Golden Dragon tattoo and my shorn hair. "Look at me. Where else could I have come from?"

He smiles at that.

"Actually, when I first saw you at our door in your mantilla, I mistook you for a *Maja*."

"And what is that, Señor?" I ask, but I don't get to find out, not just yet, anyway.

"Amadeo!" barks Carmelita from the door. "Enough hanging about with the servants! The class is starting!"

I go into the studio with some trepidation. The other students are there, setting up their easels. Since they are putting boards on them, to which sheets of paper are attached, it is plain that the class will be in drawing. They look at me with some interest as I enter.

Before reporting for duty at the studio, I had been taken upstairs and shown my bed in a small room that I will share with Paloma. It looks comfortable enough — better than the hard ground upon which I have been sleeping, that's for sure. Paloma, herself, plump and round of face and black of hair, seems to be a cheerful sort and I know we will get along. *Gracias a Dios* that I don't have to sleep in the same room with that mean Carmelita.

I am introduced to the others and give a slight bob of the head at the mention of each name. I have put my wig back on so as not to attract any more attention than I already have. Paloma has lent me a servant's white mobcap, which I perched on top of my fake tresses. I decided to leave my mantilla up in my room, figuring it would be in the way. When I saw the work that had to be done, I knew that I was right in thinking that.

After the introductions, I am led by Amadeo to a workbench on the other the side of the room and shown how to grind pigments into paints.

"Here. You see the glass plate here? You'll note the surface has some tooth, some roughness to it. *Bueno.* Now you take this spatula and ladle over some of this color. It is yellow ochre. Maestro uses a lot of it. And we put it right there."

I look on attentively. Oil paints! I have never worked with oil paints! Not that I'm likely to be allowed that pleasure here, but we shall see.

"Then we add some oil . . ."

He takes a flagon and dribbles a bit on the bright powder.

"Not too much . . . That's it. Now you take the spatula and mix it up into as smooth a paste as you can make."

I take the tool and whip it back and forth through the puddle of color. Looks good enough to me, but I find it is not.

"Now, Jacquelina, you must take the muller to it," he says, and he grasps a thing that looks like a squat potato masher, except that the handle, sticking up from its back, is off center. He grunts a bit as he lifts it and places it flat down on the mess of powder and oil, and then he starts to spin it around and around. It makes a *swoosh*ing sound as it does its work.

"You see, the color must be ground into the oil or it will not be smooth. Here, you try it."

I put my hand on the handle and attempt to move the thing around like Amadeo did, but it does not move. I grind my teeth and try again, but it is just too heavy. *Madre de Dios! This thing must weigh half as much as I do! What do they expect of me?*

"Here, *chica,* let me help you," says Amadeo, coming around behind me and putting his arm about my waist and placing his hand over mine on the muller. He starts it spinning again. "See, you just have to get it started and then it goes a lot more easily." He takes away his hand, and wonder of wonders, I am able to keep it going. *Well, that's much better, isn't it?*

I sneak a look over at Carmelita and note that she has not missed a bit of this and is *not* pleased. If looks could kill, I would be dead.

"Keep it going for about five more minutes, and then ladle it into one of those bladders there. Then clean off the platen with turpentine, and mix the raw umber next. It's right there."

"Thank you, Amadeo," I murmur as he removes his arm. "I will try to do it to your utmost satisfaction."

Is that a growl from Carmelita? I certainly hope so.

Amadeo goes back to his easel and takes up a piece of charcoal and gets ready for the arrival of the Master.

He does not have to wait long. The door opens and Maestro Goya enters the room and is followed shortly by a large man dressed in working clothes. The big man says nothing but goes behind a dressing screen, and presently his clothing appears, looping over the screen, piece by piece. There was a red robe hanging on that screen, and it snakes over the edge and disappears. I keep grinding.

I find that by keeping both of my hands on the muller handle I can keep it going without too much trouble, but I do have to get my shoulders into it.

The man emerges from behind the screen and steps up on a low platform, his broad face impassive.

"Pose, please," says Goya, and the man drops the robe and stands there completely naked. He is very strongly built — plainly a workingman who labors with his hands and his strong back. All his muscles stand out in sharp definition, without his even flexing them. His legs are like the trunks of trees, his arms like truncheons, his chest as broad as a barrel. Indeed, a fine figure of a man . . . and a perfect male model.

"With the spear, Jorge," orders the Master, and the man picks a spear from the rack of props on the back wall and assumes a gladiatorial posture. Goya adjusts the pose slightly, and then says, "Begin."

I finish up the yellow ochre and turn to the dull brown raw umber. As I mix and grind away, I watch the progress of the students — they are all quite good — and I listen to Goya's advice to each.

I am getting the hang of this grinding business, and I am glad of that, for I always like to do my duty, and do it well, but . . .

But what I'd really like, in my heart of hearts, is to be at my very own easel, with my own piece of charcoal in my hand, and my own eye on the model . . .

Chapter 14

Dinner involves the entire staff of Estudio Goya. It is cooked by Ramona, of course, and is served by Paloma and by me, at a long table at the far end of the kitchen, just off the pantry. I had been relieved of my color-grinding duties after the drawing class was over, and I stumbled down the stairs to the kitchen, my shoulders and elbows aching.

"Here, *muchacha,* set out the glasses and pour the wine," says Paloma, upon seeing me enter. She hands me a tray of glassware. "Over there."

I see, at the end of the kitchen, a large, heavy oaken table that is already set with plates and utensils for a goodly number of people. Wearily, I set out a glass at each place and then look about for the bottles of wine, but there is only an empty pitcher on the tabletop.

Paloma sees my confusion and points to a large cask set into the wall, with a wooden spigot sticking out of it.

Comprehension dawns. I take the pitcher and stick it under the spigot and turn the handle so that the rich red wine spills out. Looking about and seeing that the other kitchen help is occupied, I let some spill over my thumb and then stick my thumb in my mouth. At least I'll get a little, anyway.

Ummmm . . .

Whipping thumb out of mouth, I turn to pouring the wine into the individual goblets. When I am done, I turn to Paloma for further instruction.

"Here. Put out the food," she orders, and bowls of steaming dishes are thrust toward me. I take them and place them about the table.

The rest of the household pours into the room. A tall man, mustachioed like many men in this country, and dressed in a suit and tie, goes to take his place at the head of the table. That would be Manuel Garcia, Goya's manservant. It is plain he functions as butler also.

Carmelita Gomez comes in, cuts me a glance, and sits at the foot of the table. In an English household, that would be the place of the head house-mistress, in charge of all the maids. Here, I don't know what she is.

The students then wander in, laughing and joking, and they, too, take their places.

I stand about, waiting to be told what to do.

Carmelita points to a chair, three places from her, on the left side of the table.

"You sit there."

I am a bit taken aback at this, but I go over to place the Faber bottom in the chair as instructed.

Well, why should the help not sit with the others? The students are really just apprentices, and the practice of art is merely a trade, like any other.

Paloma, her duties done, comes to sit next to me. The young student Cesar is on my other side. Amadeo is farther down the table, as is Asensio, who is next to him. Ramona eventually comes to sit opposite me.

When all are seated, Señor Garcia leads the grace recitation, preceded and followed by everyone making perfunctory Signs of the Cross. The bowls are passed and all begin eating, and needing no further encouragement, I dig in, too. It is all wondrous good — there is a thick mutton stew with gravy with mashed something or other, maybe parsnips, maybe potatoes, and good thick and crusty bread. Butter, too.

Well, this is a bit of all right, I'm thinking.

I'm tucking it in, trying to stay inconspicuous for a change, when the boy Cesar pipes up with, "You are from America, Señorita? Could you tell us something of that place?"

I take a sip of wine, dab the lips on the cloth provided, and say, "Of course, young sir, but first you must call me Jacquelina, or rather Jacky, as that is how I am called in America. Can you do that, Cesar?"

He gives it a try. "Jack-ie. How's that?"

"It will serve, if I may call you Cesar?"

"*Por supuesto,* Jack-ie."

"*Bueno.* Now tell me about Maestro Goya, and I will tell you about America. Did he come from a rich family; was he — ?"

"Oh, no, Miss," says Cesar, eager to tell the story. He is a pleasant-looking lad, slightly built and about my height — curly dark hair, good straight nose, yes, all in all, a quite presentable young man. "He comes from Fuendetodos, a very poor part of Aragón. His father was a simple gilder, a man who puts gold leaf on things to make them pretty. One day, when Maestro was a boy, he was out tending pigs and he took a burnt stick from a fire and drew a pig on a nearby wall. A priest going by asked Goya how he learned to draw so well and Maestro replied that no one had taught him. So then the priest arranged for the boy to be educated and he was apprenticed to the studio of a local artist named Jose Luzan to take art lessons."

"Must have been some pig," I murmur, my nose in my stew. I am ignored.

"Then he did go there and later on to here in Madrid, where he worked even harder, made some good connections, got some good commissions, and now he is the greatest artist in all of Spain, one who paints kings and queens," concludes Cesar, plainly proud to be a member of Goya's studio.

The Faber ears perk up at that. *Hmmm . . . Kings? Queens? Perhaps . . . perhaps I shall stick around for a bit. Where there is royalty, maybe there will be a chance to do my duty for King, Country, and General Wellesley . . . and, possibly, opportunity for some mischief of my own.*

"They tell the same story about other artists," says Asensio Julia. "Giotto, for one. Do not believe all you hear, boy."

Asensio sits to Amadeo's right, and both have managed to get themselves into some very elegant clothes in the time between the last class and dinner — silken shirts, fancy embroidered vests, tight black trousers tucked into fine leather boots. I sense that they have something planned for the evening.

I also sense that Cesar doesn't like being called *boy.*

He looks up, resentful. "They will go to El Café Central, Jack-ie. It is the favorite place of the *Majos*. There will be music and dancing and beautiful *Majas*, and all will be gay — and they won't take me with them."

"Someday, Pepito," laughs Amadeo, rising. "When you are grown into a man. You, too, may be a *Majo*. Asensio, are you ready?"

Asensio, a slim, dark man, with luminous eyes and straight black hair that hangs by his face, gets to his feet. He wears a thin mustache on his upper lip and a small pointed beard on his chin. He nods to Manuel Garcia.

"Señor. May we be excused?"

The butler nods assent, and the two turn to leave. Before Amadeo exits, he looks back at me.

"Perhaps, Jack-ie, you will come with us soon. I did take you for a *Maja* when first I laid eyes upon you. You might have fun."

"I am sure I would, Amadeo, but I have no fine clothes to wear."

"What does a slut need with clothes?" spits out Carmelita, standing and flinging down her napkin. "I am excused!"

With that, she flounces out of the room. I have the feeling that she is less annoyed with me than with the fact that Amadeo is going out without her.

"I hope you will forgive our Señorita Gomez," intones Señor Garcia from the head of the table. "She is high-strung. I shall speak to her tomorrow. As for you, Señorita, welcome to our house. I hope you will be happy here."

With that, he gets to his feet and goes off.

It is time to clean up, and I rise to help. As I do so, I ask of my dinner companion, "Cesar, are there any *guitarras* about?"

"*Sí, Señorita*. There are many. They are often used as props in the paintings, as background, so to speak."

"Good. Get me one that has all its strings and meet me after we are done cleaning up," I say, reaching out to ruffle his hair. "Perhaps I shall show you a good evening after all."

He looks up at me, gulps, and hurries off.

I believe I have a friend.

Chapter 15

"Will I be paid, Paloma?" I ask of my roommate. Night has fallen and she has lent me a nightdress and we are both abed. "For what I do here?"

"Oh, yes, Jack-ie. Señor Goya is a generous man and a good master. I get one *escudo* a week." I sense she is blushing in the darkness. "You will probably get more . . . for the other thing you will be doing."

Hmmm . . .

"Paloma, I hope you will not be alarmed, but sometimes I have bad dreams, so I thrash about and say strange things. I am not mad, nor am I possessed, but I have seen many bad things and sometimes, when asleep, I cannot control myself."

She replies that she will not be frightened if it happens and for me not to worry about it.

I lie there in the darkness, grateful for a warm, soft bed, and think back on the events of the day . . .

After Amadeo and Asensio had left in a state of high spirits and Señorita Carmelita Gomez had gone off to sulk, and the dishes and pots had all been scrubbed, scoured, and cleaned by the three of us — Ramona, Paloma, and I — Cesar reappeared with guitar in hand. Then he and I went back into the now quiet and dark studio and lit a lamp.

We sit on a long couch and I begin tuning the guitar he has brought me. It seems to be a well-built instrument and has all six of its strings, at least. As I tune, I tease the boy, telling him what a handsome young man he is, *so talented, I cannot believe it. That drawing of Jorge you did, it was the best in the class. I am sure that the others were very jealous. It is no wonder you have been taken on as a pupil by the greatest artist in Spain!*

I strum a chord and then begin singing *"Tú Sólo Tú,"* which always seems to go over big with Spanish audiences, and the lad is appreciative.

"Muy bueno, Señorita! Please, play another!"

"I do not know many Spanish songs, *chico,* but here is *'Malagueña Salerosa,'* recently taught to me by a bold brigand. If you will forgive my poor accent . . ."

I play the song and again he is pleased, claps his hands, and says, *Olé!,* and asks for more.

Adjusting the lower string, which had gone a bit flat, I reply, "I will do that, my bold young caballero, but first, Cesar, tell me of *Majos* and *Majas* and I shall listen."

"Well, we are mostly from the lower classes — actors, artists, dancers, musicians, singers — "

"*We,* young Cesar?" I ask, with cocked eyebrow.

"Yes, I am a *Majo,*" he says proudly. "A true son of Spain."

"And a fine one, I am sure," says I. "Now, *chico,* explain, *por favor.*"

"The *Majos* show their love of *España* by dressing in the old fashion — many colorful silks and leathers and pantaloons and flowing hats with plumes. The *Majas* dress with fine silks, too, but with lace mantillas draped about their lovely faces."

"Ah, that is why — "

"That is why Amadeo called you a *Maja* when first he saw you. Plus you were not dressed as an *Afrancesada*."

"Ummm . . . and they are?"

"They are *Madrileños,* the people of Madrid who have adopted the ways of France — the fashions, the styles, the ways of talking. The *Afrancesados* say that Napoleon has brought modern things to Spain as well as liberty from the old ruling classes that have oppressed us. That may be so, but he has also brought something very different."

"Yes."

"He has brought death and destruction to our poor country. You have heard of the Massacre of Evora?"

"Yes. Horrible, if true."

"It is true, Señorita, believe me. And *Dos de Mayo?*"

"Tell me." I sigh, expecting the worst, and the worst is what I get.

"On the second of May this year, the French tried to move some of the younger members of the royal family, the Prince and the Infanta, to Bayonne, in France, where they already had taken King Charles and his son, Ferdinand."

Cesar lowers his voice and looks about furtively, then goes on.

"The people of Spain rose up at this outrage and took to the streets. The army, too. There was much bloody fighting, but eventually the French put down the rebellion. Many, many died."

"Well, that happens," I say with some resignation. "War and death, they go together."

"But that was not the end of it, Jack-ie." He gulps. I sense he is trying to control his emotions. "On the next day, the French took out all the rebels they had captured and executed them without trial. There were hundreds, perhaps thousands, gunned down like animals."

Good Lord . . .

"There was a girl, from our very street, who went down to the center of the city on *Dos de Mayo*. Her name was Manuela Malasana and she was fifteen years old. She was taken by the French, and they tried to do bad things to her — like bad things to a girl, you know? But she did not let them do that, so they lined her up with the others and shot her dead."

The lad is overcome with emotion, and I lay my hand on his shaking shoulder.

"I should have been there . . . with her and the others," he says with a whimper. "But, to my shame, I was not. I stayed here, safe."

"No, Cesar, you should not have been there. Fifteen is too young to die," I say, thinking of that poor girl who stood before the firing squad in the flower of her youth till the pitiless bullets blew her young life away and her shattered body fell to the ground. "And so is fourteen. Best leave the butchery to the grownups. They are better at it." I am unable to keep the bitterness from my voice.

He nods, but I don't think he is convinced.

"Things are bad here, Miss. Very bad. It has affected the

Master's work. He has done some very dark sketches — horrors of war, atrocities, lunatics. Look over there — do you see it?"

In the gloom of the studio, I see, leaning against the far wall, a large canvas. It is plainly only a start — an underpainting in blacks and browns — but, still, I can see what it depicts. Men are lined up before soldiers. Dead men already lie on the ground. Arms fly up in desperation, some are on their knees, praying their last prayers.

"It will be called *Dos de Mayo*."

"But won't the Master get in trouble for that?"

"No one will see it, trust me. There is a bucket of cheap black paint over there, and Goya has ordered that it be quickly painted over should the French arrive at our door."

"I see, *chico*," I say, putting my fingers once again to the strings of the guitar. "Now, please, calm down, and I will sing you another song, one I learned in America. It goes like this . . ."

"Did you know the girl Manuela Malasana?" I ask Paloma later, after Cesar has gone off to his bed and I to mine.

"*Sí*. I would see her at market. We would talk. She was a good girl."

"Why did she die?"

"She went into the streets in all the excitement. The French say they killed her because she had a weapon that could do harm to them . . . Could spill French blood."

"Did she?"

"She had a pair of scissors," whispers Paloma. "Why would she not have a pair of scissors? She was a seamstress."

Why, indeed?

Paloma is silent for a while, and then says, "Sometimes, Jack-ie . . ."

"Yes?"

"Sometimes I get the bad dreams, too . . . Good night, Jack-ie."

"*Buenas noches,* Paloma. I hope you sleep well, sister."

Chapter 16

James Emerson Fletcher
The House of Chen
Rangoon, Burma

My dearest Jacky,
*Right now I am reclining in a pool that I believe you know
quite well from what Sidrah tells me of your time here at the
House of Chen. You will recall the turquoise tiling within, the
aromatic cedar planking around the edge of it. The steam curls
about on the surface of the bath, the hot water below soaking
out the vestiges of my pent-up anger.*

No, dear one, the exquisite Sidrah is not here in the
bath with me, not that I would mind that overmuch, but I
fear you might object. No, I am content with the ministrations of the giggling Mai sisters, Mai Ling and Mai Ji, who
apply the soapy sponges to my back and shoulders with soft
hands, kind determination, and endless barely stifled
snickering.

I have, at Sidrah's gentle insistence, been assigned to
study with the Zen master Kwai Chang. Sidrah assures me

that it will do me much good and will help to ease my mind. So, to humor her, I wrap myself each day in my saffron robe and sit cross-legged before the bald-headed little man, who, against all odds, manages to speak a kind of English. A bowl of incense smolders between us and he speaks while I listen. He has given me the name Chueng Tong — "Long Boy." Sometimes I am asked questions . . . Sometimes I am able to answer in a way that seems to satisfy him.

The potions and medicines that I had been given upon my arrival here have been tapered off as my mind continues to clear. Now I receive nothing in that regard save the instruction of Kwai Chang and the kind ministrations of the Lady Sidrah.

Till later, yours,
Jaimy

Chapter 17

The next morning, the bell of La Basilica de San Francisco el Grande tolled long and insistently as Paloma and I groaned and got out of bed, dressed, and tumbled downstairs to help Ramona make breakfast for the House of Goya.

The steaming food is on the table — *huevos revuelto, salchichas y chorizo picante, pan plano, y café fuerte.* The students came in, with Amadeo and Asensio looking a bit worse for wear. *Ah, young men off for a night on the town, and then the inevitable morning after, same as it ever was . . . except that Amadeo has a small cut over his left eye. What's with that . . . ?*

Afterwards, we clean up, and Paloma heads off to make the beds, while I go to the studio, ready to grind more paint. But I soon find that is not what I will be doing today, oh, no . . .

Upon entering, I notice right off that the model Jorge is not in attendance — the robe hangs slack over the edge of the dressing screen.

Hmmm . . . I guess it is going to be my turn now . . . Oh, well . . . Hand me the robe.

It is my turn, in a way, but in another way, it isn't.

A chair is set up on the model platform, and when Goya enters, he points and motions for me to go sit in it, which I do. He comes up and stands before me. He gestures toward my hairpiece. I catch his meaning and take it off and put it aside.

He pats my shoulder in a kindly way and says, "Pull your shirt down over your shoulders, *chica,* so as to expose your neck — a very fine neck, I must say. Lift your chin, and face that way . . . not so far . . . That's it . . . Hold that."

He turns to the others.

"So, *mis estudiantes,* commence your drawing of this lovely face. Remember, the gesture, the tilt of the head, the planes of the face."

As they start scratching away, I look off into space and hold the pose.

Ha! This is easy, I'm thinkin'. *All I have to do is sit here while they toil away, and I do not even have to grind paint! Ha! Take that, Carmelita! Lovely face! Did you catch that? Ha!*

The euphoria lasts about ten minutes. Then my bum begins to get a bit sore and I feel the urge to rutch around to get the buttocks in a more comfortable position, but I can't. My hip bones, which seem intent on grinding their way through the softness of my rump, are relentless. I flex, but it does no good.

Then my nose starts to itch and I cannot scratch the bloody thing. Why did it not want to be scratched before? Why?

I must distract myself, else I shall be seen as a worthless scrub, not even able to sit for a simple portrait.

Maybe I'll just write a letter to my sweet sister Amy, if only in my mind:

Miss Amy Trevelyne
The Lawson Peabody School for Young Girls
Boston, Massachusetts, USA

Dearest Amy,
You cannot possibly guess, Sister, where I am right now, much less what I am doing. I know, I know, you think me to be atoning for my sins in the penal colony in Australia, but I am not there. No, suffice to say I am in Madrid, Spain — can you believe it! — and am sitting as a model for portrait study in a very fine art studio. You might ask Mr. Peet if he has ever heard of a Señor Francisco Goya, the Maestro of this establishment.

Yes, dear one, I shall tell you of just how I got here when we are both once again snugged up in that wonderful hayloft at Dovecote. I can smell the warm hay now . . . Ummm . . .

It is actually a very pleasant house in which I now find myself, mostly. True, one of the students here, Señorita Carmelita Gomez, is a bit of a bitch, but I can deal with that. After all, didn't I deal with one Clarissa Worthington Howe in the past? So I am definitely an expert in that sort of thing.

There are three male students here, Amadeo, Asensio, and Cesar, and they are very nice — for right now, anyway. Very courtly — that Randall could take a lesson . . . How is that rogue, anyway? Still with Polly Von? I hope so, and I hope he's being good, which I doubt.

When I first got here, I was thinking of resting a bit, then stealing enough provisions to put me back on the road again, but I shortly changed my mind when I found that Señor Goya was court painter to the royalty of Spain, and I might be able to gain some information that could be of use to my country . . . or countries. I hear that Goya is going to the palace very shortly, and he always takes helpers with him . . . hmmm . . .

Anyway, so here I am, hired as housemaid and sometime model, so I might as well stay put.

I must tell you that my poor James Emerson Fletcher has run into a bit of trouble, both legally and mentally, all because of me, of course. He is in Rangoon, in Burma, undergoing treatment. Heavy sigh . . . Oh, why didn't Jaimy find a nice girl early in his life, one that would make him happy? Instead he is condemned to suffer the slings and arrows of misfortune because of his association with my troublesome self. Why?

Ha! That heavy sigh must have been heard and touched the Master's heart, for a break is called! Gracias a Dios!

More later, dearest Sister . . .

I get up, stretch arms and shoulders, flex poor buttocks, and then walk around to see what has been done with my face in the way of art.

Both Amadeo and Asensio have done strong, forceful drawings. Asensio's is a bit more elegant, and I smile on him for that — I think of Lisette de Lise when I gaze upon it. Amadeo's effort is more . . . well . . . *macho*, I think is the word. He makes me look as if I am, very shortly, going to do something naughty. He looks at me as I gaze upon it and he gives me a knowing smile. *Macho,* indeed. *Well, we shall see, Señor . . .*

Cesar's is equally well done. It is softer than the others, and he has taken my bodice down a little lower than it actually was, revealing a cleft between my breasts, a cleft he has not yet seen. *Ah, the imagination of a male youth, I swear.*

I give him a wink and then pass on.

Señorita Carmelita Gomez's drawing, on the other hand, is much more severe. She has portrayed me with pinched nostrils, frown, and gimlet eye. *Oh, well, Carmelita. Thems that likes me, likes me, and thems that don't, can kiss my—*

"Pose, please," orders Goya, and I am back up on the platform yet again.

So, Amy, I am back again in position. As I sit here, I think on the drawings I have seen. They are different from the portraits back in Boston, which were static, with poses held rigid. These are more vibrant. There is more movement in them. I shall take note and learn some new ways of doing things. I shall—

"Stop moving, girl," snarls Carmelita. "Can you not sit still? Is it too much to ask?"

I realize my head has been drooping and I jerk it back up. *"Pardon, Señorita.* It shall not happen again."

Back again, Amy, having just been chastised for nodding off—good Lord, Amy, I could use a nice reclining pose just now. Just lie back and doze . . .

No, now, I must stop that! Must do my job!

Ahem! Back on the line.

Anyway, dear Sister, during the last break, I spotted a piece of paper tossed into a trash can and pulled it out. It was a false start on a sketch by one of the students, but it did have an untouched area about six by ten inches on one edge. I gingerly tore out the clean piece and set it aside.

Seeing me do this, Amadeo asked, "Why do you need that, Jackie? Will you write your love a letter?"

I smiled secretly, blushed, and said, "Something like that."

I do, Amy, have a bit of a plan in my mind . . . Ah, another welcome break. Till later, Miss Trevelyne.

Your Loving Sister,
Jacky

Later, after the day's toil is done — yes, the portrait session had ended and I had been sent back to grinding paint — we once again gather for dinner. The places are set, the wine poured, the food served. As we pile into it, I sense a bit of tension about the table and I am afraid I am the one who sets it off.

"Tell me, Amadeo, of the painting sessions at the palace," says the English spy in me. "Can it be that you actually go there and paint the royals in their own quarters?"

"We used to." Asensio sneers. "But now the Master paints the French invaders. We will go there next week to paint King Joseph of Spain! Napoleon's brother! How Spanish is that?"

"Now, Asensio," warns Señor Manuel Garcia from the head of the table. "We will have none of that, young man! No politics at this table!"

But Asensio will not leave it be.

"Pardon, Señor," he says, his eyes burning. "But must we put up with the insults of the *Afrancesados?* Is it not enough that French soldiers march on our streets? Abuse our citizens? That — "

This is too much for another of our number. Carmelita speaks up, "Napoleon brought some good things to Spain! He has abolished many of the old bad ways! He should be thanked for that, at least! No more will people be burned at the stake!"

"True, Carmelita," retorts Amadeo. "Now they will merely be tied to that same stake and shot. Same sorry end."

"*Bastante!* You will all stop this talk or you shall be sent from this table, and the Maestro will be informed! Do you hear me?"

It is plain that Señor Garcia is angry, so the voices at the table subside, as does mine.

Eat your mush and hush, Jacky, and stop stirring up trouble!

Chapter 18

It is a Saturday afternoon and things are quiet at Estudio Goya. There are no classes, but there is some work to do. I have been shown how to stretch and prepare canvases for future paintings, and I work at that through the morning hours. After what proves to be a light lunch, I am left on my own and I coax Paloma — *please, Sister, just a little while* — into the empty studio, to start on a small watercolor portrait of her. I put her in a pose very much like the one I had just sat for, but just the beginning outline sketch is all I get done, for I perceive she is anxious to be off to enjoy her brief few hours of freedom. It was, after all, payday, and I myself have eight *reals* warming in my vest pocket.

I had noticed many small brushes standing about in pots and had asked Amadeo if I might make use of some of them — *with the watercolors only, Amadeo, of course, never the oils, oh no . . .*

I manage to get the basic stuff down — shape of her head, slope of shoulders, some background color — then I lay the paper aside to dry, thank her, and wave her off to the town. She is gone in an instant. *As would I be, Paloma, were I in another place, in another town.*

After I wash the brushes — an easy thing to do with the watercolors, not so easy with the oils — I wander around the studio and look at the works-in-progress that sit on five of the easels. Goya was so pleased at the drawings the students had done of me that he directed each of them to do a painting of the same pose — except this time, he set up a canvas of his own and had me put on a more elaborate top with my mantilla over my head and draped around my shoulders. They have been at it for the better part of a week and most are almost done.

As I walk around, I give the paintings my own critique. Cesar's is coming along, a little weak in the shadows of the face, but then he is young. Carmelita's is competent, but I find it is rather cold, emotionless — perhaps it helps if one actually *likes* what one is painting. Asensio's is excellent, with good vibrant color, but Amadeo's is the best of all the students' — perfect resemblance with a mischievious glint in the subject's eye. I get the feeling *he* liked painting me. When I first assumed the pose in costume, he said, "*Olé,* Jack-ie! You are now at least *half* a *Maja!*"

He says "half," I know, because, from the neck up, I am dressed in the style of a Spanish lady, but down below, I am still in Lawson Peabody serving-girl rig. I mean to change that condition, however, as soon as I put some more money together.

Half a Maja, *but all a tramp*, I heard Carmelita mutter while the others laughed and I grinned in appreciation of Amadeo's wit, if not hers.

I stand now for a good while in front of the Master's

work. It is, of course, the best of all and already completed — perfectly composed, it glows with life. I feel honored, somehow. Wherever I go in this world, whatever happens to me, this will shine on some wall and bring pleasure to those who gaze upon it. And some of them will wonder, *Just who was that girl?*

. . . and that girl will have been me.

Turning from the world of art, I grab a guitar and settle on the couch for a little practice. I do some of the finger-picking rolls Solomon Freeman taught me back on the Mississippi, and I am softly singing "The Bad Girl's Lament" when Cesar comes in to sit next to me.

> *There is a house in New Orleans,*
> *They call the Rising Sun.*
> *It's been the ruin of many a poor girl.*
> *And me, oh Lord,*
> *For one.*

"That is very beautiful, Jack-ie," says Cesar. "Please, play some more."

I do. I sing the rest of the verses and end with . . .

> *I'm going back to New Orleans,*
> *My race is nearly run.*
> *I'm going back to end my days*
> *Beneath that Rising Sun.*

"So beautiful, Señorita. So sad sounding. What is it about?"

"Oh, it's just a song about a place I used to work in," I say, idly strumming another chord and leaning back against the couch. "I know lots of songs, but mostly in English. I wish I knew more in Spanish." I give him a look. "Do you know any you could teach me, Cesar?"

"Oh, no, Jack-ie. I would love to do that for you, but I have the voice of the toad," says the lad. "Sometimes my throat squeaks and sometimes it croaks and I have no control over it."

I look over and give him a sympathetic smile. "Don't worry, Cesar, it will soon even out and you will have a rich, deep, macho voice that will cause all young female hearts to flutter. I promise."

The boy looks doubtful about that but goes on. "However, I do know a man you could listen to, and learn. He knows many songs."

"And who is that?" I ask, the Faber eyebrows upraised and very interested.

"He is an old gypsy man. He sits and plays in a *taberna* right around the corner. On La Plaza Major. Would you like to go there?"

"Does a bear poop in the woods, *chico*? Does a sailor long for the sea? Does Romeo pine for Juliet? Does Jacky long for the warmth of a good, cozy tavern? Of course I want to go!" I exult, leaping to my feet.

Then I calm myself. "But are we allowed?"

"*Sí.* We are not prisoners here. We have only to tell Señor Garcia where we are going."

"Hoo-ray!" I crow. "Then let us be gone! Come, my gay caballero, you shall be my gallant escort!"

"*Sí, Señorita,*" says Cesar, rising and extending his

hand. "However, I do not understand the thing with the bear."

"Never mind, *mi estimado*. Let us be off to the merry dance!"

"It is not a fancy place, Jack-ie, I am sorry," says Cesar as we approach the door of the establishment. A sign above the entrance proclaims La Taberna de Dos Gatos. Hmmm . . . sounds familiar.

"Do not worry, *mi querido*," I say, patting his arm, which is entwined with mine. "If I am with you, to me it will be the veritable Palace of Versailles."

His chest puffs out a bit at that. I know he enjoys walking along this grand street with me on his arm. Although he is barely fourteen and I am seventeen, we are about the same height and so we do not stand out in the crowds that throng the grand plaza.

Before we left, he had dashed upstairs, then reappeared dressed grandly in brocaded jacket, frilly white shirt, and tight black pants that had silver *conchos* running up the leg. I, dressed still in my Lawson Peabody serving-girl best with mantilla on top, dipped down in a fine, full curtsy upon seeing him in his finery. He blushed with pleasure and managed a nice bow in return.

I did notice with some concern, however, that he had a sword swinging by his side. *Hmmm* . . . The aforementioned Romeo was also only fourteen when he, too, armed in the same way, ventured out into the life of a city, and we all know what we got then, don't we — a whole pile of dead kids is what, Juliet included. But, still, it is only a late Saturday afternoon and what could happen? Besides, men will be men, boys will be boys, and *Majos* will be *Majos,* so what can I say? I'm just a stupid girl who doesn't usually rely on swords.

"It is a place where only the common people go. I go there because it is cheap and Amadeo and Asensio will not take me with them to the Café Central."

"Oh, and where is that?"

"Across the plaza. Over there."

I follow his gaze and see a crowd of people outside of what has to be a very popular place. Although it is over a hundred yards away, I can still hear the laughter and song and general hilarity that comes from the place. I also note that there are many French soldiers in full uniform scattered about.

"Never mind, Señor Cesar Rivera. Let them have their fun. I am sure this place will suit me just fine. Let's go in."

We duck in and my senses are assailed with the smell of hundreds of years of spilled wine, whiskey, and ale . . . and the oh-so-good smells of simple cooking. Yep, just my kind of place.

Cesar raises a hand, and a young girl comes over to take our order.

"So, Cesar," she says, looking me over briskly, "what will you have?"

I'm looking about for the reputed musician and say, offhand, "Some wine for me, *por favor.*"

"Uh, Jack-ie," says Cesar, pointing to the rows of huge casks lined up along one wall. "This is Spain. We have many wines."

"Uh, red and dry," I say. I go to dig in my pocket to pay, but think better of it. It would un-man him, and we cannot have that, no, we cannot.

"*Vino rojo seco para la señorita, y grappa para mi.*"

The girl walks off, swinging her hips, to get the drinks. Somehow I get the feeling that Cesar's reputation as a ladies' man has just gone way up in this establishment. Good for him. Glad I could help.

Ha. There he is. An old man, stooped and halting in his walk, has made his careful way to a chair in the corner. A guitar leans against the wall and he picks it up, puts his fingers to the strings, and begins to strum.

He starts out slowly, humming softly over the melody, then he brings up the tempo. There are not many people here — just several old couples and one table of some younger ones. It is not a big room, but the man knows how to work it, I can see that.

He has an open guitar case in front of him, and there are only a few centavos in it. He goes into his next song. It is "*Malagueña Salerosa,*" which I already know, but he does an excellent job on it, especially with the guitar, and I count that as a good sign.

I dig out a *real* and say, "Please, Cesar, let me pay for the next round. I need the change."

He nods and signals for our glasses to be refilled. The girl returns, our wine is brought, and my *real* is broken down into smaller bits of coin. She also brings us plates of *tapas,* small snacks from trays laid upon the bar. Like all "free lunches" I have partaken of around the world, they are very good — marinated olives, baby octopus, smoked sardines, jerked beef — and *very* salty . . . The more to make you thirsty, the more to make you drink, for that is where the money is in a tavern. *There is no such thing as a free lunch,* wisdom well-learned from Mr. Yancy Beauregard Cantrell, back on the *Belle of the Golden West,* where we laid out many a salty *tapa* and served many a quenching drink.

After the next song, I creep over and toss some *centavos* into the case and catch the eye of the musician.

He assesses me, then says, "Your request, Señorita?"

"Sing your favorite song, Maestro," I say. "For me."

He nods and I retreat to our table. He tunes a string, strums a chord, and then begins:

> *Los bilbilicos cantan*
> *Con sospiros de amor*
> *Mi neshama, mi ventura*
> *Estan en tu poder*

It is one of the loveliest songs I have ever heard. I *must* get next to this man. I have enough Spanish to know that the words mean:

> *The nightingales sing*
> *With sighs of love*
> *My soul, my happiness*
> *Is in your power*

"Cesar. Come, let us go to a closer table," I say, already up and moving over next to the man who had sung that beautiful song.

He runs the backs of his fingers over the strings and is about to start singing again as I kneel down beside him.

"That was beautiful, Señor," I say, breathless. "Please permit me to speak."

He nods, continuing to strum as I go on.

"I am but a poor American, but I very much want to learn the Spanish songs. I have some skill with the *guitarra*. I want you to teach me that one and any more you know. I will pay."

With that, I pull out another coin and put it in his case.

He smiles down at me. "I am willing to do that, child," he says. "But that was not a Spanish song. It was written by the Sephardim before they were thrown out of Spain. That was a pity, for they were good at songs." He looks off. "They threw out the Arabs, also, and they were good at many things, too. The Spanish are good at throwing out things."

"And you, Señor?" I ask. "I heard you were a gypsy man. Did they throw you out, too?"

He throws back his great head of gray hair and laughs. "They tried to throw us out, too, but it didn't work. It never does. We are too tough, too clever. And yes, young one, I will teach you gypsy guitar. Name the times and we will do it."

Later, Cesar and I emerge from La Taberna de Dos Gatos and blink in the setting sun.

"It's best we get back in time for supper, Miss," says Cesar. "Señor Garcia might be mad."

"Aye, *chico*, let us go," I say, giving him a hug. "It was a *most* fine day, and I thank you for it!"

"I believe I see Amadeo and Asensio coming across the plaza," observes the lad, looking over the vast space.

I shade my eyes and see that it is, indeed, the two. *Ha! You may be high and mighty Majos, but you are still poor art*

*students and not anxious to pass up a free supper, are you?
And won't you find it charming that young Cesar has a fine
escort today, has beaten your time, as it were, won't you —*

No, they won't. Not now, anyway.

For now Cesar and I find four French soldiers, fully
armed and plainly quite drunk, standing in front of us, bar-
ring our way.

"Pretty little thing you have there with you, boy," one
says in French. "I think she is much too pretty for you, little
man. What do you think, Gaston?"

"Much too pretty." Gaston burps, unsteady on his pins.

"I think she should come with us, boy. There is a nice
cozy alley over there. What do you say, hmmm? Here's a
nice coin for her." He flips a copper coin onto the street,
where it tinkles before it slips into a crack between the
cobblestones.

Cesar does not understand much of this, but he takes
its meaning, oh yes, he does. He steps back and pulls out his
sword and snarls, "Back, French pigs! Back! She is not for
you! Back, I say!"

"Whoa! The boy has a pig-sticker!" The biggest brute
laughs. "Let's see how he can handle it!"

Cesar holds his sword up before him, but I can see it's
not going to serve. I look over and see that Amadeo and
Asensio are still too far away to help.

"Away with you," says Cesar. "Go! I will — "

But he will do nothing. He thrusts at the nearest soldier
and the man steps aside, laughing, while Gaston lays the
butt of his musket to the side of Cesar's head. The boy falls
to the ground, senseless, and says not another word.

Oh, Cesar, no!

The head brute reaches out to grab my hand, but he does not get it. Instead, that hand reaches down to grab the hilt of Cesar's fallen sword and hold it up in front of the soldier.

"*En garde, cochon,*" I snarl, putting the point of the blade on a line between our eyes and assuming Position Four.

He looks startled for a moment and then he laughs. "*Un femme?* Ha! Take this, girl!*"

He makes a clumsy thrust. I parry it and slip into Sixth Position. I retreat and then advance forward in Four, with my eye on his chest. He tries another thrust, and I engage in an envelopment parry, which puts his sword helplessly to the side and our faces close together.

"*Un femme?*" I spit. "*Oui. La Belle Jeune Fille Sans Merci, s'il vous plait.*"

I come out of the parry and put the point of Cesar's sword to the man's throat.

He looks suddenly doubtful.

Amadeo and Asensio have come upon us, both with swords drawn and looking ferociously enraged.

"Do you wish to die, soldier?" I ask of the brute. "Or would you like to go back to your barracks and fight another day? Eh? What would you like, *soldat*?"

The French soldier looks about, weighing his odds, and decides it's not worth it.

He spits out some curses, thrusts his sword back in its sheath, and then calls his men off. They disappear into the darkening evening.

I let out a shaky breath.

"Pick him up," I say to Amadeo and Asensio. "Let us go back to the studio. We will tell Cesar that he defended me to the end, which is what he did. Got that? Good. Let's go."

Soon we see the façade of Estudio Goya, and it looks very good to me.

Chapter 19

It is Sunday and we are all going to Mass at La Basilica de San Francisco el Grande — all of us except for
Cesar, who is ordered to his bed to recover from his
clubbing.

"My bold, bold protector, Cesar Rivera," I gush as I apply the cool, damp cloth to his forehead. "My gallant Spanish knight who stood up to armed French soldiers in defense
of my sacred honor!" He has quite a bump there, but he will
recover. He looks up at me with big brown eyes.

"I . . . I don't remember much, Senorita, I — "

"But I do, young Galahad! Oh, how you parried their
thrusts with the mighty swings of your singing sword till
that coward caught you with a low blow from behind! May
he rot in hell for his perfidy!"

"But — "

"And seeing the bold hero laid low, the scum took fright
and ran off. Amadeo and Asensio came upon the scene and
carried you back here, on your very shield, as it were." I lean
forward and place a kiss upon his brow. "And that is how it
happened."

"I . . . I think I love you, Jack-ie," he says, reaching up to grasp my hand.

"Of course you do, Cesar." I laugh, giving his hand a squeeze. "I have found that pretty young boys find it very easy to love me. But I am also very easy to forget, so put me out of your mind, as I am not worth it. Ah, here's Amadeo, and I must be off to Mass. You rest up, you."

With that, I rise, place another kiss on his forehead, and follow Amadeo out the door.

The Basilica de San Francisco el Grande is unlike other magnificent churches I have been in. It's much larger than either Notre Dame, in Paris, or St. Paul's, in London. It is built lower to the ground, more like a fortress, and its dome is much larger. Three chapels at the sides make it even more impressive. Regardless of its size, the interior is comforting with its soft light and illuminated windows. There are large paintings on the walls, generally depicting rather gloomy things — crucifixions, floggings, flayings — but I suppose that suits the Spanish character.

I have decided to pass for Catholic — don't want to give that Carmelita any more arrows for her anti-Jacky bow. And being seen as a Protestant heretic in Catholic Spain is probably not the most healthy of conditions.

I have been to church often enough with Annie and Betsey back in Boston, and with Jean-Paul de Valdon in Paris, to know the basic moves — kneel now, stand now, up-and-down, up-and-down, sing now, pray now — and with my mantilla draped in front of my face, my mumbling lips are obscured from inquiring eyes, like those of Carmelita, for she is certainly intent on watching me.

At any rate, there was no roar of heavenly outrage as I knelt to take the Host on my tongue, nor as I took a sip of the sacramental wine. No, I went back to the pew, head bowed in prayer, hands clasped before me, a beatific expression on my face, having just been washed in the Blood of the Lamb, as it were. After all, we take Communion in Church of England services, too, so I imagine everything was all right, liturgically speaking.

Before we leave the Basilica, Amadeo says to me, "Come, Jacquelina, and I will show you something." Mystified, I follow him into a small chapel off to the side. There are paintings on the walls, but we pass them by as he leads me to stand before a particularly fine one.

"It is a painting of Saint Bernardino de Siena done by our Master, twenty years ago. Do you notice anything?"

I look up at it. It portrays the saint standing on a rock, bathed in golden light, preaching to the multitudes that are gathered about him.

"Well, it is beautifully done, of course," I say, peering closely. "And there must be a hundred people there. But what . . . ?"

"See the man to the right?" answers Amadeo, pointing at one of the figures. "That is the Master's portrait of himself."

And so it is. It is a younger Goya, but it is he, all right. While all the others in the painting gaze up at the saint in adoration — and there is a crowned king among them — the Master does not. He stares straight out at the viewer as if to say, *Yes, this is a holy saint and there is a crowned king kneel-*

ing at his blessed feet, but I am Maestro Francisco José de Goya, by God, and I painted this!

There is a certain amount of cheek in that, I'm thinking, as we walk out of the chapel.

We emerge, blinking, back into the light of a brilliant day, and Amadeo offers me his arm and I take it, with some surprise. Asensio offers his to Carmelita, and she accepts it, but I can feel her eyes burning into my back.

As we wind our way through the narrow streets on our return to the studio, I prattle gaily on, pointing out this, inquiring about that, laughing and leaning into Amadeo as I do it, just being, in general, insufferably cute. I know, sometimes I should be more careful, but it does not seem to be in my nature.

This night, after we have seen to Cesar being bandaged and tucked in, we go down to dinner and discover that the Maestro will be taking his evening meal with us. He usually eats with his ailing wife, but I have heard that sometimes he breaks bread with us. This is the first time I will be in attendance for one of his visits and I am looking forward to his company.

We all stand at our places and await his arrival. Señor Garcia has taken Carmelita's place at the foot of the table, leaving the spot at the head open. Carmelita stands next to me, seething, I'm thinking, with resentment. The tale of last night's escapade has already been related at great length, and much to my advantage.

I blush and protest that the French were simple soliders and not used to fighting with swords.

"But you are, Jack-ie?" says Amadeo with a smile.

"Well, I admit I have had a sword in my clumsy hand before, once or twice, but it was merely for play and I have no real skill at it," I reply modestly. "If you and Asensio had not come up, I would have been in real trouble."

"It seems to us that you were holding your own," says Asensio, giving me a look. "And you seem to speak French quite well, too." He has a slate in hand and is assiduously writing upon it as Maestro Goya enters the room, dressed a little better than usual. When he is working, he is not a neat man. He nods a greeting to all of us and then sits. We follow suit, the grace is said, and we all fall to.

"So what were you all talking about when I came in?" he asks. "High art, no doubt? Poetry? Literature?"

"I am afraid not, Maestro," says Asensio. He sits next to Goya and holds the tablet up for him to read. Asensio has been with the Master the longest and has worked out a kind of shorthand to quickly communicate with him. With that, and some simple gestures, the story of last night's fracas is told.

Goya, munching on a carrot, reads and then glances at me. I blush and look down, all demure.

"So, young *perros*. You were all out looking for trouble and you found it, no?" he says, looking around the table. He is plainly *not* amused. Carmelita puts on a righteous look and shakes her head — *No, not me, Maestro* — but the rest of us look slightly abashed.

"Well, listen to this," he says, pointing his fork at each of us miscreants. "I go to the palace in two weeks to paint the portrait of King Joseph . . ."

There is a sharp intake of breath around the table.

" . . . and I cannot have any trouble with that. Do you understand me? Good."

We all listen with bated breath. After a few more bites, he goes on.

"Yes, I know that our royal family has been sent off by Napoleon and that his brother *King* Joseph has been set on the Spanish throne. You know it, too, and it wounds me as much as it wounds you. But we need the money, the patronage, if our studio is to survive. *Entiende?* You will not provoke the French soldiers anymore. If you do, I will send you back home to your families. Do you take my meaning?"

We . . . *gulp* . . . do.

"Good."

Goya returns to his dinner, as do we all. Now that we have been chastised, Carmelita looks smug and satisfied.

The dinner is lamb chops with mint jelly and roasted potatoes. It is very good, and I give Ramona a wink of appreciation. After a bit, Goya takes a rib from his mouth and points it at me and says, "Explain."

I remove from my own mouth the succulent rib upon which I have been avidly sucking and look to Asensio. He cocks an eyebrow at me and takes chalk in hand and waits.

I tap napkin to lips and say, "Maestro, I have some small skill with the *guitarra*. I told Cesar that I wished to learn more Spanish songs and he said that he knew of a gypsy singer, named Django, who played in a nearby bodega. We went there and listened and, yes, the man was very good at the guitar and the songs, and Señor Django agreed to give me lessons. When we left there, the trouble arose. It was no fault of ours. Certainly not Cesar's. He is a good boy and a credit to your studio."

Asensio taps away with his chalk, no doubt distilling my many words down to a few. Goya glances over and says, "You speak the French language? Just what have we welcomed into our midst?"

Before Carmelita can offer her opinion on that, I say, "I learned in America, Maestro. At school. It was required."

More scribbling by Asensio.

"Umm," says Goya, considering. "You, Jack-ie, may continue to take the guitar lessons. Amadeo, Asensio, you will be careful. And watch out for Cesar — you have been lax in that regard. Any more trouble and you will all be confined to the house. Understood? Good."

The Maestro rises from his chair and is gone.

Looks are exchanged around the table, mostly directed at me.

What? What'd I do?

But never mind. The dinner is cleared, the dishes cleaned, and I go back to working on Paloma's portrait.

"All right, Paloma, we are almost done . . . Just a few more highlights on your lovely hair . . . there."

Paloma, meaning "dove" in Spanish, is so suited to her gentle nature. She smiles and dimples up, and I expect her to actually *coo* in appreciation when the painting is finished.

When the job is done to my satisfaction, I show it to her and she says, "Oh, Jack-ie, that is so beautiful! Oh, if I could — "

"Of course you shall have it, Paloma," I say, blowing on the last application of watercolor. "And when you are old and gray, you will show it to your grandchildren and they will look at it in wonder and say, 'Grandmother, you were so beautiful.'"

She blushes and shakes her head at the notion, and I say, "I will give it to you tomorrow, after it dries and I can find a suitable glass and frame around here. Now, off with you, Paloma. There are still a few more hours in the day, and did I not see you with a likely lad at La Taberna de Dos Gatos last night? I think I did."

I give her a wink, and she gives a bit of a giggle and is off.

Ah, boys and girls together, it is what makes the world go round.

As the door closes behind her, I regard the portrait.

Not too bad, I'm thinking. *This plan might go well. But we shall see . . .*

I turn the thick paper over, blow upon it, and when it is dry enough, I take a piece of charcoal from an easel tray and begin a quick sketch on the back.

I draw a jolly little pig, and he is dancing a merry jig and has a pennywhistle to his lips. Yes, he is the very image of the piglet on the Pig and Whistle sign that hangs outside that beloved tavern back in Boston.

When I am done with him, I slide the whole thing up on a shelf where no one will find it until it is time for me to bring it out.

That done, I head upstairs to prepare for bed.

• • •

Dear Jaimy,

I hope you are well and I pray your condition is improving.

I, myself, am not in a bad place, for a change — I am learning many new things and I have made some new friends, and, yes, it must be said, one enemy, too, but isn't that the way it always goes? Them's that likes me, really likes me, and them's that don't . . . well, they really, really don't. Strange, ain't it?

I am in nightshirt and snugged down under the covers and wishing you were in here with me, oh, yes, I do.

Ah, well, maybe someday, Jaimy. But I dunno . . . things do seem to work against us somehow.

Be well.
Yours forever,
Jacky

Chapter 20

We are in the studio.

There is a new model, a young boy, probably four-teen, I guess from the amount of fur on his slim body. He is not at all shy about being up there like that, so he must have done it many times before. He probably figures it's better than some nasty outside work, and it is my opinion that he's undoubtedly right.

Under Goya's direction, the boy is posed *contrapposto,* weight on one leg, opposite shoulder higher than the other. He holds a panpipe to his lips, so this will plainly be a fanci-ful work — a satyr gamboling about some mythical sylvan landscape. There are strings on straps wrapped around his wrists that run up to pulleys on the ceiling to help him hold the pose, else his poor arms would soon falter and droop.

Preliminary drawings are started, and I continue at my work, which is grinding more paint. The Maestro obviously has something major planned for two large canvases, about three feet by six feet, that have been stretched and primed — well I know because I was the one to prepare them.

Amadeo had to help me with the long, six-foot

stretches — he pulled while I tacked — and as we did it, he locked eyes with me and asked, "Asensio and I are going to El Café Central tomorrow night. Will you come with us?"

"With 'us'?"

"With me."

"Why do you not ask Carmelita?"

"Because she will not go. She says a lady would not go to such a place. Besides, I want to go with you, not her."

"I am glad she cannot hear this, Amadeo. She hates me enough already."

"Forget her. What is your answer?"

"Very well. I will go . . . but only if Cesar can go with us."

"*Sí.* He can come. He has proved himself."

"*Bueno.* I look forward to it."

Four more canvases have also been made up, in half-size, eighteen by thirty-six inches. I suspect those are for the students, and it later turns out I am right in thinking that.

The break is over and work resumes, and as I grind away at the paints, I muse upon my condition at Estudio Goya. Having been here for about three weeks now, I have received pay on three occasions and have been out on the town, buying some small things — castanets; a better skirt, embroidered with colorful thread about the waist and hem; a frilly black shirt, also decorated. Cesar, who has fully recovered and accompanies me on these outings, pronounces me to now be a true *Maja,* and I am pleased by his praise.

I have also bought, for a few *centavos,* a flageolet, a fipple flute very similar to my dear old pennywhistle. I never want to be without somesuch again stuck up my sleeve, like

I was on that rough trek from the border to Madrid, for I can always warble away on any foreign street corner and generally collect enough tossed coins to appease the insistent Faber belly.

After that purchase, I played a quick medly of jigs for Cesar when we got back on the street and he proclaimed himself amazed at my ability. But then, he is an easy audience, because it seems that anything I do is all right with him. Still, I like to hear it.

Sometimes there are gypsy dancers at La Taberna des Dos Gatos. Actually, the place turns out to be quite the gypsy hangout, I find. *"El flamenco,"* Django calls it. *"Both the music and the dance, little one."* I have been studying the dancers' moves, which is why I bought the castanets. Yes, some fans, too. They do a lot with those fans.

I have been enjoying my lessons with Django, and he pronounces himself pleased with my progress in the flamenco. Using thumb and first two fingers to up-pick, the rhythm goes like this: *DUM* dum dum, *DUM* dum dum, *DUM* dum dum, all the while changing chords with the left hand, mostly in minor keys, and then followed by mighty and most dramatic downward strums of the nails across all of the strings. It is most exciting and goes perfectly with the movements of the dancers. I go every chance I get to take more lessons, and Django is always there for me.

The announcement "Break!" brings me back to the present. The boy model unstraps his wrists and stretches his arms. The students also step back from their work to limber up and move about. Goya goes over to a sideboard upon which stands a flagon of red wine and pours himself a glass. He waves his hand, inviting his students to join him in refreshment. They do, with murmurs of thanks.

The Maestro has been rather kind to me of late, reaching out his hand sometimes and ruffling my hair and calling me "little mouse" and other terms of mild affection. He motions for me to take a glass, too, and I do it, coming up close to his side. I decide to make my move.

I had stuck my small painting of Paloma into my open vest, and after I pour my own wine, I pull it out to show it to him.

Ah, but I do not show him the painted side, no I do not. Instead I dangle the charcoal drawing of the little pig before his eyes. To the right of the drawing I had written the words, *Es la verdad?* I put on a questioning look and wait.

Carmelita sucks in her breath, shocked at my temerity, but Goya merely takes the paper and looks at it.

"Is it true, you are asking, little rabbit? The tale of the pig drawn on the wall?" he says, smiling. "Well, it makes for a good story, no? So we shall let it stand, whether it is true or not. Suffice it to say, I came from humble beginnings and I am not ashamed of that. Nice cartoon, though, *chica.*"

He goes to hand it back to me, but I fumble in reaching for it such that it lands on the sideboard with the portrait face-up.

"Hmmm. That is our Paloma, is it not?"

I nod, then look down, all modest and shy.

He cocks his head, still looking at the painting. "That is not at all bad. I could show you some things," he says, plainly musing.

He looks over at the grinding table. "You have done enough of that for now. Set yourself up an easel."

I knock back the rest of my wine and joyously go get drawing board, paper, and easel.

"Pose, please," says Goya, and the boy gets back in position.

"Now, *guapa*, you must first get the gesture," instructs the Master, putting his charcoal to the paper. "You see how the line of the shoulders is a slope like this, and opposing it is the set of the hips. Now . . ."

I may be a mere model and chambermaid . . . but now I am also a student of Maestro Francisco José de Goya!

Olé!

Chapter 21

James Emerson Fletcher
Student
Temple of Buddha
Rangoon

Jacky Faber
Somewhere in the World
Probably Portugal

Dearest Jacky,
    I continue my studies with Master Kwai Chang. To-
day we kneel in the temple, facing each other in front of
the statue of the Buddha. He has been giving me instruc-
tions in the basics of this religion, this philosophy, really,
and I have found it all very enlightening. Today, however,
he discusses koans — *riddles designed to free the mind*
from ingrained patterns of thought — and he poses one
to me.
    "You know the sound of two hands clapping," he says,

holding up his two hands, palms out, before me. He then claps his hands together, once, twice, thrice, and then returns them to their original position. "But, Chueng Tong, do you know the sound of one hand clapping?"

I raise my own two hands, palms out to him, and let my mind roam free.

Chopstick Charlie, my most gracious host, has judged me recovered enough to inform me of what he knows about you, and your whereabouts:

"Beloved Number Two Daughter, Ju kau-jing yi, sometimes known as the Lotus Blossom and also known as Jacky Faber, was taken to Portugal to be on the staff of the great General Arthur Wellesley, as translator, aide, and, of course, spy."

Of course, I am thinking. *What else?* Well, at least you shall be relatively safe in the camp of the commanding general. That eases my mind, somewhat . . . except that I suspect you will be up to some mischief or other. Please be good, Jacky . . . Or at least careful.

My mind, that aforementioned sponge, goes back to the problem at hand. Hmmm . . .

I take my right hand and snap my fingers, once, twice, thrice. Then I return my hand to its original position.

"That, Master, is the sound of one hand clapping," I say, managing to suppress a smile at my own ingenuity.

Master Kwai Chang considers this for a while and then says, "Very good, Long Boy . . . for a novice. But this is really the sound of one hand clapping."

And he reaches out and slaps me across the face — once, twice, thrice. I am startled and jerk back.

"Is it not so, Chueng Tong?" he says, suppressing a smile of his own. "Go now and reflect upon today's lesson."

I remove myself and go to think on this . . .

Yours,
Jaimy

Chapter 22

A still life is set up in the center of the studio and the easels are arrayed about it. There are some apples on plates, a couple of oranges, some crockery, two dead rabbits — probably dinner — and much drapery. I suspect it is all to get us proficient at filling in the parts of paintings he finds boring, or not worthy of his skill. All of the painters who maintain a staff like Goya's do it — the Master paints in the hard stuff and the students paint in the curtains and all and then the Master comes back in to touch up their labors, and then the painting is shipped off to its new owner. Sort of like a factory. Actually, this rather appeals to the hard-nosed merchant in me.

We are about to get to work on it when Carmelita speaks up.

"A still life? What are we, dull tradesmen? Trolls toiling in caves?" She sneers. "Why do we not use her? That is what she is here for." She points her finger at me. "You! Get over there and disrobe. I will set the pose."

With a sigh, I put down my charcoal stick and get up to do what I am told. Carmelita has authority around here, so

I walk over and pick up the robe, unbuttoning my vest as I do so. Before I go behind the curtain, I glance around at the others. Asensio is silent but watchful, Cesar is very wide-eyed, and Carmelita is glaring daggers at me. Amadeo, however has something to say.

"Wait, Jack-ie. Carmelita — "

"Why should we wait? She is a model. She should pose."

"I have spoken to the Master and he says he has something special in mind for her." He cuts his eyes over to the large, so-far-untouched canvases.

"Special!" spits Carmelita. "*Special?* She is nothing but a common slut! *Una puta! Nada mas!*"

"Please, Carmelita," pleads Amadeo, trying to be reasonable. "I believe Maestro is . . . amused to watch her progress in drawing and painting."

"Ha! Her *progress,*" she snarls, her voice dripping with contempt. "She is but a clever animal — a cheap trick!"

"Whatever, Carmelita." Amadeo sighs. "If you wish to argue with Maestro, then go do it. The rest of us will get to work on our assignment."

He turns to his easel and I return to mine. The evil bubbles up in me and I cannot stop it. I let my skirt brush up against Carmelita, and I feel her stiffen at the touch. I think about giving her a bright smile, but I restrain myself . . . to a degree. Instead, I go stand next to Cesar, ruffle his hair, lean down, and whisper in his ear, *"Disappointed, chico?"*

He flushes bright red and nods, gulping in boyish confusion.

Ah, Jacky Faber — a hank of hair, some skin, and pieces

of bone, and that's all there is to her. But somehow . . . some-how . . . Heavy sigh . . . Boys, I swear.

Actually, I believe I have been coming along in the way of art. Of course, my drawing of the boy-with-pipe was the worst of all the students' efforts, but still, Goya had some good things to say about it and I was allowed to proceed to the oil painting of the same subject — first the underpaint-ing, the basic brush drawing in burnt umber thinned with turpentine. It seemed a shame to spoil the pure whiteness of the canvas with my crude strokes. But what the hell, I went at it.

The next day, after our underpaintings had dried, Goya came by to critique the work of the others and to start me on my first oil painting . . .

You see, when you mix the white with the sienna, you get a nice skin tone, and, yes, put it on the forehead there . . . right, like that, but for the shadows on the face and parts of the body, you must add some of the green, the complement to the red of the sienna, just enough . . . No, that's too much . . . More si-enna . . . There, that's it. Now put that on the side of the nose and blend across the bridge . . . Good . . . See?

I work away, reveling in the fluidity of the oil colors, how they mix, how they glow, how they glisten on the pal-ette and on the canvas. Oh, yes, I like it a lot, and as I work, I look over to the side where sit the two large, untouched canvases. Remembering what Amadco had said, I know that I will figure in the painting of them — and not, I sus-pect, as a student.

But why two?

Hmmm . . .

• • •

After we conclude today's still-life work, Carmelita thrusts a fistful of her brushes at me to clean and then storms out. I clean them and carefully arrange them in neat rows on her taboret, the little table that her palette rests upon. We each have one. Amadeo, as befits a fierce young artist, is careless with his, but I try to keep mine neat. I neaten up his, too.

The palettes are rectangular pieces of varnished wood, with the colors arranged around the edges. In imitation of the Master, they go from the top left with a big blob of white, to black, then the deep browns, then the sienna and ochres, then yellows at top right corner, then to the reds along the side, and down to the greens, three of them, and at the bottom, the blues, of which there are four.

After the day's work, it is my job to wipe out the mixing areas in the centers of the palettes with a rag soaked in turpentine so that they will be ready for the next day's artistic toil.

That done, I put rags aside and head upstairs to dress, for tonight we are going to Café Central, and I, for one, am looking forward to it with great anticipation.

I meet Cesar on the stairway on the way up and put my arm around his shoulders and give him my best vulpine grin.

"Come, my bold *caballero*, let us prepare for the night's revels," I say grandly. "And none but you, Cesar Maria Rivera y Romano shall be my gallant escort! Off! Off to the merry dance with us, and let dull care be forgotten!"

Olé, indeed . . .

Chapter 23

Somewhat blearily, I start the studio work of the day. Fresh oils squeezed out onto their proper places on the palettes, the easels set up with the paintings of the shepherd boy — or faun, or satyr, or whatever he's supposed to be — on each.

I look at mine, and even though I know it's not even close to the others in the way of skill, still, I feel a certain fondness for my work. While my effort lacks definition in the lad's muscles and overall form, he does have a certain mischievous look in his eye as he gazes out at the viewer with his lips wrapped around the pipe. I believe I will keep him, if I get the chance. Might look rather nice tucked into a corner of my cabin on the *Lorelei Lee*.

And yes, we did have a fine time at the Café Central last night, oh, yes, we did!

We arrived, the four of us, in what splendor we each could manage — Amadeo looking fine in tight black trousers with silver conchos up the side, frilly white shirt, and short black jacket with silver trim. His hair was oiled and pulled back and tied with a black ribbon, and on his feet, high-heeled black boots. On the way to the bistro, Amadeo stopped by a flower seller and bought a single red rose and presented it to me with a low bow. I took it and put it to my nose, inhaling its sweet fragrance, and then held it to my breast, smiling.

Asensio was dressed in a similar fashion, as was Cesar. I could not resist giving Cesar's tight little butt a pat as we walked along; it was just so neatly packed into those pants. He did not seem to mind, he was so plainly glad to be with the three of us.

I myself was dressed modestly in my new gaily embroidered black skirt and top, and before we left Estudio Goya, Asensio came up with a high comb and fixed it atop my wig-clad head, such that the mantilla, when draped over it, made a fine display. Thank you, Asensio! Now let us fly!

We burst into the place, full of our youth and our craziness, and we threw ourselves into the wildness of the night.

El Café Central was loud and full of brightly clothed Majos and Majas from wall to wall. There were four guitarists seated along the far wall, and three fiddle players on the near one, and one of them stood up to play. It was a malagueña, *and two dancers advanced to the center as we ordered drinks. The libations were brought and we drank them and ordered more. Yes, more food, more drink, more everything!*

We watched the dancers and pronounced them good, but Amadeo raised his chin, and, in a way, raised the ante when he declared, "He was good, but I could be better."

I poked him in the side. "Aha, muchacho? *You think you can do better than that?"*

"I do," he announced, thinking, I am sure, that he would

not be called on such an idle boast — but he did not know that I have been practicing that very dance with Django and some other very good teachers down at the Dos Gatos . . .

I, however, did know that, and I rose and extended my hand, golden castanets in place at my fingertips.

"Then come, Amadeo," I said. "Let us dance."

He fixed me with his eyes and stood to the challenge. We advanced to the floor and I placed a coin before the guitarras, and said, "Malagueña Salerosa." They nodded and began to play.

I charged out onto the center of the floor, not waiting for Amadeo, for I knew he would follow right behind me.

Hands above head, expression of disdain upon face, I started the beginning moves of the dance. I snapped the castanets and swirled about in time to the music, waiting to feel the touch of Amadeo.

In the flamenco, there is a certain form. The girl goes out and twirls about, looking cold and distant, seemingly oblivious to the male lurking at the edge of the stage. There is lots of fan work here — sometimes opened and sometimes folded and held before her face.

The man soon goes to stand beside her, hands on hips, shoulders square, looking every inch the macho male. As she twirls, hooded eyes peering over the top of the fan, he starts stamping his booted heels in time to the flamenco rhythm . . . RAM, tam . . . tam . . . RAM . . . tam . . . tam . . .

They circle about each other, both seemingly disdainful of the other, until, at last, she yields to his amorous advance, and they come together into an impassioned embrace, she bent backward and he leaning over her to take a triumphant kiss.

As did Amadeo and I. And did that rose end up in my teeth as I danced? Oh, yes, it did. And not only did it lend an elegant touch to the dance, but also to a rather interesting finale.

As I took the rose from my lips to receive the kiss, one of its thorns pricked my lower lip and I sensed a drop of blood forming there. Amadeo's face loomed over mine, his gaze intense, his arm around my waist as I was bent over backward. And then his mouth came down on mine, and when our lips parted, the blood was no longer there.

Right. *Ahem.* That was last night, but this is now.

The Master comes into the studio, looks about at our work on the shepherd boy, and says, "Okay. One more session. Finish them up. Good work all around. Let's get them done."

Sure enough, Goya has rendered his shepherd boy as Pan, a satyr, prancing about on goat legs and hooved feet. *Hmmm . . .* That sort of thing might be all right here in enlightened Europe, but it wouldn't do in Puritan Boston, that's for sure. I'm thinking that Maestro had best steer clear of things that some might consider devilish, as you never can tell if there might be some sort of religious fanatic hanging about, ready to pounce and point an accusing finger, damning you to hell and perdition. But, hey, what do I know?

We all get to work, and soon it is time to knock off for the day. Goya stands and says, "There. I am done. You may all touch up as you will."

He stands and stretches and then drops the bomb. "Tomorrow I go to the palace to paint the King. I will take Asensio and Cesar. Jacquelina, too. Make your preparations. Good evening, all."

Carmelita is up before him in an instant, slate in hand. "Her? Why?"

Goya looks at the slate and chuckles.

"Because she can speak French, Carmelita, nothing more. You remember that the court is now French, eh?" he says. "Carmelita, you have been to the palace many times. Why not give her a glimpse of all that false splendor? Now, no bickering, *niñas y niños*, please. Good evening."

He leaves and so do the lads, but Carmelita remains, standing stiff, stunned, and glaring at Goya's retreating form.

"Well, let's clean it up," I say, somewhat cheered by the events of the afternoon and trying to smooth things over a bit.

It doesn't work.

"Oh, yes," says Carmelita. "Let us *definitely* clean things up!"

With that she goes to her palette and loads up one of her large brushes with a big blob of black, which she brings over to my canvas. Locking her eyes on mine, she grinds the paint into the face of my shepherd boy, destroying him, and the painting, forevermore.

"Scrape that piece of slop down, and prepare the canvas for something a bit more worthy than your clumsy scribblings!"

It is like a punch in my gut. But I take it, telling myself that it was not my canvas, not my paints, so what right have I to complain?

I take up the palette knife and scrape the canvas down, dumping the now muddy paint into the trash.

Goodbye, shepherd boy, I rather liked you.

After the cleanup, I go out into the hallway, and I again meet Carmelita, standing there steaming. It seems she is not yet done with me.

"So what do you want, Carmelita?" I ask warily. "It seems you have won the day. I stand here in front of you, as completely destroyed as my poor painting. What more do you want of me?"

"I want you gone, you common piece of garbage, that's what I want!" she snarls. "That's really what I'm wishing for!"

"Why's that, Carmelita?" I ask. "I am insignificant. How could I possibly be a threat to you?"

"You . . . you come here and you make everybody love you while they . . . ignore me. Me, Carmelita Ysidora Gomez! And you, a common piece of dirt!"

"But what have I done, Señorita? Besides doing my job as best I can?"

She clenches her fists.

"It is your way . . . with Amadeo . . . He used to be — "

"Ah. You think you and he might be . . . *simpatico?* Is that it? Rest your mind, Señorita. I have no interest in Amadeo, other than as a friend, which he has proved to be."

"A *friend?* Is that all he is? Out dancing with you late last night?"

"I do not covet Amadeo."

"Maybe that is true, but he covets you."

"Perhaps you should have agreed to go out with him when he asked you."

"I am a lady! I do not go to such places!"

"Maybe you should stop thinking about being a lady, if you wish to someday be happy with a man who loves life. Perhaps, if you were . . . softer . . . acted more like a woman — "

"Act like you? With the simpering tongue, the batting eyelashes? Like that?"

"Sometimes it helps. They are men. We are women."

"I will not lower myself to do that."

"Perhaps you should."

"Perhaps you should just pick up and go away."

"I will gladly do that. When I feel it is time for me to go. I am just a simple girl trying to make my way in the world."

"You are not a simple anything. I thought you were . . . just another guttersnipe, but no, I was wrong, very wrong about you." Her eyes narrow and fix on mine. "No. You are a dirty little whore who has come here and sullied our household. And tomorrow . . . tomorrow . . ." she says, gagging on the words, "you will go to the court, instead of me. Good God! That a slut should gaze upon a king!"

I have had about enough. A red rage descends and I lift my knee and cram it into her crotch, at the same time bringing my forearm across her throat, pinning her to the wall.

"Listen to me, bitch," I hiss, my breath hot on her face. "I've had just about enough out of you! Come at me again in any way and I will make you pay! Do you understand, *perra?*"

175

She struggles in my grip, but I think she gets the message. Her eyes show fear — mine do not.

"Know this, Carmelita. I have been many things in this life, but *slut* is *not* one of them! Remember that when you talk to me!"

She whimpers and cries, but I do not let her go, oh no, not yet, I don't.

"And remember this, too. I have, in the past, been many times in the company of some very rough men, desperados, even . . . and among them I was sometimes known as *Bloody Jack*. And believe me, Carmelita," I snarl through my clenched teeth as I pull back her head and gaze deep into her frightened eyes, "I must admit I was very well named. Do you take my meaning, *bruja?*"

She quivers and nods and looks down. I release her and she staggers against the wall. I do not look at her as I walk away.

That's for my little shepherd boy, bruja!

.

Chapter 24

James Chueng Tong Fletcher
The Noble House of Chen
Rangoon

Jacky Faber
Location, God only knows

Dearest Jacky,
   This morning I made so bold as to request a favor of Kwai
Chang as we sat cross-legged, facing each other.

"Master," I said, "I have been as grateful of your instruction as a starving man is thankful for food, a drowning man
for air. It has sustained me in my hour of great need."

"Yes, my son?"

"However, you do know that I have been a naval officer,
a soldier."

He nods.

"And, as such, I am a man of action," I continued. "I
would like something . . . physical to do. Something active."

Yes, Teacher, I think I need more exercise than just chasing the shrieking Mai Ling and Mai Ji around the turquoise pool.

Master Kwai Chang considers this, then says, "Yes. That can be arranged, and I think the study of a different discipline would be good for you."

I bow my head in thanks.

"Am I correct in assuming you have fought with a sword?"

"Yes, Master. I have been trained in the use of that weapon."

"Then, I believe it would be good for you to pursue the Way of Bojutsu."

"Worthy Master will now tell Unworthy Student what that is," I reply.

"Worthy Master perceives that Unworthy Student employs edge of cheap sarcasm in his speech. However, I will respond: In the past, our country has been conquered many times by powerful men at the head of powerful armies. After they had subdued the populace, they outlawed the use, or even the possession of, weapons. No spears, no swords, not even knives. So the people developed ways of protecting themselves — fighting with bare hands and feet — and common things, like canes, like sticks."

"Sticks?"

"Yes, Long Boy, sticks. You are too old to learn the Kung Fu, the fighting with bare hands, and our way of fighting with swords is . . . ah . . . beyond your expertise. There is a Shaolin temple nearby. I will arrange for one of their monks to give you instruction in Bojutsu tomorrow. Now you must get back to your meditation."

That evening, when we sat at dinner, Charlie told me

that they expect the arrival soon of one of his ships from Britain, which might bring us news of the conflict in Europe. I certainly hope so, as I am desperate for news of you.

I told Charlie and his daughter of my coming introduction to the Way of Bojutsu and expressed a bit of disdain at the idea of fighting with mere sticks, when steel and bullet are so much more deadly.

Charlie chuckled and Sidrah merely patted my arm and smiled.

Yours,
Jaimy

Chapter 25

Yes, on the next day, we do indeed go to paint King Joseph of Spain, newly placed on the Bourbon throne by his brother Napoleon Bonaparte of France.

Starting early in the morning, our party of four — Goya, Asensio, Cesar, and I — all pile into an open wagon, with our materials, and eventually pull up before El Palacio Real de Madrid. Or rather, *behind* the palace — true, Goya is a famous artist, but when it comes to Royalty with a capital *R*, one still goes to the service entrance. Oh well, I suppose it is easier that way — less bowing and scraping and all that. Trust the household staff to get things done quickly and efficiently, no matter what the nationality.

We are shown to a large room lined with tapestries and filled with fine furniture. Thick carpets cover the floor and ornate draperies adorn the windows. A nice light filters in from those same high windows, which I know will be useful when it comes to doing the job.

Cesar and I set up the taboret and palette as Goya and Asensio discuss the setup, the pose, pointing this way and that.

"So you love Amadeo, then, Jacquelina," says Cesar, as he attends to his duties, his head down, seemingly quite crestfallen. "And not me."

Wot?

He had been very quiet on the way here, not at all his usual self. I thought he might be sick, and I was a bit worried about him.

"What makes you think that, Cesar?"

"The way you kissed him the other night," he says, looking away, not willing to meet my eyes. "I saw you. You cannot deny it."

"Come on, Cesar, that was a dance, a performance. It wasn't real."

"It looked real to me . . . and to everyone else at Café Central. They were all amazed . . . speechless . . . at the passion shown between the two of you."

"Look, Cesar, I like Amadeo very much, but—"

"But you love him more than me. Very well," he says, taking a deep and resolute breath. "If you go off with him, to be his wife and to bear his children and not mine, I will wish you long life and happiness—"

"Cesar—"

"And I shall enter a holy order. There are many artists in the past who have taken on the hair shirt of the monk and led celibate lives . . . Fra Angelico, Fra Lippo Lippi, Brother—"

"Right, but you shall not be one of them, Cesar," I say, fuming. "Now, get yourself over here."

With that I grab his collar and pull him into a side hallway and put him against the wall.

"So what is going on, Cesar?" I hiss. "Out with it."

He flushes red in the face. "You kissed Amadeo, and you have not kissed me."

"Yes, I have. Many times. Here's another," I say, and plant one on his forehead.

"Not like that," he says, blushing furiously. "A *real* kiss, like you gave Amadeo. Like you really mean it."

"Why, you conniving little weasel! All right, here!" I say, then plant a good one on his mouth. "There!"

He leans back against the wall, a dreamy expression on his face.

"Ah, Jacquelina, your lips are soft, soft like the pillows of clouds that float across the sky on a summer's day, your breath as sweet as a breeze that drifts over a field of clover, your — "

Oh, these Spanish boys with their honeyed words, I swear!

"You get back in there, Cesar," I say, shoving him back out into the main room. "Enough of that! We've got work to do!"

So we go out and get ready . . . and wait . . . and wait . . .

Eventually, there is a hustle and many people bustle about the room — well-dressed men, men in uniforms, men holding papers, men looking anxiously to the door.

"I believe the *King* is coming," whispers Asensio out of the side of his mouth, his voice dripping with contempt.

I give him a bit of an elbow and hiss back, "You be good now, Asensio! I know what you are thinking. Shush."

As for myself, I stand back and listen, for much of the babble is in French. *Hmmm* . . . I'm thinking, *I was sent here as a spy and I shall have to get some of this down on paper.*

That Field Marshall with all the medals on his chest is saying, *"Yes, Murat will move the First Fusiliers to . . ."* and *"Junot is in position to strike at . . ."*

I cannot be seen actually writing things down, but I will remember, and when I get back to the studio, I will record what I hear. I am, after all, a girl who does her duty.

El Rey! El Rey! is announced, and the people in the room line up against the walls. A door opens and a man walks in. All bow low, as the King strides to the center of the room.

He is dressed *afrancesado,* of course, and not only looks like, but also is dressed very much like, his brother, Napoleon Bonaparte. Blue jacket, gold sash, white trousers, black boots. Among other medals, he has the Legion of Honor on his left breast. I'll wager I did more for that bauble than he ever did, but so it goes.

"I am ready. Let us get this done," he says in French, and he strikes a pose.

He does look a lot like his brother, I'm thinking. I'm also thinking, as I look over at Goya, that the pose will not do. The master shakes his head and says, "Please, Majesty, if you would stand a little to the left there, so that the light . . ."

His Majesty does not understand, because Goya spoke in Spanish. Seeing that, the Master motions to me. I understand and step out.

"Please, your Majesty, forgive me my impertinence," I say softly in French. "But if you would place your left foot there, and bring your right foot over there. That's it . . . Now put your weight on your left leg . . . Oh, yes, magnificent."

I look over at Goya and he motions with his hands that the King should turn a bit more to the right, and I spin my hands about in front of King Joseph to get him to do it, but it doesn't work.

I look to Goya, but he shakes his head. All right, only one way to do this.

"Excellency," I say. "I ask your permission to touch your person."

He looks down at me, incredulous, but as I do not seem to be much of a physical threat, he nods.

There are gasps as I grasp the kingly hipbones in my hands and turn him several degrees to the right. I position his feet with gentle touching of my toes, and say, "Chin up, milord," with the backs of my fingers brushing the underside of his jaw. I look to Goya.

He smiles and nods and takes up his brush.

Goya works fast, laying in the underpainting with broad strokes of burnt sienna, which he then tempers with more narrow lines of burnt umber, and then finishes it with finer touches of black. He works fast for two reasons, I'm guessing: One, he'd rather be back in his studio working on what *he* wants to do, and two, kings are famously fidgety and impatient when it comes to sitting for a portrait. Goya had already painted King Carlos IV and Queen Maria Luisa and a whole gang of their children, so he knows quite well the process.

I stand by, ready with rag, brush, and thinner. Colors, too, when needed. As I do, I look out over the room and I think about things — yes, there are important people in this room. There are ministers of state and generals of great armies, that is true. However, if my friends at Estudio Goya expect me to be overawed by all the greatness, all the splendor, then I am afraid they will be disappointed, for I am not.

Have I not been presented to King George III of Britain only a few months ago? Did I not ride with Napoleon Bonaparte at Jena Auerstadt? What would you say, King Joseph, if you knew that I had fallen asleep in your own brother's lap in that coach in Germany? And did I not sit at the same table with United States President John Adams at Dovecote? I actually did. 'Course he wasn't President at that time, but who cares . . . A president is a president, as far as I can tell. Hmmm . . . I must request that Amy Trevelyne set up a party with Thomas Jefferson so that I can fill out my dance card for this period in history, at least.

Ah, the session is coming to a close. The King is bored, and Goya is done for the day. The underpainting must dry, so we get to leave and come back another day.

As I clean up the brushes and palette and stow all away for the next time, I look about me and reflect that, yes, a cat . . .

"A cat may look at a king!" I crow as we come to dinner that night. "And I did look upon him!"

Great laughter breaks out all around the table.

Goya has joined us, and we exult in the events of the day.

"We shall go back in four days," he says. "The imprimatura will be dry by then and we may proceed. Yes, Carmelita, you will go with us. Try not to sulk."

Señorita Carmelita Gomez has been very silent since our little confrontation in the hall. I am sure she is not used to being handled so roughly. Well, she sure had it coming, and to hell with her. She eats, head down, and says nothing. Fine. I'd rather have her that way than constantly carping at me.

"And you, Cesar," I tease. "We did not see much of you there, you know. Could it be that you snuck a young princess off into a secret alcove for a bit of . . . this and that?"

Cesar reddens.

"Well, there was a girl who was most impressed with our artistic skill," he says.

"'Our artistic skill'? Your tight little *culo,* you mean, *chico!*" Asensio says, then laughs. "Tell me, did you prance about in front of her? Was she covered in jewels?"

"Well, she was very finely dressed," allows Cesar, sinking deeper into his chair.

More laughter. Asensio has been diligently scribbling away on his slate and Goya enters into the fun.

"Do you think you could ask her to pose, Cesar? We could portray her as a nymph. We need some of those."

"Oh, no, Master. I'm sure her father would object. He seemed to be a very important man. At least, I thought that when he discovered us and dragged her away . . . and not very gently at that."

Ribaldry swirls about the table.

"Oh, ho, Cesar! A conquest!" crows Amadeo. "And you so young! Your first! Congratulations!"

"I am sure she will treasure the memory of her gallant artiste!" I say, grandly waving around an imaginary brush. "Until the last of her days, he will live in her heart, and she will think on what might have been!"

"Or until the next pretty boy comes by," says Asensio, casting a glance at Amadeo.

"A very exciting day, all around," I say, taking a sip of my wine and glancing sideways at the sullen Carmelita. She does not respond.

"Exciting?" says Amadeo. "Ha! I'll tell you what's exciting. It's next week when truly exciting things happen. I cannot wait!"

I am curious.

"And what is that, Amadeo, to make you exult so?"

"Why, Jacquelina, don't you know?" he replies. "It is the beginning of the bullfighting season!"

I put down my glass.

"I do not like bullfighting. It is cruel and not fair. The bulls do not have a chance. There is no honor in it."

"Maybe not in the ring, Señorita," he says, smiling over at me. "But there is a time when the bulls do have a chance for revenge."

"And when is that?" I ask, mystified.

"It is called the Running of the Bulls, Jack-ie," says Cesar proudly. "It happens every year, right outside our balcony."

What?

"Yes, Jacquelina," he goes on. "The bulls for the ring are run through the streets before La Corrida de Toros! You should see it! *Los toros* are magnificent in their power and strength! And the young men run with them to show their bravery! And this time, I am old enough, and in your name, I will run with them!"

Wot?

Chapter 26

"That is, without a doubt, the stupidest thing I have ever heard of, Cesar, and you shall not do it," I say with deep resolution, as we walk down Calle de Embajadores, on our way to a used-clothing shop that he knows of. It is payday, and I have some things I wish to buy.

"But, Jack-ie, love of my very life, I must prove myself to you," he says. "If I do not do it, you will think less of me, and that I could not stand." He puffs up. "I must have your love and respect."

I laugh and clasp the lad to me. "You already have my love, *mi querido,* but you will not have my respect if you do that crazy thing! *Madre de Dios!* You weigh one hundred and twenty pounds and those beasts weigh fifteen hundred pounds each. And there will be seventy of them, all very angry. In that narrow street? *Loco,* that is what it is. No, I forbid it."

"We shall see, Señorita, just what you will forbid," he says, chin up, with some of his own manly resolution. "I am the man, and you are the girl."

Oh-ho, we shall see about that, little man . . .

"Ah. Here we are," he says as we stop in front of a little shop. "It is not a fancy place, but it is where I buy my clothing. I am but a poor student of art."

"I know that, Cesar," I say, sweeping into the place. "You are poor, but have the heart of the lion, and that is what is important. And I am sure this shop will be just the thing."

And it is.

"*Buenas dias, Señorita*," says the woman who approaches us. "What can I find for you?"

"I want a pair of trousers just like his," I say, pointing to the pants Cesar wears, all black, tight, with silver *conchos* up the sides and embroidery across the butt. "And the jacket, too."

"Señorita wants to dress as a matador?" asks the woman, aghast.

"It is for a private party, Señora. All girls. There will be no scandal, I assure you."

She shrugs and goes to find the items. While she searches, I spy a nice little hat on a shelf — wide brim, round crown, black, of course, and brightly decorated. I try it on over my wig, and it fits just fine. "Good, I'll take it," I say, reflecting that money does not ever stay long in the Faber pocket. "And, oh, a nice pair of pumps, too."

"What are you going to do, Jack-ie?" asks Cesar, puzzled. The proprietress returns with the requested garments over her arm, and I take them up.

I see a dressing screen and head for it, saying, "In the States we call it 'blackmail,' *chico*. You shall see."

I duck behind the screen and begin shedding clothes. When I am down to my skin, I pull on the pants — oh, yes, good and tight, just the way I like it — and button the high waist over my frilly white shirt. Then the short jacket — nice fit around the shoulders, yes, the woman has a good eye for sure — pumps on feet and hat on head, and I step out.

"Ta da! *Viva el matador!*"

Cesar's jaw drops, as does the jaw of the shopkeeper.

"Madre de Dios!" she whispers, shocked.

"Madre de Dios!" echoes Cesar.

"Cuanto para todos?" I ask, prancing around, preening.

It turns out, the price is right and Cesar carries my bundle for me as we head back to Estudio Goya. I even have some money left, and so I push Cesar into La Taberna de Dos Gatos for a treat.

I signal for wine and tapas, nod at Django, who sits playing quietly off to the side, and settle in.

When the barmaid brings the food and drink, I order a glass for Django as well, and he nods in appreciation and begins playing *"Los Bilbilicos,"* which he knows is my favorite.

"So what is this 'blackmail' of which you speak, my heart of hearts?" asks Cesar, not to be denied an explanation.

I pop a nicely marinated baby octopus in my mouth, chew, and drop it down the throat before replying.

"You see, *pepito,* it is like this. When you know something about a person, something that person does not want to be generally known, you send him a letter saying that you will expose him if he does not do as you say. Hence, the 'blackmail.' It usually is a demand for money, or position, or some desired action. Like 'You'd better leave my daughter alone or I will tell the world that you absconded with the church funds and have been copulating with goats!'"

"That is terrible and awful, but what does that have to do with us, *mi querida?*"

"Simply this, my heart. If you and Amadeo and Asensio run with the bulls, then so will I, and I cannot run in a dress. Simple, eh? Why should you boys have all the fun?"

"But you cannot," he protests. "You are a woman! It is not allowed!"

"We will see what is not allowed, my sweet little puppy," I retort, placing my finger on his nose. "But that is the deal nonetheless: You run, I run. *Sin duda!*"

"Jacquelina, it is . . ."

Suddenly a shadow falls over us as a man, a large man, comes up beside us and pulls out a chair.

Startled, I look up, and Cesar reaches for his sword and goes to rise. The man puts his meaty paw on Cesar's head and pushes him back down.

"Calm yourself, little man," growls the intruder. "My business is not with you."

"Montoya!" I exclaim, recognizing the solid and very dusty guerrilla.

"*Sí, Señorita,*" he says, smiling through his thick mustache. "It is, indeed, I."

"About time, Señor," I say, miffed. "Where the hell have you been? You were supposed to deliver my poor self to Madrid and you disappeared when there was only a little bit of trouble, leaving me on my own. Some macho strongman . . . Ha! I have known better men among urchins on the streets of London!"

Montoya smiles and picks up one of my octopuses and places it in his mouth, his big teeth grinding on both the *tapa* and my insulting words.

"I was recovering from a bullet in my side, *mi guapa*," he says, his eyes on mine. "My men dragged me away. I could do nothing for you then."

"And what will you do for me now, Pablo? You see I managed to get here without your help."

"I know you are a *muchacha* of great resolve. A fine piece of female flesh, but also tough as a strip of leather," he says, and then hooks a thumb at the astounded Cesar. "Who is he?"

"He is a fine *Madrileño*. A brave boy, and a true son of Spain. Anything you want to say to me, you can say in front of him."

"Hmmm," says Montoya, regarding Cesar with some doubt. "Very well, do you have anything to report to our superiors?"

"Only that I have gained entrance to the palace and have been in the presence of King Joseph and heard many things said by his ministers and generals that might be of interest to our . . . superiors."

His bushy eyebrows go up.

"The very palace? You do have your ways, *chica*."

"I have been told that before."

"*Bueno*," he says, rising. "Write out what you have discovered and I will get it to our people. I will meet you here tomorrow at five—"

"At seven, *hombre*."

"Seven, then. If we fail to meet, you can find me at 435 Calle de Ocho, Room 21. It is right around the corner."

"I will do that, Montoya. Tomorrow then. *Adiós.*"

"*Adiós, compadres,*" he says, smiling on the both of us. "*Viva España.*"

He straightens and strides to the door. On his way out, he puts his hand to his brow and says, "*Hola, Django.* It is good to see you again."

I wonder about that as I settle back and begin to explain things to a very bewildered Cesar.

I put my hand on his . . .

Cesar, it is like this . . . I am not altogether what I seem to be . . .

Chapter 27

Since we have a bit of a breathing spell from the palace — after all, even kings and princes cannot make paint dry any faster than it will — we return to our own pursuits.

In the studio, the chatter is all about the running of the bulls and the law that I have laid down concerning all that macho silliness.

I am sure that Carmelita would want to say something in regard to that, but since our confrontation in the hall, she has not said a single word to me. I wonder what she is about? Is she cowed, or is she up to something? One thing I do know — I must be careful.

As I go about setting up the palettes, I notice that there are only four taborets set out and one of the big canvases is up on a large sturdy easel. There is a green couch resting on the model platform. It has one high end — a bolster, like — and has several big pillows and sheets strewn across it. On the bed sits some folded clothing, as well.

Hmmm . . .

I look to Amadeo and raise my eyebrows in question.

"You will pose today, Jack-ie," he says, blushing slightly. "Maestro wants you to put on those clothes there and then lie upon the couch." He gives out a bit of a dry cough. "With the wig on, *por favor.*"

I nod and go to do it.

I have noticed that, since our torrid little dance at Café Central, Amadeo's glances at me have grown ever more warm. *Hmmm . . .*

I take the clothing and duck behind the screen. I look at what I am to wear: a loose, somewhat transparent white gown with a low-cut bodice, a red satin sash to wrap around my middle, and a top that is gold brocade with filmy gold sleeves and black net cuffs. I sigh, drop my regular serving-girl garb — all of it — and put on the outfit. With all this *Maja* finery upon the Faber body and golden slippers on the Faber feet, Jacky Faber, model, steps out just as Maestro steps in.

"Good, Jacquelina," he says upon seeing me properly decked out. "Please lie on the couch with your feet to this end."

I go, place my silk-clad bottom on a cushion, swing my legs up and over, and then rest my back against the bolster. I look to Goya for further instructions.

"Yes, now slide a little farther that way . . . That's it. Tuck the dress between your legs. Good."

Well, even though I'd rather be painting, the pose is easy.

"Now raise your arms above your head."

Uh-oh . . . not quite so easy. Oh, well . . .

"*Bueno*," says Goya, going to his canvas and picking up a stump of charcoal. "Look directly at me. That's it. Let us begin."

As they scratch away, I pass the time thinking about the events of the past two days.

The first night after my surprise meeting with Montoya, I found some discarded paper and, by candlelight, wrote down everything I could remember from the overheard conversations at the palace, anything that possibly could be of value to Wellesley, or whoever else is in charge of British forces in Portugal and Spain. When given a task, I tend to do my duty, if I perceive the cause to be worthy, and, I suspect, the liberation of Spain is a worthy goal. I wonder if Amy Trevelyne would agree? And what would she think of my harem outfit? Ha! I have to suppress a smile.

My nose begins to itch, as it always does when I am not allowed to scratch it. I wiggle it around a bit, but that doesn't help. *Put your mind on something else, girl, for you will be holding this pose for a long, long time.*

Yesterday, after I had passed the papers to Montoya and he had left the Dos Gatos, I spent some time with Django. We shared some wine and he showed me some more moves on the guitar. We talked, and he told me more stories of the *Roma*, the traveling people we call gypsies — tales of the great caravans, the beautiful women, the wild singing and dancing around blazing campfires in new and strange lands, always new places, always the winding road stretching out ahead of the brightly colored wagons. He laughed when he described it all, and I listened wide-eyed and rapt. The life of the Roma appealed to the wild side of my nature, that's for sure.

But how came you to be here, Papa? Why did you leave the road and all its charms?

Ah, chica, *it was the stiffening of the bones. After I could not keep up, I had to leave . . .*

I had observed Django trying to walk upright and straight, without limping, and failing at it. Poor man, I thought, for I knew, from my time with Dr. Sebastian, that it was creeping arthritis and there was nothing to be done about it, except suffer its presence. Well I remember Jemimah Moses, my cook back when I ran the *Nancy B.* down to the Caribbean, how she would grind her fist into the small of her back and groan, "Oh, my Lord, when Uncle Arthur comes to visit, he don't *never* go home."

But I was fortunate, Jacquelina, in that it only affected my legs and not my hands, so I am able to play the guitarra *and sing and make my way for whatever time I have left in this world.*

He put his fingers on the strings and played a piece I had not heard him do before.

I have never heard anyone play as beautifully as you, Django, with as much . . . feeling . . . so much soul.

He put up his guitar and looked upon me, fondly, I believe. He chuckled and reached into his vest pocket.

You are a good girl, little one. Here, take this.

He handed me a smooth chip of wood, about two inches square. On one side is carved a symbol, something that looks like a *J* contained in a circle. Into the carved grooves is rubbed a yellow pigment, and it is all smoothly glossed with oil.

What is it, Maestro?

He took a sip of wine and said . . .

Keep that with you always, Jacquelina. If you are in trouble sometime and the Roma are nearby, show that to them. It was my sign when I was chief of a great caravan, before I was brought low. They will recognize it. Trust me.

I will, Jefe, *and thank you.*

I stood and placed a kiss on his forehead and left to go back to the studio. I was walking along, somewhat subdued, thinking on what Django had said, when I was startled to see Carmelita come striding along on the other side of our street. I ducked back around a corner to watch.

Hmmm . . . Carmelita almost *never* goes out — except to Mass with the rest of us. She looked a bit furtive as she swept by and entered the studio, and I leaned back against a wall and wondered . . .

Where did she go? She had no packages under her arm, so she did not go shopping . . . and why did she not take one of the lads with her? Most girls in Spain don't go out without escorts, not girls of Carmelita's class, anyway. Where was she coming from?

I looked down the street and saw, way down at the end of it, across the plaza, the Basilica de San Francisco el Grande.

Could she have gone there? To pray, to offer Confession, to say the Act of Contrition for being such a miserable . . . Nay, much more likely she was praying for the salvation of her precious soul and the damnation of mine.

• • •

"Break."

I stand and stretch, and rub my traitorous nose with the palm of my hand, and then walk about to ease my poor joints and to check out the progress on the paintings.

The students are using *velos* — open frames of wood on which are stretched black cords to make a grid. The *velos*, which are proportional to the canvases on which they are working, are set up on separate easels a few feet from each student. They have made use of T-squares to pencil in similar squares on their canvases, and so are able to transfer the reality — me lying there in all my supposed glory — to the two-dimensional surface of the canvas. Like, in the top right square is part of my face and so they put that part in, and then the next square, and so on and so on. I have been told *velos* have been in use since the Dark Ages, and I find them fascinating. When I set up my own studio, I shall employ them. Anything to make life, and work, easier is all right with me.

Goya, of course, does not use the *velo* but charges right on in. He is, after all, the Master.

I pause at Cesar's and he looks up and I give him a bit of a wink. The other day, after our first encounter with Montoya, I had to tell the lad that I was a freedom fighter, giving my all for the liberation of España, which was not quite true, but he ate it up and has been filled with patriotic zeal ever since. *You and I,* mi apasionada, *we shall fight together in the cause of* libertad! I swear him to secrecy and he promises to button his lip. I thought to tell him of my credo, "Oftimes it seems to me, 'patriotic' rhymes with 'idiotic,'" but I don't bother. He is much too fired up.

I review Amadeo's and Asensio's drawings, compliment both, and then . . .

"Pose, please."

Heavy sigh as I mount the platform yet again.

Anyway, Jaimy, as I was saying . . .

Chapter 28

James Fletcher
Somewhat Bruised
House of Chen
Rangoon
I Don't Care What Date

Jacky Faber
In Spain, as close as I can figure
But it could as well be Zanzibar, if past history is any clue

Dearest Jacky,

Tonight, before dinner, I lie face-down on a mat while the lovely Sidrah kneels by my side. I try to suppress a groan as she rubs the aromatic and very soothing unguent into my poor abused muscles.

The young Shaolin monk Sifu Loo Li was presented to me today in an open green field close by the Buddhist temple. Master Kwai Chang made the introductions, we all bowed to each other, and Master Chang left the field.

Sifu Loo Li carried with him two bamboo sticks, each as long as we were tall, and about one-inch thick. He handed me one, bowed again, and stepped back about ten yards. He whipped his stick around himself in very fluid motions and ended up in a position very much like the "lunge" movement in our own Western sword technique, except that his staff is tucked under his right arm, while his other arm is extended straight out, palm open before me.

I suspect this is the ready position, the en garde, as we barbarians know it. *Well, we shall see, China boy . . .*

I take my staff in both my hands, sort of like what I have seen in paintings of the knights of old, with their two-handed broadswords, my left hand lower on the stick, my right hand higher, and advance toward him.

When we get about six feet from each other, he whips his cane from under his arm and whirls it around over his head. I lunge forward, using my training in the saber, and seek to strike him on his open left side.

I don't even get close.

His stick is a blur as he brings the end down, turns completely around, and brings it up under my staff, to lay it hard against my chin. Had he put any force into it, he would have broken my jaw.

He bows again, steps back, and assumes his original position.

I hear a chuckle behind me and, slightly bewildered, I see Master Chang reappear, leaning on his own staff, coming to sit on the grass to the side.

"You see, Long Boy, it might be a bit more complicated than you originally thought, eh?"

I nod in agreement, quite chastened.

"Sifu Loo Li will now show you the First Position, 'The Opening Flower,' it is called."

"A gentle thing, a flower," he goes on. "It smells sweet, but beware what lies within."

The lad comes up next to me and motions that I take my staff and . . .

. . . the instruction goes on for several hours . . . several grueling hours.

"When one learns through pain, Long Boy, one learns the lessons twice over," says the Master, and I grit my teeth and endure both the pain in my body and the shame of the novice. "Now you must learn 'The Strike of the Silver Snake' . . ."

At dinner, Charlie informs me that the ship bearing news of the fight against Napoleon has not yet arrived.

"Unfortunate, that," says Charlie, eyeing the two of us, Sidrah and myself sitting across from him, she kneading my still-aching shoulders. "Perhaps it is time for you to return to the barbarian world, as I think your mind is in order now."

"But, Honored Father, I believe Jai-Mee-San needs a bit more . . . rest," says Sidrah softly.

Charlie snorts. "Ha! Rest! I am sure that is what he has been getting, the dog! But that is not what causes me concern."

"And what is that, Honored Chen?" I ask, as Sidrah places a pink shrimp to my lips.

"I fear the wrath of Number Two Daughter, Ju-kau-jing yi, should Number One Daughter, Sidrat'ul Muntaha, enter into connubial bliss with Honored Guest," he says, casting a knowing eye at the two of us. "And if he should never again return to side of The Little Round-Eyed Barbarian, I am certain she would demand the head of poor old Chops on a plate."

Charlie pauses, picks up the pipe of his hookah, and takes a deep puff.

"This match I would not mind, as I have found you, Chueng Tong, to be a rather fine fellow, and I compliment the Lotus Blossom on her taste. However, should I ever give up Sidrah, I have a rich Burmese prince in mind, much more advantageous to the House of Chen than a poor, penniless Brit, however charming he might be."

Sidrah cocks a knowing eye at her doting father, knowing full well he would never do anything to cause her any unhappiness.

I nod, knowing that, in spite of all the kindness extended to me here, I will get back to Europe and I will find you, Jacky.

Yours,
Jaimy

Chapter 29

There is great excitement within the walls of the House of Goya, for today the bulls will run through the streets of Madrid, and stupid young men will run with them.

After breakfast, I go to my room to change.

Paloma is out doing up the other chambers, so I don't have to explain to her just why I am climbing into this outfit. Doffing my usual serving-girl garb, I fold it and put it in my seabag. Yes, I had bought material last payday and had stitched up a new one, and am stowing all my meager belongings in it. *Jacky Faber can be off and gone in five minutes* has always been my watchword, and it has stood me in good stead many times. It is only when I forget to be prepared that I get in trouble.

The one thing I do not keep in the seabag is my wineskin — that useful item I have filled with water and it hangs from a hook next to my bed, ready to grab should I have to run. I well remember how thirsty I got on the flight from Portugal to here.

Since the bulls do not run until noon, I have some time to reflect on the past weeks . . .

Yes, the work on the King's portrait goes well, and in my role as spy, I am able to glean more information that might prove useful to British Intelligence — overheard conversations betwixt military types, ministers, and such. I do not judge the value of the content, I just send it on to Montoya. I certainly do not let any at the palace know that I am fairly fluent in French. It brings a smile to my lips to think that my dispatches might possibly get back to dear Higgins, since, as far as I know, he is still on the staff of General Wellesley and working closely with the spymaster and cryptographer. I put a tiny JMF in one margin just in case he might be watching.

One thing has been a bit worrying in that regard, however. On two occasions when I was out to take my lessons with Django, I sensed that I was being watched. Turning around suddenly when I felt eyes upon me, I twisted about abruptly and thought I caught a glance of a black-robed figure ducking behind a corner. I could have been mistaken, but still I asked Montoya on our next meeting if he had his men out watching me and he replied that he did not. *I have most of my men camped out beyond the city,* muchacha, *only a few here.*

Hmmm . . . Well, I must be careful, I'm thinking, as I have no wish to end up strapped into the embrace of *el garrote,* a particularly ghastly form of execution by strangulation employed by the Spanish. Considering this, I had Cesar deliver my packets to Montoya at his digs at Calle de Ocho. I gave him strict instructions:

If you are caught, you tell them some foolish girl gave you five reales *to take the package to a man at that address. You don't know his name. You thought they were love letters. Do you understand,* chico?

Yes, my dearest one, but I shall not deny you! Never! I will die for the glory of Spain and for you, my heart! My last words shall be "Viva España, Viva Jacquelina!" I will die with your name on my lips!

Geez, and I thought I was a hopeless romantic.

Earlier, upon coming to live at Casa Goya, I had, of course, thoroughly scouted out the place. I noted that there are three levels — dank basement, studio and kitchen down, living quarters up. It faces on the grand plaza, but to the back and sides of it are narrow streets — alleys, really. And wrought-iron balconies extend over them, both from our building and the ones next to us.

After I had taken some lessons from Django, it had become my habit to come out on the right-side balcony to play very softly upon my borrowed guitar, so as not to disturb anyone — not anyone in our house, nor the people across the street, who also like to sit upon their own balcony on a sweet warm night.

One evening, as I sat out there strumming, I was pleased to see Amadeo come to join me. He had two glasses of Madeira, one of which he placed on the railing at my right hand, making it most plain that this was not a chance encounter.

"Thank you, Amadeo," I said. "You are very kind."

"My pleasure, entirely, Jacquelina," he said, leaning on the rail and surveying the cobblestones below.

I put the guitar aside, took glass in hand, and rose to stand next to him.

"So that is where the bulls will run?"

"*Sí, Señorita*. Right down there. It is quite a sight. Just you wait."

"I think it is stupid," opined the hypocrite Jacky Faber, who had, in the past, given herself up to many a wild, chaotic night. "You have heard what I told Cesar?"

"*Sí*. But he is only a boy and hopelessly in love with you. He may do as you say and not run with the bulls."

"But you and Asensio?"

"We are not little boys like Cesar, Señorita," he whispered. "And we do not think you will carry through on your threat . . . Not after you see the bulls coming. You are but a girl — a brave one, to be sure, but after all, still just a girl."

All this time, he has been angling his face ever closer toward mine.

Hmmm . . .

Amadeo is very handsome, and he *has* been very kind to me . . .

He put his fingers under my chin and gently inclined my face upward.

"You have not forgotten that kiss, that very special kiss, *caro mio?*" he whispers, his breath hot on my face. "That kiss we shared that night as we danced and the world fell away, leaving us alone, just the two of us . . . and the music, the rose, the drop of your precious blood?"

"Ah no, Amadeo," I breathe. "How could I forget that?"

"Then another little kiss, *chica*, on this warm and lovely night, one that was made for soft love and gentle kindness?"

Well, when you put it that way . . . why not?
Ummm . . .

As for Carmelita, who has yet to say a single word to me since our confrontation, rest assured that I'm watching her with a wary eye. She attends to her work, and is diligent in it. Her painting of me in *Maja* costume is competent and complete. It is cool and detached, and shows no inkling of the dislike I know she feels toward the model. *I am painting an insignificant girl, dressed up like the slut she is,* Carmelita was surely thinking as she worked away. I could see it in her eyes.

Fine, I say. *Let her stay well away from me. However, there had been one other time . . .*

I was out on the side balcony one night, in the cool of the evening, strumming my guitar softly, when I happened to glance down and notice Carmelita emerging from a side door below. She gazed furtively about, then headed off in the same direction I had seen her come from before . . . But this time she had a folder beneath her arm, like a small portfolio. What was she up to? Selling artwork on the side? Can she have purloined some of Maestro's discards to peddle them off for her own profit? I don't know, but, certainly, I will watch.

Oh, well, enough idle thoughts. *Into the tight toreador pants with you, girl, and yes, the frilly white shirt and the neat little top.* I pull my black embroidered skirt from my seabag and pull it on over my trousers. No sense in scandalizing anyone more than I have to. If the lads are good, it will stay on, if not . . .

I go down to join the others on the balcony, to watch the Running of the Bulls.

They are all there, the students, the staff, Goya, yes, and even his wife, Josefa, in a wheelchair, poor thing, but still seeming to enjoy the excitement of the day.

Cesar comes over next to me, his gaze hot.

"You will not let me do it, Jack-ie? You will not let me prove myself a man?"

"You are already a man, Cesar," I say, lifting my skirt a bit to show him the cuff of my trousers below, with its implied threat. "You do not have to prove yourself to me."

He says nothing to that, but I sense his frustration. So young, so full of bravado, to be denied release . . . *Oh, well, it's for your own good, lad. Maybe next year.*

I look over at Amadeo and Asensio. They are both dressed in *Majo* splendor, in outfits similar to mine, with red sashes about their waists. Paloma, also dressed in her best, has placed out trays of snacks and glasses of wine, and I go over to help pour.

Amadeo lifts his glass to me. "To love and beauty," he says, taking a drink. I lift my own glass and return the toast.

"To love and happiness," I say. "And to the health and safety of those about me."

All around drink to that, but Cesar does not miss the glances that are exchanged betwixt Amadeo and me. No, he does not, and he is not at all pleased. *Rest your mind, Cesar, it is nothing. You'll see, my dear little fellow, you'll see . . . It is just a harmless dalliance betwixt good friends, that's all.*

Looking across the street, I see that the balcony opposite us now contains three *Majas,* all dressed in the finest of garments. As I watch, I see that they are joined by two young men, dressed very *Majo,* and very *macho.*

They look across and bow.

We bow back, and then . . .

. . . then there is a tremendous trumpet blast! *"The bulls are coming! The bulls are coming!"*

I look up the street and see, at the far end, a crowd of young men running down the street, laughing and shouting. Behind them is a wall of bull — hump-backed bulls, red-eyed bulls, black-faced bulls, bulls snorting red steam out of their nostrils. Well, it sure looks red to me, anyway, as I stand trembling on that balcony.

My attention is diverted by another movement across the street. The two young men on the opposite balcony have vaulted over the railing to land in the street. They turn and bow to the ladies above them. The girls cheer and clap and throw roses down on their lads.

I feel Amadeo quivering beside me.

"Don't do it, Amadeo, *please!* For me!"

One of the young men, his lady's token rose now in his red sash, looks up at my own lads and calls out, *"Vamos, hermanos! Vamos! Arriba! Arriba! Ándale! Ándale!"*

When Amadeo and Asensio stay standing on our balcony, the man below changes his tone. "Ha! Weaklings! Cowards! *Maricóns!"*

It is too much, to be called that. Too much for Amadeo and Asensio, who quickly strip off their jackets — and even too much for Cesar.

Damn stupid male pride!

The three jump down into the street as the mob of bulls and men draws ever closer.

Well, they asked for it! I fume, as I unloosen my skirt and whip it off. *Just a girl, eh? Well, we'll see!*

I whip off my wig and toss it to the astounded Paloma, and then I, too, am over the rail and standing in the street next to Cesar.

The crowd of men running to the front of the bulls has reached us, and Asensio and Amadeo disappear in their midst. I notice that some of the bull runners have flattened themselves against the side walls, and after seeing some men stumble in front of the advancing pack and fall beneath the hooves of the bulls, I figure that's the safest option.

"Cesar!" I scream over the mayhem. "To the wall! With me, now!"

I grab his arm and drag him to the side as the press of men and bulls is upon us. We stand, our backs to the stones and feel the crush — first of desperate men, then of crazed and maddened bulls, then, no men, just bulls, raking their murderous horns back and forth. There goes another man down, there is another badly gored, on his knees and clutching his belly.

Suddenly, I can see no more as a rough, heavy, barrel-chested and hairy body is pressed against my face. *Good Lord, I can't breathe, I can't . . .*

The beast moves away, and I gulp down a breath. I still have Cesar by the arm and I screech at him, "We cannot stay down here! We'll be trampled! Follow me up!"

The bull, which had us momentarily pinned, stands stalled in front of us, pawing the ground in bullish frustration, unable to move forward because of the crush. I reach up, grab a handful of hair, and pull myself up to straddle his back, right behind the hump.

I thrust my hand down to Cesar and he grasps it, and I pull him up behind me.

"Watch your legs! Other bulls may gore you!"

He pulls his legs up high on the flanks of the bull, as do I — almost, my crazed mind remembers, jockey-fashion, and I am once again on the back of the Sheik of Araby, except that the Sheik liked me, and this bull definitely does not.

Before, the bull was merely snorting out his displeasure, now he bellows with rage at feeling us on his back. He charges forward, finding a hole in the pack and lunging through it, bucking madly.

"Hang on to me, Cesar! If you fall, you are dead!" Cesar glances back at the herd behind us and needs no further encouragement. He locks his arms around my waist as I clamp my legs as tightly as I can against the bull's heaving ribs.

We can't stay here forever. If we get to the plaza, the bull will have room to really buck and we will not be able to hold on! We will be lost.

I see the light from the open plaza at the end of the street and despair. But then I see something else — a long, low wrought-iron balcony looming ahead.

"Cesar!" I cry. "Stand up! On the bull's back! Put your hands on my shoulders. That's it! See that balcony? Jump up and grab it when we get under it! You jump first, and I'll grab the other end! Ready? Go!"

I feel him get his feet under him and then, yes! He leaps up and grabs the iron and swings away, out of harm's way.

My turn now.

As we gallop beneath the deck, I gather my strength and . . . *There! That loop of iron, there!*

I leap, but while my fingertips touch it, I cannot make it and I fall back down on the bull, as we burst out into the square.

Sure enough, given room, the bull proceeds to buck wildly, swinging his great head back and forth, leaping in the air to come down on stiffened forelegs, using all his tricks to get rid of the annoying burden on his back.

Oh, Lord, I am lost! If I hit the ground, he will turn and gore me with his terrible horns, he will . . .

He won't do that at all, as salvation comes in the form of a *picador,* a man riding a thickly padded horse and carrying a spear.

"Up behind me!" the man shouts, and he brings his horse alongside.

I need no further instruction. I grab a strap on the back of his jacket and pull myself aboard.

Thank you, Lord, thank you, I whisper as I lean my head into the man's back.

"Look, *chico,*" he says. "You are the hero! The one who rode *el toro!* See them cheer!"

I look out over the plaza and see other *picadors* rounding up the bulls and guiding them to an open gate at the side of the *corrida.* They are holding up their spears and waving them at me, shouting something. There are people leaning out of windows on the plaza, also cheering.

Viva, Viva el Rubio! Viva el Rubio!

The Blonde, herself, does not quite believe that she is still alive, let alone being cheered.

But, what the hell, I'll take it. I do love applause . . .

I direct my lovely *picador* to take me back down my street, and there we go. I make so bold as to struggle to stand behind my rescuer, smiling and waving at the crowd as we go.

Showoff? Yes. I'm afraid it's in my nature. Sin of pride, I know, but what can I do? I am helpless . . .

Eventually, we arrive under our balcony. I leap up, grab some iron, and soon am back on the balcony of Casa Goya.

"Well, now," I say to the astounded members of Estudio Goya. "That was a little bit of all right. *Olé?*"

Chapter 30

Hoo-ray, it was payday again! And the job at the palace was done! King Joseph had pronounced himself pleased with his portrait, so Estudio Goya packed up and decamped from El Palacio Real, gold *escudos* in the Master's hand. When we got back, all were given an extra packet of coins, and the freedom of the day as well.

Of course, I was off shopping, with Cesar by my side, me joyous, and him, I noticed, moping a bit.

I gave him a poke. "So why the long face, Cesar?"

"It is you, Jacquelina," he stammered. "I fear you love Amadeo and will go off with him. I could not stand that."

I gave him a knowing look . . . and a smile. Then I put my arm around his waist and held him to me.

"I am going off with nobody, my fine young lad, and though it is true that I *like* Amadeo very much," I said, planting a kiss on Cesar's frowning face, "it is you that I *love,* my bold *toreador.* And even though you disobeyed my wishes and ran with the bulls, I shall always remember how your strong arms came about my waist when we were on the back of that raging beast and how you held my frail self firmly to keep me from falling 'neath those awful hooves."

He looked at me a bit dubiously, as if he was recalling that time somewhat differently.

" . . . and it is my hope you have gotten that nonsense with the bull running out of your system forevermore."

He flushed with pleasure and said, "That was a grand thing, and I shall remember it always." He paused, and then went on. "But the next time I run with the bulls, it will *not* be at the side of the now famous *El Rubio*. No, I shall stand on my own, as a man worthy of you, heart of my heart."

I gave him a look and a poke. "How you do go on, Cesar Rivera! In truth, I have never met your equal in the laying on of the words of love."

Except maybe for Amadeo . . . and that Flaco Jimenez . . . Hmmm . . . Maybe it is part of the Spanish character. They do say that "Spanish is the Loving Tongue, Soft as Music, Light as Spring," and I do believe it to be true.

We went into a goldsmith's shop, where I picked up a light gold chain on which to place Django's safe-passage charm. My other chain, the one that holds Jaimy's ring, is back in the seabag that Higgins holds for me, and a good thing, too — had I been wearing it when I was ambushed by those French deserters, I surely would have lost one of my most cherished possessions.

Having gotten the chain, I threaded it through the hole at the top of the talisman and hung it around my neck.

"Clasp me up, Cesar," I said, leaning over such that he might do it. I feel his fingers, then I sense his lips on the back of my neck, somewhere in the vicinity of my Golden Dragon.

217

Oh, Cesar, you are such a hot little fellow! When you are grown, I fear for the reputation of any woman within your reach!

"Now, now, *caro mio*," I said, straightening up and adjusting the necklace. "Enough of that. Let us be off to Dos Gatos for refreshment . . . and some music, and maybe dance. Would you like to dance with me, *mi corazón?*"

But that was yesterday, and yesterday's done.

Today, after breakfast, I go into the studio to find that blank canvases are already on the easels, the exact doubles of those set up for *La Maja*, the painting I had just posed for. I look around . . . Again no canvas for me, just the five — the big one for Goya, the smaller ones for Amadeo, Asensio, Carmelita, and Cesar.

There is a fire in the fireplace, when there has not been one before. It is warm in here and I think I know why. I go about putting out the charcoal sticks they will use to start the painting, and wait.

Presently Goya comes in and looks about. "All ready? Good. Jacquelina, the same pose but . . ."

I am halfway to the dressing screen when he completes his sentence, ". . . *desnuda, por favor.*"

I knew it was coming, but still it gave me a bit of a shock to finally hear it. *Oh, well, girl, that is why you were taken in and given shelter and food, it is what you were hired for, so go do it. Remember, you have always said you are not shy about this sort of thing, and now is the time to prove it.*

Behind the screen, I doff my wig, hang it on a hook, then pull off vest and shirt, unfasten skirt and drop it to the floor. I toe off shoes, pull down drawers, and replace wig.

Taking the red robe from where it hangs over the screen, I put it on, tying the sash about my waist. After giving my cheeks a bit of a pinch to pink them up, I step out.

Well, Jacky, if you like being the center of attention, you sure got it this time.

I go over to the sofa and, facing away from them, undo the robe and let it slide off my shoulders. I turn around and face them as it falls to the floor with a thump.

A *thump?* Cloth does not fall to the floor with a thump. *What . . . ?*

I look over to see that poor Cesar lies crumpled on the deck.

"Que caramba!" exclaims Asensio. "He has fainted!" Asensio quickly dashes to the sink and comes back with a wet cloth to hold to the boy's flushed face. "Ah, Cesar. *Pobrecito.* All the blood has gone to your head!"

"It is not to his head that the blood has gone," laughs Amadeo.

Goya, too, laughs at Cesar's distress. "Jacquelina, your beauty has brought our lad low. Are you not sorry?"

If there had been a certain amount of tension in the room, it is gone now. Knowing that he cannot hear, I merely lift my palms heavenward and shrug, then give him my best foxy grin.

It seems to please him as he puts his arms about himself and shakes with laughter.

Asensio gently applies the wet cloth to Cesar's face. "Come, *muchacho,* in your life as an artist, you will see many such as her. She is merely your first. Come now, pick up your implement and let's get to work."

More roars of laughter from Amadeo. "His *implement!*

Bad choice of words there, Asensio, *mi hermano!* Oh, yes, how he would so devoutly wish to pick up his *implement!*"

Boys, I swear . . .

"Please, please," says the Maestro. "Enough. Let us get on with it. The fire wanes and we do not wish for our *Maja Desnuda* to get cold, do we? Amadeo, throw another log on the fire."

I am for that, as it is getting a mite chilly in here. Maybe at my best, I am somewhat presentable, but certainly not if I'm all covered in goose bumps. I turn to the couch and put a knee on it, to climb into position. Carmelita is situated nearby on the left, and as I mount the sofa, I contrive to make sure she gets a good look at my bare tail as I climb on — a good, close look. *Take that, Carmelita. I hope you enjoy.*

Cesar is brought back to his senses and propped up at his easel again. I settle into the cushions and raise my arms above my head, as I had done before in the clothed version of this pose.

Perhaps emboldened by all the ribald humor flying about, the evil wells up in me. I catch Carmelita's disapproving eye, then I take a deep breath before thrusting out my chest a bit more and give a bit of a wiggle as if settling into the pose. *How do you like them, Carmelita? Are yours as pert and saucy?*

Well, if she didn't like them, someone else certainly did.

The partially recovered Cesar gasps, backs up from his easel, and bolts from the room, hunched slightly over.

Amadeo and Asensio are convulsed with laughter.

Goya, too, is amused, but after a few moments, he says,

"No, we must proceed. Get to work, the rest of you. And, oh yes, you may leave off the tattoo."

I sneak a look at Carmelita, and she glares at me with such a level of unremitting hatred that I must look away . . . and I suddenly realize that I have been reckless and must now be good. *No more foolishness, girl — no sense in making your enemies more bold than they already are.*

After a bit, Cesar comes back in, shamefaced. He picks up his charcoal and commences working away with the others.

I settle in with a sigh . . .

Dear Jaimy,

You'll never guess what I'm doing right now, and maybe it's good that you don't. Someday I might tell you about it — but I probably won't, your being so set in some of your ideas of propriety. But then again, perhaps someday, when the world has come to its senses and is at peace, you and I will take the Grand Tour of Europe, and maybe in some magnificent museum in Spain or in Italy or some other lovely place, we will stand before Goya's painting and you'll say, "That looks rather a bit like you, Jacky," and I'll say, "Awww, go on with you, Jaimy. You've got too much imagination, you have. Who would hire such as me for a model?" I hope I'll be able to suppress a blush. "Let's move on . . . What's this? A painting by Amadeo Romero. Oh, it is very fine . . . and another naked lady, too. Naughty, Jaimy, to be looking at pictures like that, and here's another by . . ."

Oh, yes, maybe someday, Jaimy . . .

Chapter 31

And so the days stretch on to weeks and the weeks become months . . . It is now October and there is always a low fire in the studio hearth, whether I am down to my skin or not.

Yes, I do continue to pose, and in my natural state, as it were, and for paintings other than the *Majas,* too, and soon it's just as natural as breathing. I pose *desnudo* for other works — the usual *Girl With Water Jug On Shoulder;* the *Girl Seated On Bed Washing Her Feet In Small Basin;* the *Girl Standing In Tub Washing Lower Limbs.* Wouldn't mind *Girl Lolling About In Nice Hot Tub,* but I don't get that — the water too quickly cools. At least I don't have to do *The Rape of Europa* — guess they couldn't book Zeus for that gig.

Someday, when I am long dead, people will stand before one of these paintings, maybe in a fine house, or in a palace, or perhaps hanging on the walls of some national museum and think to themselves, "Just who *was* that girl?" . . . and that girl will have been me, and I like that. It's a kind of immortality, as I see it. Perhaps the only immortality I will ever get . . . but, hey, I'll take it.

I am not always a model. Sometimes I do the grub work around the studio, and sometimes I have a canvas of my own to paint some other model standing there in my place. Goya has been good to me, continuing my instruction in the art of painting, and I am grateful for it. I apply myself as best I can.

I see, Jacquelina, that you have some trouble making the eyes look like they belong together on the same face. Here is a trick: After you have one eye drawn, you look at that eye as you draw in the other one. Let your side vision work. Try it.

I try it and it works.

Very good, little one. You see there are many tricks in art — and the public thinks it is magic, and it is, in a way. But it is the magic of the magician, the trickster, and not that of the sorcerer.

I take that to heart.

I continue to take my lessons with Django, and he pronounces himself pleased with my progress. We work on new fingerings, new dance steps, new songs — one especially, *La Paloma,* is my favorite.

Cesar, full to the brim with puppy love, ever more now since I have been posing in my natural state, accompanies me on these outings to Dos Gatos.

Jacquelina, mi amor, we must be married. No longer can I stand to be separate from your divine self! We must be as one!

You speak of marriage, Cesar? You are a foolish boy to

consider one such as I to enter with you into that holy state. Here, have some Madeira to calm your ardor.

You are the love of my life, my heart. I do not have much, but what I have is yours, mi corazón.

And what will your family say, when you bring me into their midst?

They will welcome you as a cherished daughter and worthy consort to their son.

I'll bet they would. Ha! You may ask me again when you are eighteen, Cesar, when you are ready.

I am ready now.

Sí, but I am but a girl of only seventeen years and not yet ready. When you are eighteen, I will be an old woman of twenty-two and you might not want me then, having already conquered the most beauteous young Majas *in all of Spain, with that honeyed tongue of yours,* mi vaquero valiente.

After the lessons, I sit and talk with Django and listen to his gypsy stories.

And the time we sold whiskey to the Austrian army back in '94 and they ended up shooting each other rather than the Turks! Ha! What a time it was, Jacquelina, what a time!

At one meeting, I asked him, "One time before, when I was in this place, I saw you nod to Pablo Montoya. Do you know him?"

He does not reply right away. Then he says, "*Sí, Señorita.* I know him. And I realize that he knows you, as well."

"Yes?"

"Be careful, little one." He takes a sip of his *grappa* and continues, "He is a good man, engaged in a good fight. But I warn you, *chica,* he is also a very *hard* man."

And he would say no more, but I take his words to heart.

Today, Amadeo and I stand, side by side, in front of Goya's *The Naked Maja,* working on various parts of the painting. I work on the cloth sheets to the left, and am proud that it has been entrusted to me. True, I find it somewhat strange to be working on a picture of oneself that is not a self-portrait, but, hey . . .

Amadeo works to the right, touching up the pillow's fringe. We each have what I call the "thumb palette" — a thin board with a thumb hole in the far end and a blunt end to tuck up against your chest to hold it steady. The colors are arranged around the edge, we mix the colors in the open space in the middle, and there is an oil cup hanging off the end. The brushes are entwined with our fingers. In the beginning, it's rather awkward, but you get used to it.

"You know, Amadeo," I say, mixing up a bit of bluish rose color and applying it to the sheet in a middle-tone area and blending it into an adjacent dark fold. "The painting you have done of me is spot on — it really looks like me — but this one here, done by the famous Goya himself, does not. He has given me considerably more flesh, and the face, while close, does not really look exactly like me."

Amadeo smiles as he works away. "Perhaps he had someone else in mind as he did it."

"Oh. And who might that be?"

"Maybe the Duchess of Alba. There were rumors . . . of a possible liaison, and it does somewhat resemble what she looked like."

What? The Maestro had stepped out? The hound! Men. I swear!

I fume a bit over this — using *my* body to portray somebody else? I feel . . . used, sort of.

"Actually, Jack-ie," Amadeo goes on as we work away, "the Master could get in some trouble over this painting."

"What? How?" I ask, dumbfounded.

"Because of that," replies Amadeo, pointing with his brush handle to the spot on the painting below the figure's belly and between the upper thighs.

"What? The maidenhair?"

He gives out a slight cough, perhaps shocked a bit at the directness of my words. He continues.

"*Sí*, Jacquelina, that very thing. It is very daring of the Master to put that in."

"But why? A couple daubs of paint can get someone in trouble?" I ask, also pointing to the area in question. "Every girl's got one of those, you know. Even nuns."

He chuckles. "Yes, I do know that. But somehow it is not done. It is forbidden."

"But surely, in all the world, there must be some paintings of girls that include that little bit?"

"None that I have ever seen, and I have traveled some. I have been to Italy and seen the wonders of the Renaissance."

"Huh!" I say, not believing it. "And no female fur there, not in all of Rome, not in all those centuries?"

"No, none, my plainspoken love. And there were thousands of nudes, both statues and paintings," he says. "Actually, now that I think of it, I do recall one, Botticelli's *Birth of Venus* . . . No, no, I'm wrong. She, too, was covered in that area. I saw it in Florence. Wonderful painting. You know, we should get a large clamshell and have you step out of it, onto a snow-white shore, the waves rolling in behind you. Oh, yes! I am sure we could beat the Italians at that one."

Like Cesar, Amadeo's attentions to me have doubled in ardor since I have been posing in the nude. Amadeo's pursuits, however, have been much more . . . pressing. And I know he would like to press me up against the wall right now, but there are others present, and actually, when in the studio, he has been good . . . mostly.

"Never mind, Amadeo, I'm sure we shall get to that one shortly, but for now . . . *Hmmm* . . . So Maestro could get in trouble over this?" I ask, in some wonder at the lunacy of mankind. "But with whom?"

"With the Church, for one," he says, finishing up his pillow fringe and putting aside his brush and palette. "But do not worry, *chica*. Maestro will not get in trouble over this painting. Both of the Majas are going into the collection of Don Manuel de Godoy, and they will go to his palace and will not be seen by anyone except the Prime Minister's own broad-minded circle of friends."

Hmmm . . . Somehow I am not quite so sure of that . . . *Why does my gaze stray to Carmelita, who sits working on her own painting, pointedly ignoring us?*

Without warning, Goya enters the studio and comes up next to me and looks at what I have done.

"*Bueno*," he says, and reaches for my brush and palette. I give them up and he loads the brush and makes some changes to my work — all to the better, I see — and then he goes to Amadeo and does the same thing. I notice that he makes fewer changes to Amadeo's work than to mine, but that is how it should be.

Goya tosses the palettes and brushes onto a side cart, saying, "Very well, it is done. Amadeo, make them ready for shipping to Palazzo Godoy."

Both Amadeo and I back up and bow.

"*Sí, Señor.* It will be done."

After the Master has left the room, Amadeo leans into me and says, "Tonight, the Café Central, Jacquelina?"

"Yes, with pleasure, Amadeo. We shall dance and sing and we will be gay and all will be right with the world."

I sneak a look over at Carmelita, who has heard all and sits stone-faced before her painting. With a shiver and some foreboding, I think, *Actually, I don't really know about how right things will be, Amadeo. Oh no, I do not.*

Chapter 32

James Emerson Fletcher
House of Chen
Rangoon
Burma

Dearest Jacky,
My days here at the House of Chen have fallen into a
certain rhythm. In the mornings, I take instruction from Zen
Master Kwai Chang.

"If you cannot let go of your anger, Chueng Tong — and
I sense you do still have much trouble inside your mind — you
will always lose in any endeavor, whatever it might be . . .
fighting, yes . . . love, yes . . . and even the mundane things
of life . . . health, business, caring for family, honoring ancestors. But, if you can empty your mind of those kinds of feel-
ings, you might see how the way of Zen could lead you . . .
perhaps to victory over those less open to the Way. You must
let the Zen lead you on the proper path. Come, Long Boy,
you have progressed a considerable distance on the Path of
Enlightenment. Open yourself to further release. It will hap-

pen if you let the anger go, if you will let your sense of self go, if you will walk the Path of the Buddha."

In the afternoons, after lunch with Charlie and Sidrah, I go to the practice field with the Shaolin Monk Sifu Loo Li.

Today we worked on the move known as The Windmill of the Silken Moth, over and over again, till I get it just about down. Sifu Loo Li and I bow to each other and break for a rest and go to sit next to Master Chang. He always comes to watch us practice, sitting quietly by the side to observe and translate if needed.

Tea is brought by a boy in saffron robe. He pours and we take the small cups and it refreshes us and I am thankful for it. It is a warm day and Sifu Loo Li wears a tunic, a gi, that is armless, and I note there is a tattoo of a dragon on the inside of his left forearm.

"Master Chang," I ask. "Does that mark mean that Sifu Loo Li is a master at Bojutsu?"

The Master chuckles and says, "No, Long Boy, it means that he is a novice."

A novice? This man who could take his stick and beat me down to the ground in an instant is merely a novice? What must a master be like?

Sifu Loo Li stands and we get to work on yet another move, The Strike of the Angry Mongoose, and yet again, I end up flat on my back with Sifu's stick at my throat . . . most times . . . but not all times.

I will get this, I will . . . I swear.

Yours, though thoroughly bruised,
Jaimy

Chapter 33

I am in a washtub in the laundry room next to the kitchen, up to my chin in hot soapy suds. I'm chattering away with Ramona, she who heated up all this lovely water on her stove, and who is now folding towels as we talk.

We have just come from Mass, had lunch, and since there is no work of an artistic nature to do, I thought a nice bath would be just the thing, and I was right. *Ah, yes, I do love a good soak!*

The service at the Basilica was magnificent. Those Catholics really know how to lay it on—all that high-sounding Latin, a huge roaring chorus, colorful priestly costumes, the statues, the paintings, the whole scene. I enjoyed it all very much. And during one of the times on my knees, I offered up heartfelt prayers for Jaimy and, yes, for poor Richard Allen, too—I do so hope he has recovered from his wounds—and for all my other friends, too.

We were missing one of our number today. Carmelita had begged off, saying that she was sick. Ha! Probably she couldn't stand listening to us laugh about our riotous time at El Central last night. Oh, well, I for one certainly didn't miss her.

Hmmm... The water is getting a mite tepid, so it is time to get myself out of it. *Rise, Venus, and step out of your shell and onto the shore and dry your heavenly body.*

I stand and step out of the tub. Ramona hands me a towel and the door opens and Amadeo walks in.

"Amadeo!" I exclaim, clutching the towel to my chest.

"Good afternoon, my lovely one. We lack only a seashell on which to place your delicate little foot and the tableau will be complete. We don't really need the angels, do we?"

"Please leave, Amadeo. You are embarrassing Ramona and you are making me *very* uncomfortable."

"But why, *mi querida?*" he asks, smiling as he comes over to me.

"Because I am naked, that's why," I reply, stating the obvious. "You must go."

"But, Jack-ie, I have seen you in that state almost every day for the past many weeks. Somewhat drier, I will admit, but still the same. Come, little one." He puts his arms around me and pulls me to his chest. "I beg but a kiss."

Heavy sigh... *You know it's your own fault that you get in situations like this, girl. You should be much more restrained in your taking of pleasure.* I will try to remember that in the future... *But it was just a few caresses and gentle kisses on the balcony in the moonlight... that was all.*

"That is different, Amadeo," I say, rigid in his embrace. "That is work, what I do to earn my keep. This is... personal. It is real life. Please let me go."

He stands back, perplexed.

"But you came to us as a tramp. You have free-and-easy ways. You pose before us in the nude. You must have had many men. Why not me?" His face assumes that hurt look that boys put on when they think someone else is getting something from a girl that they are not.

"I have not had *any* men. Not in the way you mean."

"I do not believe it," he replies, his face dark now.

"I do not care if you believe it or not. It is the truth. And I am not a tramp."

"What are you, then?"

I puff up and my anger overcomes my good sense as I say, "My name is Jacky Faber, Lieutenant in His Britannic Majesty's Royal Navy. I have served at the Battles of Trafalgar, Jena-Auerstadt, and Vimeiro! I have been dispatched as an undercover field operative to Madrid to gather information that might be useful in the fight against Napoleon! That's who I am, Amadeo Romero."

"Of course you are," he says, laughing at what must be a joke, and his disbelieving laughter defuses the tension in the steamy room. "I am sorry to have disturbed you, Señorita. I did not understand. Adiós."

He bows, turns on his heel, and walks out.

Hmmm . . . I could have handled that better, for sure . . .

I spend the rest of the afternoon at guitar practice in my room, needing a bit of privacy after what happened earlier. Everyone needs to cool off a bit, even me. Paloma is visiting her family, so I'm not disturbing her with my endless repetitions of musical phrases and figures.

I'm about to pack it in and head down to dinner when there is a light tapping on the door.

"Come in," I say, wondering who it could be.

Amadeo pokes his head in and says, "Pardon, Señorita. Do not be alarmed. May I enter?"

"Yes, of course, Amadeo," I say, rising from my bed, where I had been sitting. If I am to endure another wrestling match with an amorous male, I certainly don't want it to be on a bed.

"Again, I apologize for my behavior today. It was rude and not worthy of you."

"Oh, don't say that, Amadeo. You must know I like you *very,* very much. It's just that . . . Oh, I can't explain," I say, knuckled fist to mouth, big eyes tearing up.

"You do not have to explain, *mi querida.* However, by way of making it up to you, I wish to present you with this." Saying that, he reaches out in the hallway, pulls in a stretched canvas, and hands it to me.

I gasp to see that it is his painting of me as The Naked Maja, glowing in the waning light of the day. It is plain that it has been freshly varnished to bring all the rich colors back to their original brilliance. The golden figure fairly bursts with vibrant life.

"Oh, Amadeo, it is magnificent! You cannot—"

"Yes, I can, Jacquelina. It will give me great pleasure to know that you shall have it in your possession."

"Oh, thank you, *mi amigo.* I shall treasure it always! Here, let me hang it on my wall!"

I go to my wineskin, which hangs on a hook, and pull it off and fling it to the floor. I hang the painting in its place.

"There! Is it not wonderful? You are verily the Prince of Painters! A kiss for you on that, my prince!" I get up on tiptoes and plant one on his cheek. "Thank you for that, Amadeo . . . and thank you for . . . understanding."

He nods and gives me back a kiss of his own, on my forehead. Then he turns to regard the painting.

"So. We have had *The Clothed Maja,* and then *The Naked Maja* . . ." he says, smiling on me. "And now we have *La Maja Virginal,* do we not not, my dear?"

Yes, we do, oh yes we do!

Later, as I lie abed, I gaze up at the painting, gently illuminated by the moonlight filtering through the window.

What would you think of that, Jaimy? I hope you will like it, but I suspect you might be scandalized. Why don't we make a copy of it for your mother, hmmm? Now, Lord Richard Allen, you, I know, will like it, you dog, and I hope you are recovered enough now to enjoy it.

Where shall I hang it? Perhaps in Amy's lovely little room at Dovecote? No, I am sure that Randall would steal it, his love of Polly Von notwithstanding. Hey, maybe I could get Polly to pose for me and we shall make a La Maja Cockney *for the randy lad. I am sure she would do it.*

On the wall of my cabin on the Lorelei Lee? *No, I'm afraid it might destroy discipline. Hanging in the tea room of the Lawson Peabody School for Young Girls? Oh, sure . . . Mistress would faint and Clarissa would draw a mustache on it.*

Ah-ha! I have it! Over the bar at the Pig and Whistle for all to enjoy. That's it! Perfect!

Let all lift their glasses and toast The Virgin Maja!

Hear! Hear!

Chapter 34

James Emerson Fletcher
House of Chen
Rangoon
Burma

Jacky Faber
Madrid, Spain

Dearest Jacky,
In the early evening, before going in to dinner, I usually bathe in the turquoise pool and Mai Ling and Mai Ji rub the soreness from my shoulders and back.
Yes, that is the usual routine . . . but not today.

Today Sidrah enters the bathhouse bearing a silver platter and on that plate is a letter.

"The ship from Britain has arrived, Jay-mee," she softly says. "And this is a letter for you. I hope it brings you good news."

I am out of the tub in an instant and, sitting on the edge of the pool, I rip open the letter and read . . .

John Higgins
Horse Guards Barracks
Lincoln Fields
London
September 1, 1808

Mr. James Emerson Fletcher
The House of Chen
Rangoon, Burma

My dear Mr. Fletcher,

It is my most sincere hope that this letter finds you in good health and restored spirits. I will now relate to you the happenings as regards our Miss Jacky Faber since your rather hurried departure from Britannia's shore.

After seeing you off safely in the care of Mr. Chen, both Miss Faber and I were assigned by Naval Intelligence to the staff of General Arthur Wellesley, recently embarked to Portugal to take command of British forces in the fight against Napoleon on the Iberian Peninsula.

We arrived, in the company of Cavalry Captain Lord Richard Allen, with whom you are acquainted, I believe, in time for the Battle of Vimeiro.

Miss Faber was employed as messenger and liaison between the high command and various partisan fighters. She emerged relatively unscathed from the fight, but I regret to report that Captain Allen was grievously wounded in the field and was sent back to England, under Miss Faber's orders, to be placed under the care of Dr. Stephen Sebastian.

After the battle, Sir Wellesley was relieved of command and replaced by several generals superior to him in rank but much inferior to him in experience and skill on the battle-field. Before going back to England to contest his demotion, he, having already discerned Miss Faber's considerable abilities, bade her go to Madrid, under the protection of one of the more prominent guerrilla leaders, a Pablo Montoya, to gather information about the French occupation of that city for when he would return to command and continue the war against Napoleon.

She agreed to that and set off in the company of what I perceived to be some very rough fellows. I was forbidden to accompany her, and was sent back to England to continue on Wellesley's staff. Her entourage, however, was ambushed by the French, suffering heavy losses, and Miss Faber was separated from her escort, feared lost, and not heard of for some time.

However, I am pleased to report that some reports have been coming out of Madrid, and it appears that Miss Faber is the one sending them. One of the missives had a small anchor drawn over the letters JMF in the margin, so I knew that it was she. It is plain that she did manage, on her own, to get to that city and establish herself in the studio of a well-known artist. She has managed, against all odds, to actually get into the palace of the usurper, King Joseph, and supply critical intelligence to our operatives. She does have her ways, as I am sure you will agree.

Apparently, General Wellesley felt it best that she stay in place for the time being, but rest assured, Mr. Fletcher, that should the situation change, we will bend every effort to bring her out.

I am glad to report that Captain Richard Allen is recovering nicely under the care of Dr. Sebastian. He continues to improve and is hard to restrain.

Should you be recovered—that is, of course, our fondest hope—and should you wish to return to England, I counsel extreme caution. Miss Faber's fanciful plan to substitute Flashby for the Black Highwayman worked in the short run—and Mr. Flashby did spend some very unpleasant time in Newgate—but it will not work in the long. He is already out of prison and back with Naval Intelligence. There was no way to prevent it—Flashby does have his supporters.

Long story short, when you come back, I suggest deep disguise. Please, Sir, no barging in, swinging your sword, and calling for Flashby's blood, as is your usual wont. Caution, please, I implore you.

I hope I have brought you some comfort with this letter. I am, always . . .

Your Most Obedient Servant
John Higgins

"Is it good news about our Lotus Blossom?" asks Sidrah, as I fold the letter and put it back on the tray. "This one hopes so."

"Yes, dear Sidrah," I reply. "It is. She still lives and is abroad in the land of Spain. I must go to her."

"I know, dear Jay-mee, but you must listen to Father first. Shall we go to dinner?"

Indeed we shall, Sidrah, but there are passages from the letter that make things boil inside me—"In the company of

Lord Richard Allen" is one, and "Captain Allen is recovering nicely."

Yes, Master Chang, I know, I know. The anger, the jealousy, the rage, must be put aside . . . but . . . but . . .

I must get back!

Yours, but with teeth clenched,
Jaimy

Chapter 35

I'm at the kitchen table with a chopping board, bottle of brandy, a small goblet, and a saucepan. Studio time is over for the day and dinner has been served and cleared away, and I'm trying a bit of an experiment. Late evening sunbeams still stream through the kitchen windows as Ramona fusses with hanging up her precious copper pots, their bottoms once again all nice and shiny.

I take two of my dried-up mushrooms and chop them into tiny pieces. They are quite leathery, but they do mince up easily. I dump them into the low saucepan and add a bit of water from the pitcher that always stands on the sideboard. I stick the whole mess on the still-hot cook stove and wait for it to come to a boil. When it does, I give it a bit of a shake and see that the contents have turned a deep purple. *Hmmm* . . . I recall there was a lot of purple haze on that particular, and very peculiar, afternoon in the company of Brother Bullfrog and his brethren.

"Still hungry, Jack-ie?" asks Ramona. "There's some bread and cheese in the cupboard."

"No, dear, and thanks," I reply. "I'm just doing a color

experiment. Maybe I'll come up with a new pigment for Maestro Goya. Who knows?"

She shrugs, and finished with the final cleaning of the day, she wipes her hands on a dishrag and goes off.

I take a sniff of my brew — but not too big a sniff, believe me — and it just smells, well, mushroomy.

I take my pan off the stove to cool and pull a tea strainer off the wall rack and place it over a clean wine glass. When the contents of the pan are tepid, I pour it all into the strainer — a pure, clear, purple liquid drips down and fills the bottom half of the goblet. I give the stuff up in the strainer a bit of a squeeze with my fingers and I get a few more droplets.

Hmmm . . . I'm thinking . . . prolly all the weird stuff that was in those mushrooms was destroyed by the drying and the boiling. Ah, well, we shall see. I uncork the brandy and fill the rest of the glass and give it a stir. It assumes a most pleasing violet hue. *It is very pretty, anyway.*

Turning away from my experiment, I dump the mushroom residue into the trash and wash the saucepan and strainer. As I am hanging up the latter, and making a bit of a clatter with the pans already hanging on the rack, I do not hear someone entering the kitchen.

However, when I turn around again, there stands Amadeo, grinning at me . . . with an empty glass in his hand, one that still has a few deep purple droplets clinging to its inner sides.

"Ummm," says Amadeo, running his tongue over his lips and looking at me with a good deal of warmth in his gaze. "You knew I would come seek you out and you prepared a fine drink for me. *Gracias, mi amor.* It was most delicious — a fine concoction of brandy with a hint of what . . . musk? Ah, yes, perfect . . . but why do you look so startled, *mi quierdo?*"

"Oh, nothing," I say with a grimace. "I just hope you're not doing anything for the next hour or so."

If I was thinking the mushrooms' potency was ruined by the boiling, I was dead wrong. Ten minutes later, I am dragged by an exultant Amadeo out of the kitchen and up the stairs.

"Come, Jacquelina! We must fly up to the roof and be with the stars! To be with the gods!"

"Amadeo! Please!" I bleat, his hand on my wrist. "You must be quiet! You will rouse the household!"

"I do not care if I awaken the entire world!" he exults. "I have been reborn! As a god, and gods shake the world!"

Geez, Amadeo, all I did was see white rabbits and Jesus, and talk to a bullfrog. 'Course, he dropped down the contents of two mushrooms, while I only ate the one. Perhaps the alcohol intensified the effect . . . More study is definitely required.

First floor, second floor, third, and then onto the roof. Since this is Spain and it does not snow here — or rain all that often, either — the roof is flat, tarred with gravel, and painted white. Amadeo releases my arm and goes to spin about in the center of the roof.

"See the stars, how they whirl and twirl, see how they pour down on us in a silvery stream," he says, ecstatic. "I must feel them on my skin, I must!" He strips off his shirt and flings it aside, holding his face up to bathe in what he must perceive as a cascade of stars pouring down over him.

In spite of myself, I smile on Amadeo, standing there in the moonlight, his arms outstretched, his body smooth and, though the night is cool, glistening with a sheen of sweat. He turns from his celestial shower to leap over and gaze again upon me, still grinning a foxy grin.

"Jacquelina!" he exclaims, grabbing my shoulders. "Heart of my heart, I must kiss you . . . I must . . ."

A beatific look comes over his face and he whispers, "When you smile like that, *pepita,* I want to . . . I want to . . . lick your teeth."

Wot?

Before I can turn my face, I feel his tongue run across my upper tusks, and then thrust deep into my mouth.

Ummph!

I push him back, giggling in spite of myself. "Amadeo, you must stop with that!" No use telling him to get ahold of himself, 'cause that ain't gonna happen for a while yet, I know.

He spins away from me, laughing. "Oh, Jacquelina, when we kissed, I felt the earth move! Did you feel it too, *guapa?* Did you feel the very earth move under us?"

"Well, maybe a little, Amadeo, but — "

"The stars! The stars! They fall down upon me as the gentle rain from heaven! I must feel them all over my body!"

'Tis plain he's listening to the gods and not to me, as he reaches for the buttons on his trousers, unfastens them, and pulls both pants and underwear down and off. He stands naked in the moonlight, and in all his glorious young manhood.

"You must feel them, too, Jacquelina!" he exults, coming back to grab my shoulders. This time I keep my apparently quite lickable teeth hidden behind pursed lips and he merely places a wet kiss on my forehead.

However, the lickability of my teeth is not his demented intention this time, oh no. As was my usual practice when not modeling in the studio or off on the town, I had worn this day my Lawson Peabody serving-girl rig, except that I had left off the rib-hugging vest, as the evening was warm.

"Jacquelina, Jacquelina, how the name trips off my unworthy tongue!" he says, as he pulls the flimsy blouse I wear off my shoulders and down to my waist. I gasp as that unworthy tongue finds itself on my breastbone.

"Amadeo! You cannot!"

"Yes, I can, my heart," he breathes. "Ah, thy breasts, there before me, on either side . . . two white doves, two perfect white doves with pink noses. I shall kiss their rosy little noses now."

"No, you shall not, Amadeo," I say, drawing back and stifling a laugh. "You shall calm yourself. We must get back, we must — "

"No, *mi querida,* what we must do is fly up to the stars and become one with them!" he shouts, standing straight and pointing heavenward. "We shall ascend to the cosmos and become a new constellation, a new sign in the Zodiac! We shall be the Jackamadeo constellation and our Sign shall be Two Hearts and Bodies Entwined and we will rival Aquarius and The Mighty Hunter Orion and The Bears and The Ram and, oh let us fly, fly up to the sky!"

With that, the holy fool begins dragging me to the edge of the roof with the full intention of the both of us leaping off and upward.

"Amadeo! Stop! I am not yet ready to be a constellation!" I yelp as we approach the edge of the roof. There is a rail about the perimeter of the roof, but it is only about waist high and it certainly doesn't look very sturdy.

"No, Jacquelina, we must go! Lovers throughout the ages will look up and admire us and sigh and swear eternal promises of love everlasting! I shall go first and you will follow!"

He lets me go and runs to the edge, his thighs against the railing, his arms raised and ready to take flight. I leap after him, grab him about the waist, and hang on.

"Please, Amadeo," I plead, looking down at the hard pavement three storeys below, for I know that is *exactly* what he will fly to if he does launch himself off the roof. I sink to my knees for better leverage in holding him back, my arms tight around his thighs. I bury my face into the small of his back. It is slick with sweat, but I hang on and say, "Amadeo, for me . . . for Jacquelina . . . please turn around and stop this."

He still seems intent on leaping and I redouble my pleas. "Amadeo! Your paintings . . . the ones you have not yet finished . . . the one of me . . . the ones you have yet to paint . . . the others this world wants to see! Amadeo . . ."

He shakes his head and turns, confused.

Ha! He is probably coming down a bit, maybe . . .

He looks down at me.

"Jacquelina . . . ?"

"Yes, Amadeo." I sigh, relieved. While Amadeo's body is very smooth overall, he does have a nest of hair on his lower belly, and into that I thankfully press my face. "It is me, and . . ."

. . . and just then others burst on the scene . . . The house has indeed been roused. Asensio is suddenly beside us and . . .

Oh, Lord, how this must look!

I get off my knees, climb to my feet, and pull my shirt sleeves back up onto my shoulders.

"Asensio," I manage to say. "Please see Amadeo back to your room. He has had an . . . interesting evening."

Asensio gives me a searching look and goes to Amadeo. Recognition comes into Amadeo's confused eyes.

"Asensio?" he asks, dazed and weaving slightly.

"*Sí, mi hermano,*" says Asensio, softly, as he puts his arm about Amadeo. "Come, let us go to bed, brother."

As they disappear through the doorway, I sigh and go to pick up Amadeo's discarded clothes, as he will need them tomorrow. Neatening myself as much as possible, I go to the door and am startled to find that Asensio was not the only one awakened, for there stands Carmelita, in a nightshirt and a state of pure fury.

She says nothing, but only gazes into my eyes and then spits on the floor between us.

She did not speak, but she was most eloquent.

Chapter 36

The day's work is done and Cesar and I turn out in the early evening, arm in arm, on our way to Dos Gatos for a quiet evening of song and maybe dance.

It has been several days since The Night of Celestial Revels and thanks be to God that Cesar did not awaken that night. I'd have had a hard time explaining away that scene to the poor lad. Oh Lord, I am so glad I did not have to talk my way out of that one.

At breakfast the next morning, Amadeo had appeared a bit confused. I can well imagine the look on his face when he awoke in Asensio's arms and not mine. Asensio, on the other hand, seemed most content. A bit smug, even.

Later that day, I made up more of my Magic Mushroom Potion — one half brandy, one half Essence of Purple Mushroom — but this time I kept a close eye on it. Never can tell when something like that might come in handy, now that I don't have any Tincture of Opium, otherwise known as Jacky's Little Helper, at hand.

I tightly corked up a bottle of it and stored it in my seabag. I did, however, keep three of the mushrooms in their dried state to show to Dr. Sebastian, should we meet again.

"A lovely evening, Cesar," I say, breathing in the soft night air as we walk along.

"All the more lovely for being by your side, *mi amor*," replies my constant consort. We are proceeding down a side street toward the plaza. I am wearing my finest *Maja* gear — white lacy shirt, embroidered jacket and skirt, with gold sash about my middle — and Cesar is similarly dressed, a dashing and bold young matador, by God!

"Ah, Cesar," I say, giving him a bit of a poke. "You would find, if you had the time, that a little of Jack-ie Bouvier goes a long, long way."

"I hope to have that time, *mi corazón*, but I should never tire of you. I — "

A figure appears before us. It is a woman dressed in black with a black veil across her lower face, her head covered with a black shawl.

She raises her hand and points to me.

"That is her. Take her."

Before I can even wonder at this, some men, also dressed in black — four of them, I think — come from a side alley and swarm over us.

"Get the girl! Gag her. Quickly!"

What?

Hands are put on me and I am pushed to my knees. Before I can scream, a rag is stuffed in my mouth and a bag is thrown over my head. I struggle, but in vain — my arms are pinned to my sides. I feel myself lifted up and tossed into — *what?* — a cart, yes, for I can smell horse.

"Let her go, damn you to hell!" I hear Cesar cry out.

"Hit him! Club him down! We don't need the boy!"

"By God, I'll — "

There is a dull thud and Cesar speaks no more.

Oh, God, please!

God does not answer — not me, anyway — as the cart starts forward, its wheels creaking as we go along.

What can it be? Am I found out as a spy? Is it torture and finally the garotte for me? Oh, please.

I lie in deep despair, but soon the cart draws to a stop. *Hmmm . . .* My rational mind figures we must not have gone far . . . *Where can we be?*

I am gathered up and held tight in someone's grip. I give a few kicks in what I feel would be the proper direction, and though I am rewarded with a few *oooffs*, it avails me nothing. I sense that I am carried to a doorway, for there is the sound of a latch being opened and a heavy door swinging out. Then, from the gait of the man carrying me, I figure that I am being borne down a staircase, a *long* staircase. It is as if we are descending into a pit — a cold and dank pit in the belly of the earth. In spite of the cloth wrapped around me, I shiver.

Eventually, my short journey as a senseless burden ends, and my long journey as a helpless victim begins . . .

I am thrown onto a rough platform and I feel straps being wrapped around my ankles. Then the ropes are taken from my arms, and my wrists are pulled up and each wrapped in restraints of their own. There is a cranking sound and my arms are drawn up above my head and my legs are stretched out straight.

Abruptly, the hood is yanked from my head, my eyes adjust, and all is plain. I am in a circular, windowless room, and I sense that I am far underground. My crazed eyes cast about and see stone walls curtained in deep red drapes. There are strange symbols drawn upon them, but I cannot tell what they are. And there are hooded figures about me, dressed in deep red robes. Have I been taken to a witches' coven? Have I been . . . ?

Then I see, high on the back wall, a moss-covered plaque, and it reads:

MORS CERTA
SOLUM TEMPUS
INCERTUM EST

I ain't got much Latin, but I know the first line reads, *Death is Certain*. If I ever had any hope in getting out of this, I lose it right then upon reading that.

The man who took off my hood leans over me such that I might see his face under his red hood. He has a tight mouth, long nose, and sunken cheeks. His eyes gleam with an unholy light. He smiles beatifically at me and announces, "You are a very lucky girl. You see gathered about you the Tribunal del Santo Oficio de la Inquisición. It is possible that we might be able to save your immortal soul."

"What!" I exclaim. "The Inquistion? Are you joking?"

"No, my dear," he says softly. "I assure you the Holy Office does not joke."

"But the Emperor has banished the Inquisition! How — ?"

"God is our Emperor, not that little man. Shall we proceed?"

I look about and see another red-robed figure at my feet, and yet another at a large cogged wheel. Lifting my eyes, I am able to dimly perceive a narrow balcony on which stand perhaps a dozen silent men, each in a similar red robe and hood, looking down upon me. Off to the left and affixed to the wall is what appears to be a large silver scythe.

"We must know more about the nefarious actions at the House of Goya."

"What? We are an artists' studio! We paint pictures and sell them! Nothing more! I swear!" I say, desperate. "Please, you must let me go!"

"We know he has painted a picture of you."

"Yes, he did. What of it?"

"He painted you naked."

"Painted me naked? Señor, there are thousands of paintings of nude people. Check out the Vatican in Rome. I am a model. That's what models do. Why are you doing this to me?"

"Because Goya painted your sex, and you allowed him to do that."

"My sex? Yes, I'm a girl. Ain't it plain? Half the world is, you know."

"Yes, and that is a pity. However . . . that dirty old man, Goya, has offended us. He painted your sex and the painting will be shown to the public and base desires will be inflamed. For that reason, it is forbidden. There are no paintings like that, not in all the world — not the civilized world, anyway."

I well recall the conversation with Amadeo, that day

back in the studio. *I guess you were right,* mi amigo . . . *and I so wish you were here with me right now . . .*

"What? You are talking about my maidenhair?" I demand of my Inquisitor. "*Incredible!* A few strokes of brown paint and you have me here for that? That paint is made out of burnt umber, which is a color taken from the earth, and oil. God's good earth, God's good oil. Nothing more. What is the matter with you? How can that be evil?"

"It is for us to decide, not you."

"How do you know all this?" I ask, damned uncomfortable being laid out as I am and plainly getting the worst of this one-sided conversation. "You could not have seen those paintings. They were private and not for the eyes of such as you."

He lays his hand on my forehead in an almost fatherly way. "Ah, you see, a good Catholic girl has shown us. Last Sunday, she let us in, and we gazed upon the wretched paintings and were aghast at what we saw."

Carmelita! That's why she didn't go to Mass with us! She was the woman on the road, the one who betrayed me to these fiends!

"Yes, and we saw other things. Depictions of monsters, grotesque beings that could only have come from the mind of a heretic. Like these . . . Here's one of Satan biting off the head of a man."

He holds a sheaf of papers before my eyes and I recognize them as Goya's. He had done so many of those dark drawings, he would not have noticed these few missing.

"Carmelita Gomez stole those!" I shout. "Damn her to hell for her treachery!"

"Ah, it will not be she who is going to hell, it will be you, minion of Satan," he says. "But not before you tell us some things about Señor Goya. We must know more."

"But why me? Carmelita must've told you all the lies you wanted to hear."

"Ah, yes, she has told us many things," he says. "But you see, we must have more testimony — more than just that of one young girl — to bring an important man like the despicable Goya to trial before the Inquisition."

He nods to the man at my feet, who puts his hand on the great wheel and gives it a turn. The straps tighten and I am stretched out to my full length. He takes this opportunity to pull down the waist of my skirt.

"Yes, there it is, just like she said. The mark of the devil's pitchfork. And the heathen symbol on her neck."

He pushes my head roughly to the side.

"Ah, yes, that, too! Good God, my fingers tremble at the touch!" he says, his voice full of loathing. "Now tell us, Whore of Babylon, everything that goes on in that place. Do you have a cabal? Is Goya the warlock? Are you one of his witches? Tell us and your pain shall end — your pain in this world, anyway."

"No! I swear! We just paint pictures, that's all!"

"A quarter turn, Brother Bruno."

The wheel is cranked and I am lifted from the platform and hang in the air. My elbows and knees cry out in pain.

"Yeow! Stop! Please!"

"We will stop when you admit your guilt and the guilt of those within that house of sin," he says. "Will you do so? Did you see goat men prancing about, witches casting spells?"

"No! Nothing like that!" I shout. "Please don't — "

"Another little turn, Brother Bruno."

Screeeech! No! Oh!

"It is time for our Vespers, brothers. Let her stay here and reflect upon her sin. Brother Ignacio, you may release the scythe."

The red-robed monks file out of the room, heads down, hands in sleeves. Brother Ignacio is at the end of the line, and as he exits the pit, he pulls a lever. The others, who stood on the balcony, also file out, chanting an ominous chorus.

Dies irae, dies illa
Solvet saeclum in favilla,
Teste David cum Sybilla.

Quantus tremor est futurus
Quando iudex est venturus
Cuncta stricte discussurus.

Tuba mirum spargens sonum
Per sepulcra regionum
Coget omnes ante thronum.

In my misery, I hear a *swoosh*ing sound and look up to see . . . *Horror!* There is a great crescent-shaped blade on a long pendulum that swings slowly back and forth. It describes an arc of about twenty feet and takes about five seconds to complete its passage from one apex to the other. At its low point, it passes about six inches above my belly.

Whoooosh!

There it goes again, and I swear it is closer to me than on the last pass. The monks did not find my shiv when they strapped me down, but, though I twist in the bonds and try to get it, I can't . . . I can't . . . !

Whoooosh!

I am right in thinking that it comes closer with every swing. I sight on a point on the far wall, and, sure enough, I see that the blade has, indeed, come closer to my poor self. It must be on a ratchet, such that it drops down a half inch on each pass.

Whoooosh!

I can see the blade close up now, and it looks sharp as a razor. It fairly whistles as it goes by, now a scant three inches above me.

Whooosh!

Another pass, and I squirm under the sweep of the pendulum. If I could only get to my shiv, but I cannot, I cannot! The straps hold me too tight. *Oh, I fear I am done!*

Whooosh!

The blade now clears my stomach by a mere two inches . . . Now one inch, now one half, now . . . Oh, Lord, now it slices through the waistband of my skirt, and it is so sharp that the fabric does not even shudder as the razor cuts through it.

Whooosh!

The sides of my skirt fall away, destroyed, and my stomach lies white and bare and defenseless before the relentless descent of that awful blade.

I cannot stand it, and I scream, "I am a good girl! Oh, God, save me! My belly is supposed to have babies in it, not a cruel knife! Oh, please, God, do not let it happen!"

Whooosh!

Screech! I look down and there is a thin red line of blood across my middle! And, as the scythe swings to the side, I can see a smear of my blood on its edge. *Oh my God! I am going to be gutted! I—*

But no, that is not going to happen, not just yet. Even worse things are in store for me.

Fra Gilberto comes back into the pit and stands by my side.

"Brother Bruno, please stop the pendulum."

Bruno grabs the lever, and the scythe comes to rest against the far wall, ready, at any moment to swing again. The former occupants of the balcony once again take their places.

Fra Gilberto leans over me and whispers, "Come now, girl, tell us. Did you see horrible, devilish things happening at Goya's house? Did you yourself copulate with goats, did you—"

"No, no nothing like that, please, no!"

He turns aside in disgust.

"I see that you are still in the grip of the Horned One. Brother Ignacio, please bring the cleansing water."

I feel the rack on which I am lying lean back and my feet are raised high above my head. *What is going on? Cleansing water . . . What?*

Brother Ignacio appears in my vision, grinning and holding a pitcher of water.

"Proceed, Brother," says Fra Gilberto. "Let the Holy Water of the Mother Church shrive her soul."

With that, Brother Ignacio lifts his pitcher and pours the water into my nostrils.

I buck and gag and try to rise, but I cannot. I can only choke and beg for mercy.

"Please . . . please . . . stop!"

Fra Gilberto nods again and more water is poured into my nose and a hand is put over my mouth.

Oh, Lord, I am drowning and it hurts, it hurts, I can't stand it! Please take me! Take me now! Oh, God, please!

The hand is removed from my mouth and water streams out as I hack and cough.

I have been hurt before, but nothing like this. *Mercy!*

"Will you tell us now, to save your soul? If you confess, we will end your suffering."

"Anything . . . anything . . ." I manage to gasp. "Please just stop."

"Describe the obscene rituals you have observed. Did the heretic Goya lead them?"

"What? No."

Fra Gilberto again signals Brother Ignacio and he tilts his jug.

"No!" I scream. "I mean, yes! Whatever you say! Yes, rituals! Dancing! Blasphemies! The Devil himself! Goya, too! Yes, all of us!"

"Good. That is very good, girl. You have confessed. You might just have saved your very soul," says the monk. "You will find out very shortly. Brother Bruno, begin the auto-da-fé. Let the blade take her."

The sonorous chant from the gallery above begins again as Bruno walks toward the lever that will free the scythe. *Oh, Lord, I am coming . . .*

But Brother Bruno does not pull the lever. In fact, he does little else in this world.

There is a splintering crash from the door behind me and I hear shouts . . . then shots, and Brother Bruno falls to the ground. I am suddenly surrounded by grim-looking men — men with bandoleros across their chests, men with guns and knives in their belts — and one of them is Pablo Montoya.

"Kill them, brothers," he shouts, and they do it. Brother Ignacio is cut down, screaming, by a sword thrust through his gut. The water jug crashes to the floor.

More shots ring out and several of the figures in the choir slump over, and they sure ain't singing anymore, no they ain't. They're too busy dying.

"Hold that one," orders Montoya, pointing at a very stricken Fra Gilberto, who still stands by the side of the rack. "Help the boy get her loose. Hurry. Some of those up there got away. They will spread the alarm."

One of the men pulls the rachet on the rack's wheel and it relaxes its grip on me.

Oh, thank you, God!

In my daze, I realize that someone is fumbling with my wrist straps and muttering curses.

"Rotten bastards! May they all rot in hell!"

"Cesar? Is it really you?"

"*Sí, Señorita.* When they took you, I followed them to the Basilica and then ran for Montoya. I am sorry we took so long getting here, but he had to gather his men," says Cesar. "Oh, *pobrecita,* what agony you must have endured!"

The last of the bindings is removed and someone sits me up. I am groggy, but I manage to get up and throw my legs over the side.

"Yeeeow!" I cry when I stand and the pain hits my joints. Cesar catches me on my way to the floor.

"Pick her up," orders Montoya, and Cesar gets one arm under my useless legs and the other under my shoulders and lifts me. I put my face against his chest and sob, all strength and pride gone.

Montoya looks up at the blade hanging ready.

"Anselmo, Fernando. Put him on his foul machine and strap him down."

"*Sí, Comandante*," say the men, taking the suddenly comprehending Fra Gilberto and putting him on the rack. When the straps are around his wrists and ankles, Montoya goes to him and rips open the front of his red robe.

He leans down and speaks into the Inquisitor's stunned face. "You will now go to your god, false priest, and you will be judged. Augustin! Pull the lever. *Vamos, compadres!*"

As I am carried through the door, I hear a very familiar sound . . .

Swoooosh!

. . . followed by a very long scream.

"We must flee the city, *chica*," says Montoya over his shoulder. "They will be after us." I have been put up behind him on his horse and we clatter through the darkened streets.

"Yes, Pablo, but not yet," I say, clinging to him. "I must go back to Casa Goya. There are things I have to get . . . and something I must do."

"Very well, girl, but you must be quick about it."

My mouth is set into a grim line.

Oh, I will be quick, all right . . . very quick.

Cesar and I burst into Estudio Goya to find an astounded Master, Amadeo, and Asensio. My strength had returned to me on the way here, and the pain in my joints has lessened.

"Carmelita has betrayed all of us to the Inquisition, especially you, Maestro," I say, my chest heaving. "Where is she?"

"Upstairs," says Amadeo, perplexed. "But I don't understand."

"You will," I say, as I bolt up the stairs. "Cesar will explain."

I dash into my room, grab my seabag, and pull out my toreador pants. Stripping off skirt and drawers, I examine my belly.

Good. It is only a thin graze, but the next swing of that awful blade would surely have opened me up. Food for future nightmares, but now I must be off.

I am stuffing myself into the trousers when Amadeo comes in.

"This is terrible, Jack-ie. I cannot say how sorry I am for what you have suffered," he says.

"It is all right now, Amadeo. How is Maestro taking it?"

"He is moving the household. We will be gone by midnight. Carmelita will be sent back to her family."

"Good. It is what she deserves. Now, Amadeo, please take your painting of me off the stretcher bars and roll it up. I wish to take it with me."

"You are not coming with us, Jacquelina?"

"No, Amadeo, I am not," I say. "Remember when I said I was a British spy and you thought I made a joke? Well, it is the truth, and I must flee for my life. Put the painting in my bag there, then set it out in the hall. I shall pick it up shortly."

Taking my wineskin from my bedstead, I stride with great purpose to Carmelita's room.

"*Madre de Dios!*" she exclaims as I enter to find her sitting on the edge of her bed in her nightclothes. "You!"

"Yes, it is I, Carmelita," I snarl, advancing on her. "The one you betrayed and sentenced to an awful death. It gives me great pleasure to inform you that Goya has been informed of the full extent of your treachery and you are to be sent back to your family in disgrace."

She gasps and puts her knuckle to her mouth as I advance on her.

"Get away from me!" she says, shrinking back.

"Oh, I will get away from you," I say with a smile, as I pull my wineskin from my shoulder. "But not just yet. You see, I want you to experience something before I go . . . something for you to remember me by."

"No!" she cries, as I leap upon her and force her back on the bed, such that her head hangs over the side. Sitting on her chest, I uncork the wineskin.

"This is what it felt like, you miserable scheming bitch!" I snarl, sticking the nozzle of the skin into her right nostril.

"No, please! I am sorry! I—"

But that's as far as she gets as I give the bag a good hard squeeze. I am gratified see her eyes fly wide open as she gargles on the water. She gasps for breath as I pull the spout out of her right nostril and put it in her left one.

"And that's not all they did to me, Carmelita, oh no. They stretched me on the rack and they pulled me apart, but you see I came back together. They cut me, they did, and they hurt me, but this was the worst of all."

I put my hand over her mouth and squeeze again. Her eyes are now bugging out in a most satisfying way.

"Hurts, doesn't it? Feels like you're drowning, don't it, sweetheart? Here, have another."

This time I take my hand off her mouth and am gratified to see her vomit the water and what looks to be her dinner all over herself. I sling the wineskin back over my shoulder and stand, leaving her gasping and choking on what once was her bed but shall be her bed nevermore.

"They called you a good Catholic girl in that dungeon, for your betrayal of the House of Goya. Huh! Well, the next time you are on your knees in the confessional, I suggest you confess it all, Carmelita. Maybe God will forgive you, but I certainly shall not!"

With that, I turn and see Carmelita Gomez no more, and of that I am glad.

I run back to my room and find Amadeo standing by my bag.

"Thank you, *mi amigo*," I say. "One final kiss for you, my good friend, and then I must be off. I did enjoy your company."

I grab his collar and pull him to me. An avid kiss is given, breathlessly received, and I am off down the stairs.

The place is in a turmoil of hurried packing, but Cesar is there waiting for me, looking stricken.

"They say you are leaving, Jack-ie."

"Yes, Cesar," I say, my hands on his shoulders. "But you must remember this, my bold young man, you are my one true love at this place, and I mean that. *Adiós, mi corazón*."

I plant a kiss, a real kiss, on his lips and head toward the door and out to where Montoya waits for me with a horse. I bound up into the saddle and wave to those assembled on the steps to see me off.

"Goodbye, Maestro, you were so good to me. Adiós, Asensio, Cesar, Paloma, Ramona . . ."

I lift my hat and put my heels to my mount and call out, "*Viva España!*"

PART III

Chapter 37

We pounded out of Madrid in the dead of the night, leaving a very shocked Spanish Inquistion behind us . . . and a stunned Estudio Goya, as well. I know the studio will get over it. I hope the Inquisition does not.

It was an hour's ride to the guerrilla encampment, and my bones cried out from their recent exercise under the kind care of the Holy Office, but I managed to make it without too much whining. Nothing broken, so nothing spoken . . . except for a few whimpers, *but oh, it hurts, it hurts* . . .

There is a campfire burning as we rein in, outlying guards having already announced our arrival. We dismount and I manage to stand as I meet the other members of Montoya's band. I had already met Augustin, Anselmo, and Fernando in the dungeon pit, but now I have been made known to Primitivo, Rafael, and the brothers Andres and Eladio . . .

. . . and to Pilar Montoya.

This Pilar looks me over with a certain amount of disdain. She is a stocky woman of about forty years. She, too, is adorned with bandoleros and pistols. About her waist is a thick leather skirt. Below that, heavy boots. There is no nonsense about her.

"So, Pablo, you have brought back a foundling," she says, her voice cold. "Just what we need."

"She is not what she seems, Pilar," says Montoya. "*Jacquelina, mi esposa, Pilar*," he continues by way of introduction.

I bow, since I'm not wearing a skirt in which I might curtsy, and murmur, "*Con mucho gusto, Señora Montoya*," but it seems to have little effect.

"So what are we to do with her?"

"She must be taken back to the English army in Portugal."

"Must she?"

"*Sí*. She works for them."

"What of the fight, Pablo? Eh? What of our cause? Have you forgotten?"

"The British will pay us well if we do it. I sense she is valuable to them."

She looks at me and snorts. "That?" she says.

It is becoming plain to me that it is this Pilar and not her husband, Pablo, who really runs things around here. Maybe that is why he spends so much time in Madrid.

"*Sí, Pilar*," says Pablo, somewhat abashed. "They will give us money and we will be able to buy better weapons . . . guns . . . powder . . . to better fight the French pigs."

"*Humph*," grunts Pilar, unconvinced.

I step forward.

"I will not be a burden on you and your fine men, Señora. I can ride and I can shoot. I am used to the hard life in the field."

She gives an exasperated sigh of disgust. "Very well. You can cook and clean up after the men until we can dump you off and—"

I turn and leap back into the saddle. "I will not do that, Señora," I say, looking down on her. "I shall ride with you and I will fight, if it comes to that. But I will not be a scrubwoman."

My bag is packed and sits behind me. I can be gone in an instant. "Pablo, and you others, thank you for saving my life today." I stick my finger in my side pocket and pull out a few coins and toss them on the ground. "That is for the horse. *Adiós, mi amigos!*"

I turn the horse's head and prepare to ride off, but Pablo reaches up and grabs the horse's halter and looks to his wife.

She shrugs and mutters, "*Muy bien, ella puede permanecer.* But if she causes any trouble"—she cocks her hand into the shape of a pistol and points her finger at my face—"she is gone."

Pilar fixes me with her hard gaze and pulls the imaginary trigger.

And I know exactly what to expect from her.

And so I now ride as a member of Comandante Pablo Montoya's guerrilla band, my legs clasped around a very good horse, my hat on my head, no wig for me now, oh, no, for El Rubio now rides as *La Rubia, The Blonde Partisan,* two pistols held high, a cry of *Libertad!* on her lips.

Well, sort of like that . . .

Mostly I ride into any encounter firing my *pistolas* into the air, shouting revolutionary slogans, prancing about, and trying not to kill anybody.

Generally, we ambush small French convoys from whom we take supplies — food, powder, small arms. Once, we managed to capture a good-size cannon mounted on a caisson. Perhaps it will come in handy.

While I try not to kill anybody, men are indeed killed and left by the side of the road. It is war, after all, and men will die. Some of ours, some of theirs . . .

After one such encounter, birds circle in the sky as we withdraw from the scene of the violent action, leaving dead men on the ground.

As we ride, I look up and Pilar sees me doing it. She smiles grimly.

"*Sí, muchacha,*" she says as we push back into the hills. "It is said that Napoleon loves his soldiers . . ." She pauses to spit on the ground. "But, you see, the buzzards love them, too."

I think of my Clodhoppers, the French boys in my squad back at the killing fields of Jena Auerstadt. *I hope you all went back home after that carnage, I hope that with all my heart. Laurent . . . Dubois . . . all of you fine boys. I would hate to think of any of you lying still and open-eyed beneath the pitiless Spanish sun, beneath those descending carrion-seeking birds.*

The men call me *La Apasionada,* and it pleases them to do so, so I do not mind. At night, by the campfire, I sing, I dance . . . A fiddle has been found for me and I play upon it, and all cheer and shout; and joy, however short-lived, reigns.

And so my legend grows . . . Why, I do not know, but it does, in spite of me . . .

Chapter 38

James Emerson Fletcher
Shaolin Novice
House of Chen
Rangoon, Burma

Jacky Faber
By All Accounts, Somewhere in Spain

My dear Jacky,
     Today I received both an honor and some very good news.
     Early in the afternoon, Sifu Loo Li and I face off. We bow and go to the en garde position, which now I know is called Waiting Dragon, our Bo staffs resting on our shoulders, our knees bent in lunging position. He initiates the bout by going into the Attack of the Angry Butterfly, in which his stick is held low to the ground and then whipped around to attempt to strike me at the shoulders. I parry with the Whispering of the Willow Wand and come back with Awakening of Sleeping Bee.

I find the Shaolin names for these moves quite charming. In our own British Navy Manual of Arms, a saber swing at the neck of an opponent, hoping to open his jugular vein, is called Attack in Position Two, while in Bojutsu, it would be named something like Gentle Caress of Sharp Banana Leaf. Very poetic . . . but just as deadly.

Sifu Loo Li and I fight to a draw. A break is called and we take tea with Kwai Chang, cross-legged on the grass. There are several other Shaolin monks in attendance as well, and all have been watching our bout. These monks do not wear the novice dragon tattoo that rests on Sifu Loo Li's forearm, no, they have one on each arm, entwined with vines and flowers. These are the true Masters of Bojutsu.

"We are quite pleased with your perfomance, Chueng Tong," says Master Chang. "You have come a long way in your time here . . ."

. . . *for a barbarian,* I think, silently filling in the unspoken words.

" . . . in both mind and body."

"Thank you, Master," I say, my head bowed. "I owe you much. I owe you my very self."

He says nothing to that, merely nods.

"Ah, they are ready to resume the match."

Sifu and I arise and go to the center of the field, bow to each other, and assume the Waiting Dragon. Soon we are fully engaged.

The Kick of Drowsy Lion parried with Alert Jaw of Jackal and then an attack in Devious Swan, fended off with Beguiling Perfume of Precious Peonies, and . . .

And then I see an opening. Sifu, recovering from my

last attack, seems a little off-balance. I know it could be a trick to draw me into a fatal error, but I go for it anyway. Thrusting my stick between his ankles, I leap into the air and twist around, giving my Bo a hard yank.

There is no poetic name for what I just did, but Sifu Loo Li goes down all the same.

I whip my stick around and place the heel of it at his throat. His eyes go hooded and he nods in defeat.

I have won. I have won!

We get to our feet and bow to each other. I think the day over, but I am wrong. Master Chang takes me by the elbow and leads me to the Shaolin masters.

"Go with them, Long Boy," he says. "You will not be disappointed."

I follow them, and I am led into the Shaolin temple. I have been in here many times with Master Chang, but not with these men. They take me to the main altar, where bowls of incense and myrrh smolder. Hands reach out and take off my gi, and I am left standing only in my loincloth. They gesture for me to kneel and I do it, wondering just what is going on.

It does not take me long to find out.

A monk comes to my left side and places a sort of small bench, more of a footstool, really, next to me and then takes my left arm and puts it on the bench, inside of forearm up. He opens a packet he has by his side, and I see needles and vials of color.

He takes a long needle and sets to work, the black color first, then the gold, then the green.

When I leave the temple, I have the Mark of the Red

Dragon on my arm. I have been made a novice of the Shaolin Monastery, and never have I felt more pride in an accomplishment.

That night, after Mai Ling and Mai Ji have expressed their joy and admiration over my new decoration — and dear Sidrah has placed a soothing ointment on it to ease the prickling pain — Chopstick Charlie smiles upon me.

"Honored guest," he says, puffing on his hookah, "and you are truly honored now — the Shaolin do not give those things away, you know — I have something to tell you, something that might give you great joy . . . and perhaps distress the heart of my dear daughter."

She and I look up expectantly. Charlie hands the hookah to me, and I take a long drag and wait.

"There is a ship moored in the harbor, and she is headed back to the West. It is the merchant *Mary Bissell.*"

There is a sharp intake of breath on both my part and Sidrah's.

"My associates inform me that she is sound of timber and well-captained. I assume you will want to sail away on her? Hmmm?"

"Yes, Honored Host, I would like that," I say, my pulse beginning to race. "I must get back."

"Umm," says Charlie. "I suspect you must. However, the *Mary Bissell* sails under American colors and is headed back there, not to England."

I sit quietly, taking this all in, while Charlie goes on.

"That might be just the thing for you, Long Boy. I have told you that the very worthy John Higgins has also written to me, and he is of the opinion that England is not a very safe place for you right now. It seems the populace has not forgotten the depredations of the Black Highwayman. Hmmm?"

I have to grimace at that, and admit the truth of it.

"Besides, the object of your affections just might find herself back in America. From long discussions I have had with Number Two Daughter, I know she feels safe there, and it is to that place she consistently returns."

That is true, I'm thinking. *And it might be months before a ship comes here, one bound for Britain, that is.*

I will take it! It will be easy to get from the States to England.

I collect myself and say, "Where in America is this *Mary Bissell* headed?"

"New York, I believe, but I do not have her list of ports-of-call right now. Tomorrow, I will. But Boston is not all that far from New York, I see from my charts, and . . ."

And what?

"Think on this, Long Boy. It would be well for you to be in disguise for a while, considering, well, you know . . ."

How well I know . . .

" . . . and when we brought you here, you had no clothing other than shirt, trousers, and boots. Oh, yes, and that big black cape . . . and a mask . . ."

Don't rub it in, Chops, I know what I did . . .

"So what I propose is this: We can tie back your long black hair, maybe shave your forehead a bit, and outfit you with a noble Chinaman's attire. If you affect a slight halting of speech, like English is not your first language, you could easily pass for Eurasian — Yankee missionary father, Chinese mother, all that."

"And to what end, Honored Chen?"

Charlie smiles his cat-that-swallowed-the-canary smile. "To establish a branch of the House of Chen in the New World will be the purpose. It is time for me to expand into that area. You will be given money to do that and I want you to set up that shipping company — Oriental Enterprises, I think we shall call it . . ." — he pauses, as if relishing a private joke — "in Boston."

I, too, have to smile at that.

"Won't that put a bit of a twist in the tail of our little Lotus Blossom, hmmm?" says Charlie with a grin. "To have a rival company that already has a firm grounding in the spice-laden Orient, perhaps even right across the street from Faber Shipping Worldwide, hmmm?"

I lose my reserve and laugh out loud at that. It just might, Charlie, and I must admit, the thought of a little twist in that particular tail is not all that distasteful to me . . .

Chapter 39

We sleep out in the open most nights when the sky is clear and it does not rain, but sometimes, when it is not clear, we commandeer a farmhouse — sometimes with the blessing of the owner, sometimes not.

Those who resist pay a price, mostly in material goods, as the Montoya band is not needlessly cruel. That, in fact, is where my fiddle came from. The previous owner, landlord of a big estate, proclaimed himself *afrancesado* — we are near the French border, and so there are many sympathizers in this area — and added that we were a bunch of dirty scoundrels and that we should go away. Brave man, yes, but stupid, too. Unwashed we are, but away we don't go. We are also well armed, so his violin now rests in my seabag when I am not playing it for the joy of my compadres. The owner was lucky to escape with his life, and perhaps in the future he will watch his mouth when facing an unruly group of desperados.

Tonight we sleep under the stars, my head resting on my saddle, the seat of which has been well polished by my bottom. As I lie here by the campfire, I think on Jaimy and

Richard and all my other friends around the world, they who have taken me in and protected my poor self, and I pray for their safety and health. As I am about to drift off, with my knees pulled up to my chin, my blanket wound tightly about me, I think about my present companions — Montoya and all the lads . . . and Pilar, too.

Hmmm . . . One good thing about having her stern presence around is that I do not have to put off advances of an ardent nature from any members of the band. She has made it quite clear that she would consider that disruptive to our mission, and so no one is to mess with me in an amorous way, especially not Pablo. *Ah, no more honeyed words of romance from that stalwart guerrilla, oh, no.* Napoleon is to be feared, but the wrath of Pilar, even more.

Sleep is about to come, and I hear the deep breathing and, yes, the snores of those gathered about me, and it gives me some comfort to be in their midst.

Yes, Jaimy, I am once again amongst friends and am safe, sort of — at least as safe as one can be, being a member of a guerrilla band — but I —

Suddenly, there is a shrill whistle from outside — the danger signal from one of the sentries! In an instant, we are all on our feet, grasping our weapons. Pablo and Pilar are standing together with pistols in hand and looking in the direction of the alarm.

Two short whistles are heard, and everybody relaxes . . . to a degree. Two whistles means "friend approaches," but still we are watchful . . . and we wait.

Presently, a rider appears out of the gloom, reins up, and dismounts.

"Hola, Pablo, Pilar!" says the man. "I bear orders from Comandante Guzman!"

"Joachim!" exclaims Montoya. "Welcome! *Compadres,* bring refreshment for our brother-in-arms!"

I stand back to watch this exchange. Pablo grabs the intruder by the shoulders and gives him a bear hug worthy of Mississippi Mike Fink.

"What news do you bring us? Tell me Bonaparte is dead and in the ground!"

"Not yet, Pablo!" The messenger laughs. I can now see he is a very young man dressed like the rest of us — black garb with crossed bandoleros on his chest, black hat thrown back and hanging on his neck by a cord. His teeth flash in the firelight as he looks about. "But soon, I swear it! I will shovel the dirt on him myself!"

I hang back, watching. This Joachim looks somehow familiar.

"Ha! So what is the news? What are the orders?" asks Pablo, releasing the man.

"You and your gallant freedom fighters are to blow up the bridge at Siguenza."

"Over the Henares River? *Pero porque?*"

"We have word that the French will be sending many divisions of soldiers over that bridge. It will hinder their advance if there is no bridge there to carry them over."

"But, Joachim," says Pilar, "we have no powder, no explosives."

"Ah, but we know of a shipment of such material that is coming soon and right by here. We shall take it and use it to destroy that bridge and cause confusion to our enemy!"

This young man does not lack for words, that's for sure, I'm thinking, as I step out of the shadows to warm my hands at the fire.

"Yes, the convoy will arrive on — But what's this, then?" asks this Joachim, as his eyes fall upon me. "Ah!" he exclaims, catching his breath. "Can this be *La Rubia* herself? *La Apasionada* in person? We have heard of her! I am astounded, I am in awe!"

He drops to one knee and bows his head to me. "Bless me with your touch, divine one!"

Pilar snorts. "That is her, all right. We are taking her to Lisbon, and good riddance, I say."

"But such a shame," says the young man, rising and extending his hand to me, "to let one such as this slip away from us!"

I laugh and take his hand. "I am neither divine, nor will the loss of my company be much of a shame, but I am pleased to see you again, Joachim, nonetheless."

"Again?" he says, confused. "We have met before? I am sure the memory of that meeting would have been seared into my very soul, but I — "

"You were the one who picked up my poor battered self on the battlefield at Vimeiro and took me to hospital. Do you remember now?"

"Of course!" he exults. "The poor little *muchacha,* fallen on the field of battle. But then your face wore a veil of our precious blood and I thought for sure you had given your very life for the cause! I cried over you as I carried you off!"

"You can see that I did not die, Joachim," I say, grinning

in spite of myself at his glowing words. *These Spanish lads, I swear . . .*

"Enough pleasant talk," growls Pablo Montoya. "What of this caravan?"

Joachim avidly kisses the back of my hand, leaving it a bit wet, and then releases it. He turns to the Montoyas. "It will be here in two days and will pass down the road right here. It is well guarded, but with our courageous fighters, and *La Apasionada* by our side, we are certain to take it. And then we will use that powder to blow up the bridge."

I listen to their plots and plans, but one thing I know—I will not be taken to Lisbon until this job is done. And I will have to help do it.

Chapter 40

"They are not Grand Army Regulars," I say, squinting through Montoya's spyglass. "Maybe the two riding off to either side are, but the rest are new conscripts." I am lying on my stomach, peering over the ridgeline at the coming convoy.

"How can you tell, *chica?*" asks Joachim, who lies by my side.

"Because of their uniforms. They are cheap and ill fitting. Remember, I was once a member of that army."

"Are you sure?" asks Pablo, who lies on my other side.

"*Sí.* They are just the kind of soldiers sent on a dismal mission like transporting tents. They do not even have outriders."

Joachim nods. "Our informant tells us that the explosives lie under the tents. For cover. It is possible the guards do not know what they are carrying."

"So they should be easy to take," asserts Pilar with a certain air of grim determination. "Who would die to protect tents?"

"*Sí, Señora,*" I say. "But any of them could get off a lucky shot if we just charge at them blindly. Some of us could be hurt or killed. And all of them would be dead. It could cause reprisals. They could send out a division to hunt us down."

"So what do you suggest, wise one?" asks Pablo Montoya. "That we just let them go on their way, whistling a happy French tune?"

"Nay, Pablo," I reply, handing him back his glass. "We must have the powder. I know that. But perhaps we can do this with a minimum of bloodshed. Look down below there, at the curve in the road. Do you see the little stream there?"

"*Sí.* But what — ?"

"I intend to wash my feet, as they sorely need it," I say, and outline my plan.

"Good one, Jacquelina! An excellent idea," exclaims Joachim upon hearing it. He gives my rump a slap before rising to his feet to prepare for the action.

Men, I swear . . . Present them with a female all demure in a dress with modestly covered head, and they are all, *So pleased to meet you, Miss* and *À votre service, Mademoiselle* and *En su servicio, Señorita,* but put that same girl in pants and all fine custom disappears, and all she can expect is a rude slap on her tail. *Geez* . . .

Actually, I have been enjoying a bit of fun with this Joachim. Since he is from another band, he is not completely under Pilar's stern control, and, therefore, he can be on more friendly terms with me. Oh, she still puts her gimlet eye on us as we sit close, laughing and singing by the campfire. He has a fine tenor voice and we have a good, warm time around the campfire at night. He has with him a *cuatro,* a very small guitar, and we sing all the songs we know to each other, and for the enjoyment of the others.

I sing the *"Malagueña Salerosa"* and dance in the firelight, castanets clicking, while Joachim plays on his *cuatro* and all cheer and shout.

At the end of the evening, I take the little guitar and play the beautiful *"La Paloma."*

> *Si a tu ventana llega Una Paloma,*
> *Trátala con cariño, que es mi persona.*
> *Cuéntale tus amores. Bien de mi vida,*
> *Coronala de flores. Que es cosa mia.*

The song refers to the legend of a time when the ancient Greeks were fighting the Persians, and while the victors were watching the sinking of the defeated fleet, they saw swarms of white doves lift into the air. They decided that those birds were the souls of the dying seamen heading back home, where they'd beat their white wings on the windows of their beloved ones as a last message of love. Of course, that sort of lyric hits me right where I live, and I put my heart and soul into it.

Joachim gets into the spirit of the thing and joins me in singing the whole chorus.

> *Si a tu ventana llega Una Paloma,*
> *Trátala con cariño, que es mi persona.*
> *Cuéntale tus amores. Bien de mi vida*
> *Coronala de flores. Que es cosa mia.*
> *Ay! Chinita que si!*

Ay, que dame tu amor.
Ay, que vente conmigo.
Chinita a donde vivo yo!

After we sing the refrain one more time, all turn in for the night.

A little kiss at the end of evening? Well, maybe . . . But no, I do not sleep with him . . .

Even though I do sleep next to him, rolled up in my own bedroll.

I now sit by the side of the stream, facing the road. My feet are in the water, and I am washing them. Actually, it feels quite good, the cool water flowing over my grubby hooves. *Mmmmm* . . . I have shed my matador pants and jacket, and wear only my loose white top and simple black skirt. I scan the hills that surround me and signal to those who lurk there that all is in readiness. Then I wait.

Presently, the lead rider appears at the bend in the road, followed by the rest of the caravan. I pull my skirt higher on my thighs, thrust my arms down between my knees to massage my feet, and I commence to sing.

Auprès de ma blonde,
Qu'il fait bon, fait bon, fait bon,
Auprès de ma blonde,
Qu'il fait bon dormir.

Hearing the familiar French song, the caravan comes to a halt. Hey, the song is about a man sleeping next to his beautiful girlfriend. What Frenchman would not stop for that? Especially when sung by a passably comely maid who sits by the road with her skirt hiked up.

"Bonjour, Mademoiselle!" calls out the lead rider. "It is good to hear the beautiful French spoken in this dismal land. And by such a comely *jeune fille!*"

"You are much too gallant, Monsieur," I purr, sliding my mantilla back from my head and letting it fall about my shoulders. It is the signal to those watching above to get into position. Out of the corner of my eye, I see silhouettes appearing against the sky. *Spread your men out, Pilar. Make it look like there are many more of you than there are. Place a horse between each man and that will double your number. Put a charge in the cannon, but do not load it with shot. I will be the bait, but I do not wish to die for Spain, not just yet. Remember my instruction: Show yourselves when I take off my mantilla, fire the gun when I lift my hand into the air.*

"Perhaps you will ride with us for a while," the man says with a leer. "For long enough to have some fun . . . We will make it worth your while. We have gold and silver in great store."

"Is that what you have in your wagon, my bold young man?" I simper, drawing the skirt ever higher.

"That wagon? *Non, Cherie.* Just stupid tents in there. The gold is in my pocket," he says, patting his crotch. "Would you like to reach inside and take some?"

Coarse laughter from his cohorts. *Har-har! What do you have under that skirt, girl? Enough for all of us good fellows?*

"No, sir, I will not grant you that favor," I say, rising to my feet and going to stand by the horseman. "But I will grant you an even greater favor."

"And what favor is that?" He laughs, leaning over me in the saddle.

"I will give you your life."

He looks startled. "How will you give me my life? Are you an angel?"

"*Non, Monsieur.* But perhaps you have heard of *La Belle Jeune Fille Sans Merci?*"

"What? But she is — "

"She is standing right here, *mon ami,*" I say, twirling about and sweeping my hand toward the horizon. "Look up there, all of you."

Startled, they take their eyes off me and gaze upward. There stands the Montoya band of guerrillas, dark and menacing against the sky, a rifle in each hand, held across each chest. In the midst of them stands a cannon, pointed down at the convoy.

"*Diable!*" shouts the leader.

"There are a hundred of us! Save yourselves!" I shout. "Run, my friends! Will you die for your tents? Save yourselves!"

With that, I thrust my hand into the air and am rewarded with a deep *boooom* from our cannon on the hill.

I am also rewarded with . . . *yeeeouch!* A hail of small shot rains down upon us. One catches me on my hip, another hits the flank of the caravan leader's horse. I scream, and so does the horse. The horse bolts forward and carries his rider away.

My hipbone stings and I fume, but still I go with the

plan. "Run, comrades, run! Look, they come!" I scream, pointing up at Montoya's men charging down the hill. "They will kill you! Run!"

They need no more encouragement. The French soldiers climb down from the wagon and take to their heels. Those on horseback spur their mounts and follow the others in their panicked flight.

The last of them have gone off down the road as Pablo and the others swarm over the wagon and draw the horses around. Primitivo leaps up onto the seat, picks up the reins, and gets the nervous horses started on the way back to our camp. A grinning Joachim comes running to me. Then I spot the stolid figure of Pilar.

"Pilar!" I yell, pointing an accusing finger at her. "You loaded that gun. You shot me!"

I rub my sore thigh. It hurts, but I know the spent shot did not penetrate my skin.

Pilar smiles. "We wanted it to look good, no? It was your plan, remember, girl."

I do not think her smile is genuine and I continue to look resentful.

"No matter now, *cara mia!*" exults Joachim, putting his arm around my waist. "I shall kiss it and make it well!"

Our horses are brought up and we mount. "We have the powder and we did not lose a single man, thanks to the cunning of *La Apasionada!*" Joachim shouts, standing in his stirrups.

"On to the bridge at Siguenza!"

Chapter 41

James Emerson Fletcher
Onboard the Mary Bissell
Bound for America

Jacky Faber
Who Knows Where

Dearest Jacky,
Yes, I now stand on the deck of the Mary Bissell, *looking*
out to sea. I am dressed in the finest of Oriental garb. At my
waist is a sash that holds a very sharp knife, but at my side
hangs no sword. No, instead, in my hand I hold my Bo staff,
and I think I will need naught else in the way of protection.

The sails have filled and we gain headway and Burma
fades behind me, as I look to the west with a certain amount
of cautious hope concerning our eventual reunion.

I bade farewell to my Rangoon friends last night at a
great feast put on by the House of Chen in my honor. Mai
Ling and Mai Ji were there, protesting that they shall wither

and die without their beloved Long Boy, but I suspect that they will survive.

Kwai Chang attends and eats very heartily for a monk. I must say, our own starched churchmen should take a lesson. He gives me his blessing and once again I give him my thanks for his teachings, and I ask him to tender my farewell to Sifu Loo Li.

"Tell him, Master, that I thank him for his instruction at Bojutsu," I say. "And I want you to do this when you tell him that." I look in his eye and wink my own eye very broadly.

"But what does that gesture mean, Chueng Tong?" asks the Master, mystified. "Could it be a Western koan with which I am not familiar? Is it the sound of one eyelid closing? That is puzzling, for that sound cannot be louder than that of the footsteps of a mosquito wearing slippers, walking across an elephant's testicles. Please enlighten poor teacher, Long Boy."

It is all I can do to suppress laughter at the Master's ability to turn a crude gesture into a metaphysical question.

"No, Master," I manage to say. "It is merely a sign that the one winking is not entirely convinced of an action, or a statement."

"Oh," he says, eyebrows raised, apparently puzzled. "Please go on."

"That particular wink should convey to Sifu Loo Li my certainty that he threw the fight that let me win my Red Dragon."

Master Kwai Chang laughs and says, "Oh, Chueng Tong, he would never do that. Trust me!" He chortles for a bit and then goes on. "But I will wink my eye when I tell him of your words!"

Yes, Charlie and I exchanged heartfelt farewells that night. I tendered my thanks for his hospitality to both you and me. He tut-tutted all that and said he was sure he would be repaid many times over by his new contacts in the New World. Never let it be said that Old Chops ever missed an opportunity to extend his business interests . . . or his ultimate empire. "Here, Mr. Fletcher, is a packet of money in various currencies. Use it as you wish, and invest it wisely, and I believe we both shall prosper. Regards to my Little Round-Eyed Barbarian when you see her. Bon voyage, Long Boy."

Everyone said their goodbyes that night . . . all except for one, and that one stood at the dock as the *Mary Bissell* pulled away. Sidrat'ul Muntaha waved a silken handkerchief and the same wind that billowed her bit of cloth also filled our slack sails.

Goodbye, Sidrah, I shall remember you . . .

Jaimy

Chapter 42

We are below the stone pillars of the bridge that arches above us. It is late afternoon and we strive to get the job done before nightfall because there is a report that a French battalion is marching southward toward this very bridge.

"Here. Pack them in down at the base of the pillar," orders Rafael, who seems to know more about explosives than the others, and certainly more than I.

I serve as powder monkey in this endeavor, not having much expertise in this field other than setting a simple fuse and then lighting it. Rafael takes my bag of powder and shoves it tight against the others already stacked there.

Last night was spent in celebration over our taking of the French convoy and its precious powder. There was good food found in the French wagons, and wine, too, and so we ate and drank and caroused far into the night. I danced with Joachim and sang with him, and when it was time for sleep, our two bedrolls became one, as the night was cool.

Today, however, is all work.

It seems rather a shame to destroy this bridge, I'm thinking, as I drop my bag of powder and gaze up at the underside of the structure. It looks like it's been here a good long time. I imagine it's helped many people in getting their goats and sheep across the river, and I'll bet lots of poor people have camped beneath it. Yes, it's just like Blackfriars Bridge back in London, which gave shelter to me and the rest of the Rooster Charlie Gang. Oh, well, war is war, and it will have its way.

I am going back for another bag when I hear Joachim call out. "Jacquelina! Augustin has come back from a scouting mission with news. He reports that there is a whole division of French troops marching this way. They intend to cross this bridge!"

Augustin sits there on his puffing horse, plainly proud of being bearer of this news.

"Hola, Augustin," I say, wiping the sweat and dust from my eyes. "What were they?"

"What do you mean 'What were they?'" asks the lad, confused. "They were French soldiers, that's what, and there were lots of them. What else?"

"Yes, I know," I say. "But how were they arrayed? How were they placed as they marched along? How were they dressed?"

The boy considers. "They were in three columns, with riders out to the side. The ones in front had shiny breastplates on their chests and high hats with plumes out the back."

I turn to Joachim and say, "They are Cuirassiers, the finest of battle-tested soldiers, second only to the Imperial Guard. They are not like the farm boys we scared away yesterday, Joachim. We must beware, and we must set our charges and get the hell out of here." I look around nervously.

"But why, *guapa*?" he says, once again drawing me to him. "They are far away and—"

"And they are members of the finest army ever assembled, and they will have scouting parties out in advance of the main force. Count on it, Joachim. Ignore my advice at your peril!"

I push him away and seek out Pablo Montoya.

"Comandante," I say upon finding him, with Pilar by his side. "We must get this done quickly and get away as fast as we can!"

Pilar crosses her arms and scowls at me. "Once again, the smallest one gives the biggest orders," she says, her voice thick with scorn.

"If they come upon us, we will be lost, Pilar. Count on it. They are many, we are few—"

"Stop squabbling, the two of you," says Montoya. "The French are many miles away, and evening is upon us. They will stop and camp for the night. So will we. Raphael has told me that all is in readiness. We need only to light the fuse and the bridge will be gone. It is time for some dinner."

Joachim comes to my side and takes my hand in his. "Come, *guapa,* the campfire is lit, the cook pot is on. Let us sing together again and—"

But we do not do that at all, for a shot rings out . . . then another, then . . .

"Allons! Pour la France!"

More shots, more screams, more—

"Compadres! We are attacked!"

Damn! I just knew it! We are ambushed! A French patrol has fallen upon us! *Damn!*

I grab my pistols and head into the fight. There are screams, there are shots. I fire at shadows once, twice, and yet again, crouching down to reload each time and making no sense of what is swirling around me.

I know that Joachim is by my side, and then . . . then . . . I feel him jerk. *No, God, please! Not again!* But it is true — a bullet has found him.

He falls against me and I hold him up as best I can and struggle with my burden back to the campsite, as the sounds of fighting slack off, then cease.

I see Montoya by the fire, reloading his pistols, cursing under his breath.

"Dirty cowards! Bastardos!"

I gently lower Joachim to the ground and kneel by his side and take his hand.

"Joachim. Can you hear me?" I say gently.

"Si, mi querida. I can . . . and your voice is like honey in my ear. I . . ."

But he does not get to finish, as blood burbles out of his mouth and over his cheek. It is plain that the bullet got him in the lung, and it is also obvious that he is done for. Yet again, I find myself at the side of a dying soldier.

He cannot speak, but his eyes are open and they fix on me.

"Goodbye, Joachim," I whisper, holding his hand to my chest, as tears stream down my face. "I will wait for the dove of your soul to beat at my window. I will, Joachim, and I will throw up the sash and let you in, I promise. Now go with God, *mi querido.*"

And, with a soft, shuddering sigh, he goes off.

I place his hands on his chest and reach up and close his eyes. *Vaya con Dios, mi amigo . . .*

Then I stand, wipe my eyes, and look about me. I see with dismay that there are three more still forms lying dead in a row. It is Anselmo, and Fernando, and the boy Eladio.

Good Lord, what a waste of young lives . . .

"We will blow the bridge now," I hear Montoya say. "Prepare the pig."

What?

I turn to see that the horror is not yet over. The band has a prisoner, and they mean to exact some terrible revenge.

He is a young French lieutenant, Infantry by his uniform, a uniform now stained with his own blood — he has received a grievous wound in his right side. He is tied to a tree and he is hurt, but not so bad that he cannot see what is in store for him. Racks of dry wood and tinder are being stacked around his feet.

They mean to burn him alive.

I rush to stand in front of the prisoner. "Pablo! You cannot do this!"

He does not reply, but Pilar does. "Shut up, girl! We have four dead lying there because of him! He shall pay for it with his death by fire!"

"Mademoiselle," I hear spoken behind me. I turn and look into the eyes of the prisoner who has spoken. Plainly, he senses in me someone of sympathy. *"Aidez moi, s'il vous plait . . . Donnez moi la mort d'un soldat."*

"What does he say?" asks Montoya.

"He asks for a soldier's death. It is his right, Pablo."

"He shall not have it. He leads a cowardly ambush and four of ours lie dead!" snarls Pilar. "No! When the bridge goes, so goes he. Rafael! Go light the fuse! Andres! When you hear the blast, you will light his funeral pyre."

Rafael takes a burning stick from the fire and runs off. Andres, numb with grief over the death of his brother, takes up another ember and goes to stand in front of the prisoner.

The French lieutenant is in pain from his wound, but that pain will be nothing compared to the slow agony of the flames. He looks at me with terror in his eyes, pleading . . .

I set my jaw. *No! I will not witness this.*

There is a tremendous blast from the direction of the bridge.

I have two pistols in my belt, one of which is still loaded. I pull it out and aim the barrel at the young soldier's heart. My finger tightens on the trigger . . . and I give him the release he seeks . . .

I give him the gift of death.

The pistol bucks in my hand, the bullet goes into his heart, and his body slumps in his bonds.

"There," I say, sticking the spent pistol back in my belt and mounting my horse. "You may burn him now."

"You should not have done that," growls Pilar, and Montoya looms large and scowling behind her.

"I know that, Pilar," I say, gathering up the reins. "But I did. I disobeyed your order and I know I must go. The 'little wars' of the guerrillas are too cruel for me. I lack your strength of purpose, I lack your resolve. *Adiós.*"

With that, I turn the horse's head, put heels to her flanks, and pound out of the camp. I put my fist to my mouth and let the tears flow.

Four lie dead on the ground . . . five, now, with the French lieutenant.

What did it serve?

Nada.

What will be remembered?

Nada.

What does it all mean?

Nada.

PART IV

Chapter 43

I have been riding for five days now. I push westward toward the sea, but I'm growing weary. I must stick to the shadows because I have no protection other than my two pistols, and they will not provide much in that way should I be jumped by . . . whom? Anybody, that's who. Anyone who takes a notion to do so. I have my resources, yes, but still I am a young girl alone. The sea is far away and I have very little money. There are great mountain ranges between me and the ocean, and then there are the mighty armies whose lines I must cross.

I am tired . . . and I am very, very hungry.

I mount a ridge and slide out of the saddle to give poor Gabriella a bit of a rest. I lean against her flanks as she munches on the sparse grasses that grow about — *poor girl, I should be able to provide better for you, but I cannot, not now, anyway, but be strong, something will turn up* — and I look down into the valley. As I gaze about, a yellow wagon pulls into my view, far below . . . then another one, painted red with gold trim . . . and yet another brightly adorned in blues and . . . finally, a long line of them. They seem to be pulling into a circle.

Gypsies!

I drag my seabag from Gabriella's back — off with my pants and on with my black embroidered skirt. I already have on my white shirt and toreador jacket; that should serve. I cram my dark wig on my head and drape the black mantilla over that. Back on Gabby's back, I give a gentle nudge with my heels and we head down to the gypsy camp.

As I approach, two men come out to meet me. They are young and darkly handsome and they are dressed very *Majo* — or very much like it — maybe even a little bit more in the way of sashes and headscarves.

"Pardon, Señorita, but we are not yet open to visitors," announces the man to the left. The other one does not say anything but merely crosses his arms and looks sullen. "What do you want?"

"Well, Señor, what I want is to get to the sea, and perhaps you will take me there," I say, flashing my brightest smile. "But right now I'll settle for something to eat."

"We are not open to outsiders," answers the sullen one. "We do not provide transportation, and we are — "

"What you are is Roma," I say, reaching into my shirt-front and pulling out the token Django had given me so I can dangle it in front of his face. "Perhaps this means something to you. At the very least, it should get me something to eat."

They exchange glances. The surly one spins on his heel and walks off.

"Follow me," says the other man.

"I will, if you tell me your name," I say, standing my ground.

"My name is Jan. Come."

I follow him through a space between two wagons and find a hive of activity. Food is being cooked over open fires, and tables are unfolded and set up, and merchandise — pots and pans, baskets, woven goods — are set upon them. The food smells very good, and my belly gives a low growl.

"Sit there," says this Jan, pointing to an empty table. "Medca, bring her something to eat. I shall get Zoltan."

He leaves as I sit down to wait. I am beginning to attract some attention. A group of small dark-eyed children gathers about me.

"*Buenos días, muchachos,*" I say, brightly. "*Qué tal?*"

They say nothing.

Hmmm . . . tough crowd, I see.

I reach in my pocket and pull out the three walnut shells and one bean that I always carry with me, and think of my great friend and teacher Yancy Beauregard Cantrell, who taught me the old shell game back on the Mississippi. "*Sometimes the simplest games are the best, Miss Faber,*" he would say. "*Especially when dealing with simple people.*"

"Come, *niños,*" I say, placing the half shells face-down on the table. "Play a game with me." I hold up the bean and then place it under one of the shells.

After moving the shells quickly about in a circular fashion for a few moments, I challenge one of the kids. "Where is the bean, Señorita?"

The girl points at one of the shells. I lift it up. "Alas, no. It is over here," I say, lifting another. She looks at the bean in wonder. "Try again."

We do it again, and again she fails to find the bean. I nod to an older boy. "You try it now, *muchacho.*"

Again the shells whirl and then stop. The boy points at one of the shells with confidence.

I lift it up. He gasps in disbelief.

I am spinning the shells again when Jan returns with an older man who possesses the hugest pair of mustaschios I have ever seen. He is obviously Zoltan, the boss man.

"Who are you and what do you want?" he growls.

"My name is Jacquelina Bouvier, and I want to go to Lisbon."

"We are not going to Lisbon. We are going to Granada, and we will not take you. You are not Roma."

"No," I say. "But I can be valuable to you. I can sing, I can dance the flamenco, play the guitar and fiddle . . . and do other things, as well. Do you see the bean?"

Startled, he looks down at the table. I turn over all the shells and place the bean under one of them and begin to make them dance. Then I stop.

"Pick the one with the bean, and I will go away. If you fail, you must take me with you."

"It is under there. Now be off with — " He reaches out and turns over the middle shell to find nothing under it.

"It is here, Señor," I say, turning over the right-hand shell to show the elusive bean. "Now, perhaps something to eat?"

He barks out a short laugh.

"So how is old Django?"

Chapter 44

And so I slip into the life of a gypsy, and I find it a style of living that is very appealing to my nature. We roll from village to village, sending out criers before us, calling out, *Tinkers! Tinkers! Weavers and Tinkers! Bring us your broken pots and we will fix them! Come see our fine wares, our delicate fabrics, and spices we bring from the Orient! Come! Come! Music tonight! Magic shows! Jugglers! Come to the merry dance! Come have your fortune told! Come!*

And come they do. Oh, yes, they do, although they hide their children from us as the wagons roll along. They shield the little ones' eyes, thinking we might snatch them up and make them Romani, and then the little tykes would never return to the settled lives they once knew. Babies are hidden, thinking we might sneak up in the dark of night to spirit them away. We don't do that sort of thing, of course. We've got kids enough of our own, for God's sake — the little buggers are all over the place—but that is how legends grow.

I had met the girl Medca on my first day with the Roma — it was she who had first brought me food on Jan's order. As I wolfed it down, I reflected that it did not take too much of my female intuition to sense that something was going on between Medca and Jan — hot glances, secret smiles, and all that.

Hmmm . . . let's see how that plays out.

Soon after, Zoltan decreed that I should stay until such time that I be delivered to the sea, and it was decided that I should bunk with Medca and her three younger sisters in the wagon that followed Zoltan — they being his daughters and all.

I was not immediately tossed in there, oh, no. First I had to be checked out by the matriarch of the clan, Buba Nadya Vadoma, a wizened old woman, seemingly made of nothing but leather, bone, and piercing eyes. She came on me like a winged bat, full of suspicion. First she grasps my right hand and peers at the palm. "*Hmmm . . .* It appears you have already experienced many things in your life. How many seasons have you seen?"

"Seventeen. Eighteen, soon."

"Are you a whore? Don't lie now. I will know."

"N-no, Grandmother, I am not, nor have I ever been."

"*Humpf.* Are you pure?"

"What?"

"Are you pure? Are you fit for marriage? Answer me."

"Pure? I suppose so . . . Sort of."

"I will take your word . . . for now."

She lets go of my hand and takes hold of my wrists, one in each sinewy hand. It is like being gripped by the talons of a great bird of prey. She peers not in my eyes but at the hair on the back of my arms.

"Ha!" she says, then reaches up and pulls off my wig and throws it into the dirt. "La Rubia! I thought so! You think to fool Nadya Vadoma! Ha! It is not done!"

I sit with my shorn head bared. There are gasps, but the old woman says, "She may stay. She may sleep with my granddaughters. For now." She shakes a gnarled finger in my face. "It is very lucky for you that you gained the trust of Django or you would not be here! But you will behave yourself while you are among us, and you will abide by our ways. Do you understand, girl?"

I nod, reflecting that, once again, Jacky Faber has been told to behave herself.

"Yes, Buba Nadya Vadoma. I understand."

In order of birth, Zoltan's daughters are Medca, Dika, Tsura, and Nuri. Medca is fifteen, Dika twelve, and the two little ones are eight and six. The youngest, Nuri, is a devil in little girl's clothing. Most nights, the younger ones are kicked to the foot of the bed, as little sisters have been since the beginning of time, and soon they are asleep, so that Medca and I can talk. And talk we do. At first she is shy with me, but she opens up after a few nights and we lie head to head on the pillow, telling each other of our hopes and dreams.

I tell her something of my Jaimy, and she tells me of her Jan.

"He is the one for you, then?"

"Yes, Ja-elle, I love him with all my heart and he loves me."

Buba Nadya has decreed that I be called Jaelle because Jacky sits too harsh on her tongue, and what Buba says, goes.

"So what is the problem, Medca?"

"Jan has no money. He cannot pay the Bride Price."

"Which is?"

"The money, or property, or other things a young man must give the father of the girl he loves in exchange for her hand in marriage."

"Hmmm . . . In my country it is the girl's father who must come up with the cash. It is called a dowry."

"That is not the way with us."

"Well, maybe Jan will come up with the price in the future. Will you wait for him?"

"Yes, I would wait forever, b-but I cannot. You see, Milosh does have the Bride Price. He has many cows and horses, while Jan has none. And Milosh has made his intentions known to my father."

"Your father would agree to that?"

"*Sí.* Milosh is a good man. He is older, but he would take good care of me should I come to share his bed. He has told me that he would. My father would not give me to a bad man."

"He is a good man, but he is not Jan, right?"

"No, he is not Jan."

"Why not just run away? The two of you. Start a new life somewhere else?"

"A new life for a pair of gypsies out in the world of outsiders? No, it is not done. It would bring great dishonor to our families. We could not bear it. It could not happen."

I think on this for a while, lying in the darkness and listening to Medca's breathing. I believe she is weeping as quietly as she can, but weeping nonetheless.

"I know how to make money, Medca. I am very good

at it, as you shall see. If I get up the Bride Price, would Jan take it?"

"No. It would shame him."

Hmmm . . . Complications.

I curl into her, safe and secure in the night. I like being right here, right now. The nightmares do not come, and I am content . . .

. . . for the moment . . .

Chapter 45

Mister Chueng Tong
Envoy, House of Chen
Onboard the Vessel Mary Bissell
Off Cape of Good Hope
Bound for New Bedford, Massachusetts
USA

Jacky Faber
Or Most Recent Alias
Location, I Cannot Even Begin to Guess . . .

My dearest Jacky,

We have passed through the greater part of the Indian Ocean and are approaching the southern tip of Africa. After we weather that point, it will be clear sailing to America, where, hopefully, I shall receive news of you.

The voyage to here was rather uneventful, merely a storm or two, nothing to upset a real mariner, and the captain of the *Mary Bissell* is a true seaman, if not a true gentleman in the Royal Navy sense of the term, but then I must stop thinking of men in that way—valuing them by their manners and their position rather than by their true worth. His name is Josiah van Pelt, a former whaler, and a man of few words. He does his job in ferrying cargo and passengers from the Near East to America, and that is what he does. He does not entertain passengers in his cabin, nor does he socialize with them.

All of this is fine with me. I myself maintain as low a profile as possible. As a Eurasian man of commerce, I affect a halting manner of speech when speaking English, as well as a slight limp, and lean on my Bo staff whenever I appear on deck. I am courteous to all and seek to cause no offense to any onboard.

That, however, does not seem to be the direction of my path. There are six other passengers: a missionary, the Reverend Gerald Lowe, and his wife, Hortense; their daughters, Florence and Abigail, well-behaved girls aged fourteen and sixteen; and a son, Jeremiah, who seems determined to attach himself to me. I suspect he considers me sort of exotic, expecting me to whip out a samurai sword at any moment to lay waste to all and sundry. Sorry, lad, I have given up all things vainglorious and seek only to pursue the humble path of peace and enlightenment.

The sixth other passenger is a Mr. Obadiah Skelton, a businessman from New York, who was securing some spice contracts in Rangoon and is traveling back to the States to enjoy his newfound success. All that would be very fine and beneath my notice, except for the fact that he is a boor and a braggart and distresses everyone with his loud and obnoxious talk. He centers his braying on the elder Lowe daughter, and on me . . .

"So, China Man," he proclaims at our dinner table — the passengers are given their meals at a long table on the second deck — very similar, I thought upon first viewing the arrangement, to the gun-deck table set for the junior officers on the many ships on which I served, and which saw many raucous good times. I suspect that such good times will not be held here. "How came you to be here, at the table with the white folks?"

I can sense that he has already had quite a bit to drink — probably hides a bottle in his cabin.

"I am an envoy sent by Honorable Chen to the other side of the world to set up a . . . trading post . . . ? In America."

"Har-har!" he bellows, lifting his glass to his lips. "And what will this House of Chink sell? Eh?"

"The House of Chen deals in many things," I say softly. "Fine antiquities, silks, rare spices — "

"Hell, we've got all that and more, Chinaman. You ain't got a chance," he says, and his look turns dark. "And what's more, you ain't gonna be welcome at any boardroom table, or dining-room table at any respectable house. No, you ain't gonna be welcome *anywhere* . . . except maybe to work on the new railways. Can you swing a pick, Chop-Chop?"

"Please, Sir," pleads Reverend Lowe. "He is a fellow guest here. Surely you cannot abuse him so. In our ministry we have met many noble — "

"Listen, Preacher, I am a freeborn American and I will say exactly what I want to say," sneers this man, slurring his words and taking yet another drink of his wine. "And I gotta say you got a mighty pretty daughter right there, yes, you do. Hey, maybe me and her could get together. I'm rich and you all look poor as church mice."

Reverend Lowe shoots to his feet. "I believe we are excused, Sir. Good evening." He gathers his little flock and prepares to leave the dining room.

I also get to my feet.

"Good evening, Sir." I am barely able to suppress my gorge in addressing the buffoon. "I suggest you leave that family alone. If you do not, it will be at your peril."

He looks at me incredulously.

"You dare to —"

"What I dare," I softly say, with a good deal of menace in my voice, "is for you to find out." With a slight bow, I exit, leaving an astounded Mr. Skelton open-mouthed and alone in the room.

Will this end well? I do not know. I will leave it up to fate.

Yours,
Jaimy

Chapter 46

We approach the town of Albancio. It lies on the banks of the River Turia, which, I am told, leads down to the sea — the Mediterranean Sea, to be sure, and not the Atlantic, but the sea all the same.

I sit on the driver's seat of the second wagon, next to Marko, a pleasant young man who has plainly taken a liking to me — and me to him. He is very good-looking, dark of complexion with black hair and brilliant white smile, and he is my dancing partner in the flamenco, as well. He has the reins in hand and is guiding the horse on our way. On my other side sits Gyorgy, Marko's very good friend. It is he who plays the fiddle for our performances.

"A gypsy can make a violin cry," proclaimed Gyorgy, upon our first meeting, and it cannot be denied that he is very good. I had picked up my own fiddle and played for him "The Rakes of Mallow," "MacPherson's Lament," and Mozart's Concerto no. 1 in B-flat Major for Solo Violin, and he listened attentively. When I stopped, he nodded and said, "Yes, a gypsy can make a violin cry, and you did make that one . . . *whimper* a little, Ja-elle."

I answered his cheeky comment by sticking out my lower lip and giving him a rap on the head with my bow. Then we all laughed and got back to the business of making our way across the land.

I find I do not have to worry about any untoward advances from any of the men here, for the young females, of which I am one, are *very* closely watched, and it's kind of pleasant not to have to worry about that sort of thing for a change.

Buba has taken me under her wing. Not that I want to be under there. I'd much rather be off with Marko and Gyorgy and Medca and Jan, but she insists, so with her I must go. I think it is perhaps that I am new and everyone else has heard her stories ten times over . . . and, hey, everyone likes to teach a willing student.

"Come, Ja-elle, and I will show you some things about fortunetelling. Now, first, you take their hand and look at it while shaking your head and saying, "Tsk, tsk. Ah, poor thing, you have had great trouble . . ." With your fingernail, trace their lifeline . . . like this. Everybody has great trouble in this life, and they will be quick to tell you of it. Ask a few questions and they will tell you everything. You can count on that, and from what they reveal, you can tell their fortune. Trust me, they will be astounded by your wisdom."

She also tells me of her people.

"The *Gadzso,* or 'Outsiders,' call us gypsies. The legend is that the name comes from 'Egyptian,' and the story is that we were given the name because we sheltered the Baby Jesus. As punishment for that deed, we were cast out by the heathen Pharoahs to forever roam the world."

I take that one with a grain of salt, thinking that Baby Jesus sure got around for an infant, appearing in many stories in a whole lot of different cultures, but I say nothing and remain the attentive schoolgirl.

"They say we do things that we do not do. They say we steal children and deform them to make them better beggars. Do you see any beggars here, Ja-elle, pathetic or not? No, of course not. They say that we are tramps and thieves just because we travel about to fix pots and pans for people and play music and dance for them and tell fortunes, too. And that is all we do."

She pulls out a deck of cards. "Now for the Tarot . . ."

Ha! Cards! Now, that is much more to my liking!

The wagons are once again pulled into a tight circle and we set up. Buba Nadya is at her table with her crystal ball and Tarot deck. I have my own table for the shell game, and that is what I do in the daytime. I have been doing quite well at it, and my purse begins to fill. Of course, I have to give half to Zoltan for my board and keep, but that seems fair — after all, I could be out alone in the wilderness, with neither food nor friends, and I much prefer it here.

In the nighttime, I perform. While Gyorgy plays the gypsy melodies on his fiddle, with Jan on his guitar, Marko and I dance the flamenco. We start, back to back in full glorious costume, clap hands, and go into it, feet pounding, castanets clicking, faces arrogant and held just so, but with eyes flashing and possibly promising . . . other delights.

I am not the only dancer, of course. There is Lala and Yanko, and Fifika with her Luka, and when the six of us are whirling around the campfire, well, it is all very exciting.

And since the dancing is fiery and wild, sometimes the men who come to watch get a little too excited and are rude, thinking we are loose. We are *not* loose. The Romani are very protective of their women. These men make unwanted advances to us, offering up fists full of *reales* for services other than dance. We point them to our tip jar, but sometimes they insist too strongly and Zoltan has to come up and announce that there are no women for sale here and then warn the men to leave, as the show is over. They do leave, thinking that there is probably a sharp knife up every gypsy man's sleeve, and on that suspicion, they are right. I also know that I am not the only girl here with a shiv up her own sleeve as well. They do leave, but they are generally quite surly about it and mutter curses as they go . . . *dirty gypsies . . . whores, all of 'em . . .*

At night when we are abed, I begin telling stories to the girls to help put them to sleep. Mostly Cheapside Tales, as stories of the urchin gangs of London would be closest to their experience — after all, they are often called beggars and thieves, so they can appreciate the similarity. I certainly cannot tell them of my meeting with Napoleon, or the Duke of Clarence, or any of that ilk — I would be tossed out of camp as a liar.

The kids begin to anticipate the stories and are a good audience — all except for that imp Nuri. I caught her early on trying to get into my seabag. I shook my finger in her face and warned her that she should never do that again. After all, there are two loaded pistols in there . . . True, I have removed the percussion caps and have them on half-cock so they cannot be fired, but still . . . She looks at me with her big brown eyes, sticks thumb in mouth, and promises that she will not. But just in case she tries, I have secured my bag with a far more complex knot.

After a couple of nights of storytelling, it is requested that the back of the wagon be opened so that others can listen, just like back on the *Bloodhound*.

. . . and Rooster Charlie comes running around the corner with five Shankies on his tail, howling for blood . . .

Chapter 47

We are at Valencia, beautiful Valencia, on the shore of the Mediterranean Sea.

"So there is the sea, Ja-elle," says Medca, who stands by my side, looking out over the expanse of water. "You wanted to be here. Will you leave us now?"

I look up and down the coast that lies below me and reply, "I see no great amount of shipping here, so I will go with you to Granada, if the Roma will have me. It is close to Gibraltar, and I know I can book passage from there."

She squeezes my hand. "I am glad, Ja-elle, to have you with me a little while longer."

I give her hand an answering squeeze and stand back and suck in the glorious sea air.

In our time together, Medca has told me of Granada, the beautiful city to the south, where lies the Alhambra, a great Moorish temple and place of great learning — or it was until the Spaniards kicked all the Moors out of Spain, and most of the Jews, too.

In Granada there are limestone cliffs where the Roma

have carved caves into the rock and where they spend the winter months before going on the road again in the spring.

"They are not caves like you think, Ja-elle, all dark and dank. No, the interiors are smooth and white and dry, and at the entrance of each is a portico with windows, with a small sod roof above and flower gardens all about. They were built over the years by our people because nobody else wanted the cliffs, and now they have been turned into places of simple beauty. I . . . I had hopes that Jan and I would have one some day, but . . ."

"Now, Sister," I murmur. "Let's just wait and see how life plays out, all right?"

Another squeeze of hands and a quick embrace, and it's back to the camp.

We have been here in Valencia for two days now and intend to stay for five more, as it is a wondrous city, full of life, and the money, always a consideration, is good.

When Medca and I get back from the cliff, she hurries off to see Jan, and I've got a mind to find Marko. But just then, Buba Nadya comes up and latches onto my arm.

"Come, Ja-elle, we have a job."

But I wanna stay and play with Marko! cries the little girl in me, but I meekly follow the old woman down the path to the town.

"What sort of job?" I ask, a bit surly.

"The *gadzso* woman whose fortune I told last night," says Buba, leaning on her cane and beginning to breathe a bit hard from the exertion of the walk. "She wants me to find some money."

"What?" I ask, confused.

"The outsiders believe that the Roma can find money in a house, like in a minute, so we can steal it and run away quickly." She puffs. "This woman is a widow. Her husband died last month but left no will, no money for her. She has begged me to come look. I agreed, for a quarter of the money if I find it, nothing if I do not."

"So why am I here?" I ask.

"Because I need someone young and spry. Did you know that Ja-elle means 'mountain goat' in the old language? It seems to fit you."

Hmmm . . . well, I have been called worse . . .

We eventually come upon a small farmhouse. There is a pigsty over to the side and a fenced-in garden area. There being no other houses about, the pigs are allowed to run free. I can hear the lowing of a cow coming from a run-down barn.

Buba knocks on the door, and it is opened by an old woman who says over her shoulder, "The gypsies are here, Magda."

This Magda appears in the doorway and looks at us very suspiciously. She is plainly the other woman's sister, and it is equally plain that she doesn't approve of this at all. Both are dressed in black widows' weeds. I am sure the silverware has been hidden.

"I am afraid, Brunilda," quavers Magda, wringing her aged hands. "They are gypsies."

"We must, Sister. The gypsies know things . . . dark things . . . that we do not. There is no other way. We must have Gaspar's money."

We are ushered in and Buba casts her eyes about the room. It is raftered with heavy timbers overhead. There is a kitchen on one end, a dining area with a table on the other. The stove is lit and it is quite warm in here. There is another doorway, which probably leads to a bedroom.

I stand there useless, while Buba lifts her arms and starts mumbling unintelligible words — not words in any language that I know, anyway. The two sisters cross themselves and look worried. At length, Buba stops and, with eyes closed, says, "Your husband, he was a big man."

She says this as a fact, not a question.

"*Sí, Señora.* Very big."

"And he died slowly."

"*Sí.* He was sick for a week before he died."

"Ah," says Buba, and she commences mumbling again. Then she says, "I will need something of his . . . Something he held close to him."

Brunilda thinks for a second on this and then goes to a rack by the door and reaches up and pulls down a very worn leather cap and hands it to Buba Nadya.

"It was his. He wore it every day."

Buba takes it and holds it to her forehead, mumbles a few more words, and then goes rigid.

"He is here," she whispers. "And he is not happy."

The two sisters clasp each other, eyes wide.

"He is very jealous of his money," says Buba in a more normal voice. Brunilda nods to that. "And he wants you to wait outside."

"Do not do it, Brunilda," warns Magda. "They will steal!"

"You have nothing we want," says Buba, lifting her chin and putting on a haughty look. "Either you go out, or I will not be able to find the money."

Brunilda pushes the furious Magda out the door and closes it behind them.

Buba waits a moment, then flings the cap aside and says, "All right, Ja-elle, let us get to work."

Mystified, I say, "But how can we, unless you actually did talk to Gaspar?"

She laughs. "No, he was most silent."

"But it could be anywhere, Buba Nadya — buried outside, in the field, in the garden, in the barn."

"No, little one, it is not in any of those places," she says, placing a finger on my nose. "You must learn to think . . . Think like a gypsy."

When I look baffled, she goes on.

"The man was very miserly with his money and did not trust his wife, else she would know where he kept it. Or, at least, he would have told her about it before he died. And remember, he did not die suddenly. That much must have been plain even to you."

I nod.

"He would not have buried it outside for fear the pigs would root it up. Not in the garden, either, because it was his wife who tended that. The barn? No. It is in need of repair, and workmen hired to fix it might find it. No, he would keep it in the house, close by him. But not here in the kitchen — that was her place — no, probably the bedroom, and up high."

"High?" I ask, beginning to feel like a dumb schoolgirl.

"Come, come, Ja-elle, I thought you were a bright one," she says, shaking her head and clucking her tongue before continuing. "She said he was a big man when I led her into it. And did you see how she had to reach up for his cap, she being quite short?"

I'm thinking that if Buba Nadya Vadoma and a certain John Higgins ever got together, they could form a very formidable detective agency.

"So we will start with the bedroom. Bring that chair for you to stand on," she says, moving off in that direction.

I grab the chair and follow.

"And by the way," she says, pointing down as we pass the stove. "*That* is where they hid their silverware. Do you see?"

I look over and, yes, there is one short floorboard that seems set apart from the others, lacking dust and dirt in the grooves that surround it. I am amazed.

"But how did you know?"

"With the women, it is always a floorboard." She chuckles. "And did you see that Magda glance over at the hiding place before they left? Ha! They *always* do that, stupid things, to see if all is secure, which it never is, but never mind, girl. Time for you to work."

We go into the bedroom and look about. It has the same heavy open rafter and plaster ceiling as the rest of the house.

"Start at that side," orders Buba, pointing. "And tell me why I say that."

I put the chair there and climb up on it and look down. I see nothing but the bed and a chest at the bottom for blankets, sheets, and such. We don't even bother looking through that, for we would find nothing there. Even a *gadzso* like me could figure that out. Then I get it. I nod to the bed.

"He slept on this side," I say. "It is lower there, because of his weight. And he would like to be close to his money."

"Very good, Ja-elle," she says. "Now start looking."

Standing on the chair, I begin running my hands over the top of the wall upon which rests the ends of the rafters. There is a flat area between them, and each of the spaces seems to be full of nothing but dust.

I shake my head at Buba and get down and move the chair and try the next space. Still nothing.

"Let your fingers be nimble, Ja-elle, let them search where you cannot see."

I move the chair two more times until . . .

"Buba! I feel something!"

"What is it?"

I feel an edge of something — possibly only a splinter in the wood — but, no . . . it is a groove.

"Maybe," I say, digging my fingernails into the slit. When they are deep into it, I give a pull and am rewarded with a small board, which I toss down on the bed.

"Ha!" says Buba, expectant.

Hoping there is no mousetrap nor poisoned barbs set to end my explorations, and possibly my life, I plunge my hand into the open hole and feel something . . . what? . . . slippery?

I grasp whatever it is and look upon it. It is an oilskin packet. I shake it and it clinks. It is sealed with red candle wax. I smile and hand it down to the eager Buba Nadya.

She takes it and laughs. "Ha, Ja-elle, perhaps there is

some Romani blood in your veins after all!" She goes back into the kitchen. "Replace the hidey-hole board and bring the chair back in here," she says as she goes.

When I get back in the front room, the package lies upon the table, and Buba stands triumphant next to it.

"You may call them back in," she says, and waits as I go to do so.

I poke my head out the door and say to the waiting sisters, "Please, Señoras, we have found it."

The widow and her sister waste no time in getting back into their cottage. Brunilda gasps as she sees the packet on the table.

"*Gracias a Dios!*" she exults, as she dives for it. In an instant she has torn it open and the golden coins spill out onto the table top. "*Dios!*"

"It seems your man was a successful farmer," observes Nadja Vadoma. "I am pleased at your good fortune. Now, if you will give us the quarter share we have earned, we will be on our way."

The sister Magda looks at the pile with much greed in her eye.

"No!" she shouts. "A quarter share is too much for such as these *gitanas asquerosas!* We would have found it, anyway. Here! You! Take this and go away!"

She picks up one of the thin silver pieces and thrusts it at Buba.

"Take it!" she snarls. "If you do not go, I will call *la policía* and say that dirty gypsies came to rob us poor widows of what little we have! Go!"

I look to Buba Nadya with a questioning look in my eye

and a gesture toward the shiv up my sleeve, but she shakes her head and instead snatches the meager coin and throws it on the floor.

"We made a bargain," she whispers. "And you did not keep your word." With that she makes some strange movements with her hands, hands which end up trembling and pointing at the forehead of Magda.

"Enjoy your riches, *gadzso*," she says. "For you will be dead and rotting in your grave within the month. Come, child, let us leave this house of shame."

Buba leads me back out into the light and we head back to camp. I, for one, am miffed.

"I hope that was a good Romani curse you laid on that crone's ugly head, Nadya Vadoma!" I say, with a certain amount of heat in my voice.

She sighs.

"Yes, I did, Ja-elle," says Buba. "Sometimes the magic works and sometimes it does not, but at least that hag will worry about it to the end of her miserable days."

"Well," I say. "That is a comfort. But still a waste of your time, Buba."

"Not so, little one," she says, reaching into her pocket and hauling out three large gold coins and handing one to me. "You see, we have prospered after all, in spite of their greed."

I am astounded.

"But I saw the sealed packet. How did you . . . ?"

"The stove was hot. I took out the coins — our fair share and nothing more — for I knew that they would try to cheat us. And then I just took it to the stove, held the seal against it till it melted again, and then returned it to the table as you came in. See, little Mountain Goat, see?"

I laugh long and loud and hug the old witch to me.

"Go, Ja-elle," she says. "Find one of our young men to escort you, and go into Valencia and spend your coin, for you have earned it. Go!"

Later, on the arm of the handsome Marko, I go joyously into the city. We marvel at its splendor and poke our heads in shops. I buy some things, and my good Marko puts up with my ramblings and squeals of delight. I purchase watercolors and paper and brushes . . . and, oh, yes, a new deck of Tarot cards.

When I am done, we go arm in arm to a nice cantina to eat and drink, and we have a marvelous time. We do not draw undue attention, other than being young and beautiful. He is not any more swarthy than many of the *Majos* in the cafés, and I, wearing my black wig and mantilla, fit right in. Hey, I pass just fine for a fiery *Maja. Olé!*

A good day, all around, I say, as we wend our way, arm in arm, back to our people.

Chapter 48

Mister Chueng Tong, Envoy
House of Chen
Onboard the Vessel Mary Bissell
Off Cape of Good Hope
South Africa

Jacky Faber
Or Most Recent Alias
Location, I Cannot Even Begin to Guess . . .

Dear Jacky,

    We are off Cape Town, South Africa, and it is Captain van Pelt's intent to go into that port to take on water and supplies.

I am finding the company of Reverend Lowe and his family very convivial. He is learned and well mannered, his wife is lovely, and his daughters charming. The boy, Jeremiah, has attached himself to me, thinking me to be some sort of impossibly romantic figure. He is young but enthusiastic and full of questions, and I enjoy his company.

One whose company I do not enjoy is that of Mr. Skelton. He is intemperate in his habits, drinks too much, and grows more boisterous by the day. I bear his insults, recalling the teachings of Master Kwai Chang—*They are only words, Chueng Tong, little black birds borne away by the slightest breeze. Pay them no mind.*"

Still, I must grit my teeth to keep my temper down.

Today things have come to a head on the *Mary Bissell.*

As the land of Africa looms on our starboard beam, I stand at the rail looking out with young Jeremiah. The Reverend Lowe is also on deck, with his family, enjoying the beautiful day and the fine breeze. Captain van Pelt is on his quarterdeck looking up at his sails, which are perfectly trimmed, I will give him that, simple merchant sailor though he be.

The joy of the afternoon is destroyed when Mr. Skelton comes on deck, a bit red in the face from what I am sure is what he considers his "noon cup."

"Well, isn't this a fine group of Christians . . . and one heathen," he says, opening his arms to us. He makes a circle of the deck, humming some sort of off-key tune, and then he goes to the rail between the girls Florence and Abigail. He brings his face very close to that of Abigail and says, "Hello, little church mouse, what say we take a bit of a turn about the deck, and maybe below decks, too. Hmmm?"

"Mr. Skelton!" cries Reverend Lowe. "This is an outrage! She is but a child!"

He goes to get between the man and his Abigail, but Skelton thrusts him aside. "She don't look like a child to me, Preacher. No, she don't. A man can't expect to keep his daughters by him forever, 'specially a man like you."

With that, he places his hand on the girl's shoulder. She is ashen.

"So what do you say, my pretty little miss?"

Those are the last words he says to her. He is suddenly startled to find my Bo staff pressed against his neck.

"What! You dare to confront me!"

"Do not touch the girl, Sir," I say evenly. "Do not touch any of this family ever again. Do you understand?"

"Understand?" he shouts. "Understand *this*, Chinaman!" and he pulls the sword that habitually hangs by his side.

He gets it halfway out as I turn about and go into the Attack of the Angry Butterfly, whirling my staff before me and finally bringing it down forcefully on the back of his sword hand. He cries out and his weapon falls to the deck.

I glide back into the Waiting Dragon stance and wait, knees bent in lunge position, staff on shoulder. *"It is enough, Long Boy,"* I hear Kwai Chang say. *"Let anger not rule you . . ."*

It is not yet enough, Master, I am sorry.

"Damn you to hell, you heathen bastard! Let's see how you handle this!" He reaches in his vest and pulls out a small pistol and aims it at my chest.

I glide from the Waiting Dragon and go into the Kick of the Drowsy Lion, whirl, strike, and the pistol hits the deck next to the fallen sword, and then bounces over the side.

Skelton holds his bruised hand and howls.

Jeremiah looks up at me and says, "Wow!"

Reverend Lowe gives me a look of thanks and hustles his female brood below.

Mr. Skelton, though thoroughly humiliated, is not yet done.

"You yella bastard," he snarls, plainly sinking back into his vernacular. "I challenge you! To a duel! With pistols! Like men! At dawn!"

I bow to him and say, "I believe it is your custom that I, as the challenged one, get to choose the weapons. However, I will agree to your request that it be . . . what? . . . pistols? Like that thing that just went over the side? Very well. I will meet you."

"Ain't nobody meetin' nobody tomorrow morning," says Captain van Pelt from his quarterdeck, having observed all that has happened below him. "You can settle this 'twixt the two of ye after we sail out o' Cape Town. We'll be there in the mornin', and I don't need no Court o' Inquiry as to some dead man lying on my ship with a bullet in him. No, sirs! Iffen you want to blow each other's brains out, you'll do it when we're a day outta Cape Town. Then we'll be able to throw the carcass o' the dead one over the side, no questions asked. I have spoken!"

I bow to the Captain and say, "You are wise, Captain van Pelt. I thank you. For your decision will give me some time to familiarize myself with these things you call . . . pistols, is it?"

At that, Mr. Skelton straightens up and smiles at my apparent lack of expertise with pistols.

"Yes, Long Boy," I hear the Master say. *"It is always good to let one's enemy go complacent and confident . . . for a while . . ."*

I have learned much from the Master, and, upon reflection, a lot from you, Jacky.

Yours,
Jaimy

Chapter 49

And so Valencia falls behind us, and we go down the coast of the Mediterranean to Alicante and to Torrevieja and then to San Pedro del Pinatar, and circle our wagons and set up yet again, and yet again, and then comes, *yes!* Cartagena! The Jewel of the Sea!

"There are many ships down there, Ja-elle," says Medca, looking upon the forests of masts in the harbor from our perch high above. "Will you go on one of them?"

As is our usual custom when we are close by the sea, Medca and I join hands to walk by the shore, sharing our thoughts and dreams.

"Nay, Sister, they are all Spanish — you see the flags flying at their mastheads — and I prefer to wait till I get to Gibraltar, where there will be British ships, possibly more kindly disposed to one such as me. Now, let us get back to the camp before we are missed."

The camp is in a high state of excitement, for the Roma know that Cartagena is a good place to stop, with a happy and liberal populace, free with their money and their good cheer.

I get dressed in my *Maja* gear, ready to play my fiddle and dance and sing, but it is early yet, so I go over to Buba Nadya Vadoma's table, set up, as always, just outside her wagon.

She looks up as I sit down across from her with my Tarot deck in hand and, possibly, a mischievous look in my eye.

"Tell your fortune, Buba?" I ask, all modest, with eyes cast down.

"Yes, Ja-elle," she says, her look hooded and dark. "You may show me if you have learned anything."

I shuffle the cards, as clumsily as I can without actually dropping any, then deal them out.

In the Tarot, it is not only the individual cards that matter in the telling of a fortune but also their placement next to each other. Like if *The Empress* card lies next to *The Moon* card, when all is laid out, it means one thing, but if it lies next to *The Hanged Man*, it means another thing. It is all up to the dealer to interpret the meaning, and therein lies the advantage of the fortuneteller.

But still, certain cards mean certain things.

I deal out a very favorable four cards . . . *The Moon, The Judgment, The World,* and *The Chariot.*

"Ah, Buba," I say. "It looks like good things are in store for you."

She snorts. "What else have you to show? I am an old woman and need no more good fortune."

I take the deck again, and this time I do not bother dealing out the classic array. Instead I say, "Suppose you wished to tell your sitter of . . . say . . . death."

I shuffle, turn the deck over, and deal four cards down, and then turn the fifth over. It is *The Hanged Man.*

"Then suppose you want to tell her of good fortune to come." Again I shuffle and deal. This time I turn over *The Justice* card. "Is that not right? And how about *The Lovers* card — should you have a pair of young sweethearts before you. *Hmm?*"

She looks at me, her gaze hard.

"Tell me of a card, Buba Nadya," I say, shuffling the deck and returning her look.

"*The Hermit,*" she says, watching my eyes.

I shuffle, cut the cards, and present the deck to her. She cuts and puts the deck back in front of me.

I fan the deck and pick out one card and turn it over.

It is *The Hermit,* the picture of a shrouded man bearing a lantern and a scythe, which stands for folly, arrogance, and suspicion.

She looks down at the cards.

"You have marked them," she says with certainty.

"No, I have not, Buba, I . . ." I jerk my head to the side. "I hear Marko calling me for the dance."

She cocks her head to listen and averts her gaze. It is then that I switch the decks.

I rise and shove the new deck in front of her.

"Here, Buba, you may examine."

She looks me in the eye.

"You will tell me."

"Yes, I will, Buba . . . tomorrow. But now I must go to Marko."

And I leave the very wise Buba Nadya Vadoma puzzling over what seems to be an enigma.

I sweep back into the center of the circled wagons, where we entertain the townspeople, and find Marko waiting for me.

I reflect that he is a sweet lad and very good company. I also know that he likes me for a couple of reasons, the first of which is that I am not Romani and can never be a proper bride for him. Therefore, there is no bothersome father to get in the way of a little amorous play. The second reason is that I am a good musician and up to his standards in both dance and in the playing of the fiddle and guitar.

"*Hola, Ja-elle,*" he says, as I come into the circle. "Play us a song from over these hills and far away."

I think on this and take up the small guitar that is handed to me.

"Very well," I say. "I will sing you a song of the Romani in a place called England. Yes, they roam there, too, and are called gypsies by the local people because they don't know any better."

I strum a chord. "The song is about a gypsy named Black Jack Davy, and it tells the tale of a rich young lady who, well, you'll see."

> *Now Black Jack Davy came a-ridin' along.*
> *Singin' a song so gaily.*
> *He whistled and he sang,*
> *And the green woods rang,*
> *And he won the heart of a lay-die*
> *Charmed the heart of a lady.*

I translate as I go along, so they the get the drift of it . . .

> *"How old are you, my pretty little miss?*
> *How old are you, my honey?"*
> *She answered him with a loving smile,*
> *"I'll be sixteen next Sunday.*
> *Be sixteen next Sunday."*

> *"Come and go with me, my pretty little miss.*
> *Come go with me, my honey.*
> *I'll take you where the grass grows green,*
> *And you'll never want for money.*
> *No, you'll never want for money."*

Now I pause and strum a chord progression in order to tell them that this lady is married to a high lord of the land and she's dressed really fine, and this gypsy lad ain't got nothing but his good looks and a smile, but he presses his case . . .

> *"Pull off, pull off them high-heeled shoes*
> *All made of Spanish leather,*
> *Get behind me on my horse,*
> *And we'll ride off together.*
> *Yes, we'll ride off together."*

Again I stop to say that the great Lord Donald comes home to find that his Lady Gay has run off with Gypsy Davy and he ain't at all pleased, so he says . . .

> *"Saddle me up my coal-black stud,*
> *He's speedier than the gray,*

> *I'll ride all night and I'll ride all day,*
> *And I'll bring me back my lady.*
> *Yes, I'll bring back my lay-die."*

Of course, all the Romani about me are chortling about this, knowing full well that this song could never be sung for the outsiders, for they sure don't want to hear about their women, high-born ladies or not, running off with no yellow gypsies! Oh, no, they don't!

I skip a lot of the many verses wherein the great Lord Donald catches up with his wayward bride and pleads for her to come back home, but she answers him . . .

> *"Last night I slept in a feather bed,*
> *With my husband gaily,*
> *Tonight I lay on the river bank,*
> *In the arms of Gypsy Davy.*
> *In the arms of my Black Jack Davy."*

I end with a great strumming of chords and a bow, to great applause from my friends.

Marko comes up, beaming, to lead me to the dance.

God, I love it so!

Later, much later, when all the dancing, all the singing, all the hurly-burly's done, and I lie curled up next to Medca in our wagon, I think on things, and my thoughts turn to Jaimy.

I'm sorry, Jaimy. I know I should spend more time on my knees praying for you and, yes, for Lord Richard Allen and all my friends, and not singing and dancing the night away, which is what I have been doing, but I just can't . . . My nature is to be cheerful and my foolish self is very likely to be led astray by happy, frivolous things, things of the moment, and I just can't help it, Jaimy, I can't. There is a wildness in me that can't be denied.

I hope you are well, Jaimy, and I live for the time I shall see you again.

Amen.

Chapter 50

The stay in Cartagena is in its second day and we are having a grand time. The Roma are in high spirits for they have had a fine season on the road and are looking forward to their winter homes in the limestone cliffs overlooking Granada.

Almost everybody, that is. Things are getting close for Medca's marriage to Milosh, and Jan sure ain't getting any richer. I have to comfort her each night, but I don't know if it does any good, poor girl.

I, however, have been getting richer. With the art supplies I bought in Valencia, I have set up as a miniature-portrait painter in the daytime when I am not singing, playing, and dancing, and have done quite well at it. I have, of course, done Medca and Jan, to their delight, and many other of my Romani friends as well.

And yes, we still have occasional problems with some of the local hotheads, but those are generally resolved by the appearance of mighty Zoltan and his formidable presence. We had some trouble last night, but the *Majos* eventually went away — not happily, but they did go away.

It is early afternoon, and I go to visit Buba Nadya Vadoma. But not to paint her portrait, oh no, she will not let me do that, saying she is too old for that sort of nonsense. Rather I go to answer what I know will be her questions.

I sit down at the table with my Tarot cards in my lap, unseen, so far, by Buba Nadya.

"All right, Mountain Goat," she says. "I examined your deck and found no marks. How did you do it? You are not Romani, so it is not magic. So how?"

"Nuri!" I shout, standing and yelling at the girl who is hanging about close to our wagon. "Stay away from my stuff!"

I sit back down. "That girl will be the ruin of me, I swear." Heavy sigh, and then I pick up the deck and shuffle and deal out a perfect Tarot spread: *Empress, Hermit, Moon* . . .

"All right," spits Buba. "I know you can do it. But show me how. Now."

I smile and pull the deck to me.

"You see, Buba, the deck you examined was not the deck I used," I say, lifting the other deck from my lap. "I switched them when your attention was elsewhere — like just now when I got up to yell at Nuri. Now, look at this deck you see before you. No, the backs are not marked, as you well know, but the sides are. It is what is called — at least in New Orleans in America — a *shaved* deck. Look at the stack from the side and you will see that I have sanded down the edges of the important cards so that they are slimmer than the others and I can feel them with my fingers. Some — *The Fool, The Hierophant, The Chariot* — I shave on the left side.

341

Some — *The Magician, The Tower, The Devil* — I shave on the top, and so on . . . and so on."

Comprehension dawns in her dark eyes. "So . . ." is all she says.

"Yes, Buba, just so," I say. "You have taught me, and I hope I have taught you. I give you that deck. If you practice, you will be better at it than I in a very short time. I hope you will use it wisely."

She looks at me, her dark gaze level.

"I will, Ja-elle," she whispers. "But are you sure there is no Roma in you?"

She smiles as I rise to go.

"I would be proud to have Romani blood in me, Buba, and I — "

I don't get any further, as a breathless Medca comes rushing to us.

"Trouble, Buba!" she cries, her voice full of fear. "Men from the town. They say they are the police . . . They are with Zoltan now!"

Buba Nadya Vadoma and I are up in an instant. We go to the center of the wagons, and sure enough, Zoltan stands tall and furious before six very heavily armed men. I get close and listen. A small fat man with a red sash across his chest is pointing his pudgy finger at Zoltan and speaking.

"So you see, gypsy man, this is the situation. You and your people come here unbidden and squat upon the sacred land of Cartagena! Ah, but you have not paid money to camp on the public land of Cartagena, oh, no. I am Don Pedro de Castro, *Jefe de la Policia,* and I demand that money in the name of the good people of Cartagena!"

"But, *Jefe*," says Zoltan. "We have always been welcome here. Come, good sir, have some wine and let us talk this over."

"We want none of your wine, as it is sure to be poisoned," says the oily little man, all puffed up in his importance. "What we want is two hundred *reales!*"

"Madre di Dios!" exclaims Zoltan. "We cannot possibly raise that amount of money! We are poor travelers!"

"If you do not," hisses the Chief of Police, "we shall imprison your people and burn your filthy wagons. We have the militia to do that—hundreds of soldiers. We will put your men to labor, and your women to . . . other things. Do you get my meaning?"

He grins, showing crooked teeth through a thick black mustache.

Zoltan stands stricken, but I do not. I turn away and head for our wagon. On the way, I see Medca's sister Dika.

"Dika," I cry. "Get me three oranges, cut in half and laid on a tray! Bring it to our wagon, now!"

Mystified by all that is happening, she goes to do it. I plunge into the back of the wagon, open my seabag, and pull out a certain bottle, one filled with a purple liquid. I am withdrawing the cork with my teeth as Dika comes in with the tray of sliced oranges.

I take my shiv and make cuts into the orange flesh and then pour my Tincture of Mushroom over them. The fruits seem to suck it up avidly. I recork the now half-empty bottle and toss it back into my bag.

"Thanks, Dika," I say, as I pick up the tray and head out toward the very one-sided parley.

I do not go up and offer the fruit to the *policia,* oh, no. What I do is skirt by them, as if I am trying to escape notice.

"Here!" shouts one of the armed men upon seeing me. "What are those?"

I drop my gaze down into one of complete submission. "Th-these, Sir? They are special treats for a wedding party. It is tradition . . . for the bride and groom only."

"Ha!" says the *Jefe.* "Bring them here! What need dirty gypsies of weddings? All they do is rut like dogs in ditches! Give 'em over!"

Meekly, I hand over the tray, and soon purple juice is coursing down the greasy jowls of the Chief of Police and those of his cohorts.

Wiping his face with the back of his sleeve, he announces, "So that is the way of it. Two hundred *reales* in my hand tomorrow, or the lot of you will be tossed in prison and your wagons burned. *Comprende?* Good."

He looks about, clearly enjoying his display of power.

"Now," he continues, preparing to leave, "I will take a hostage to insure that you will not just pack up and leave. Who shall it be? Someone young and comely, I hope."

His men chortle in glee at the great man's wit.

I step forward and say, "I will be the hostage."

The *Jefe* looks me over. "She will certainly do. What do you say, men?"

They agree heartily, with much low laughter and rude gestures in my direction.

"Very well," says the head man. "Let us leave this pigsty." He points his finger at Zoltan. "Tomorrow, noon, or face the consequences, gypsy."

If looks could kill, all six of the worms would lie dead on the ground before him, but looks do not kill and noble Zoltan must stand helpless before these petty thieves.

A rope is tied around my neck and I am pulled away and dragged off. But before I am gone, I lock eyes with Buba Nadya Vadoma, who stands with hands clenched and held tight to her sides, and understanding passes between us. She knows I offered myself up as hostage because I knew that if the scum tried to take a real Romani girl, there would have been riot, the consequences be damned, and it would have been a disaster for our band.

What she does not know is that I have an ace up my sleeve, one that I have already put into play. As she mutters what I am sure are dark curses upon the scurvy heads of those who take me off, I give her a secret smile and a very broad wink.

Much later, I come strolling back into camp, idly twirling the rope that had been around my neck and whistling a merry tune, which I do believe is "Whistling Gypsy," ah yes, a slightly more upbeat version of "Black Jack Davy," which I had previously performed around the campfire for the enjoyment of my Roma friends, and which seems real appropriate right now.

As I enter the center of the circled wagons, I am greeted with astonishment by Zoltan and Buba Nadya Vadoma, who seems no less astonished to see me return, apparently unharmed.

"What the hell, girl?" exclaims Zoltan. "What is going on? What happened? What . . . ?"

"Although there is no longer a threat to us from the *Jefe*

de la Policia, whom I last saw climbing the steeple of the Cathedral de Santa Maria la Vieja, stark naked and proclaiming himself to be the new mayor of Cartagena . . ." I say, all nonchalant, " . . . and although all his henchmen are now in jail or the insane asylum, and the political future of Don Pedro de Castro, Chief of Police, looks grim — he did take a few pistol shots at the present mayor on his way up the steeple — it might be better, Papa Zoltan, if we did break camp and push on."

He needs no further urging and barks out orders. Bags are packed and thrown into wagons, kids rounded up and tossed in same, horses put in harness, and the wagons begin to form the line . . .

. . . but not before Buba Nadya points her finger at me and crooks that same gnarled finger into a summons for me to meet her in her wagon. No mistaking *that* look.

I obey the summons, but not before I collect my seabag, for I know what she will be asking.

"So explain, Ja-elle," she says upon my entry. "And no nonsense about spells and such."

I open my bag and pull out the half-empty bottle of purple liquid and put it on her side table. Then I open my paper packet of three dried mushrooms and place two of them beside the bottle, keeping the third one for myself to maybe show Dr. Sebastian, or Mr. Sackett, whichever of the two scientists I happen to meet up with first.

"Now, Buba, what you must do is chop up the mushrooms very fine and then boil them in about a cup of water, strain the liquid, then add an equal amount of brandy."

She nods warily. "And what does this potion do?"

"It makes those who drink it see things somewhat . . .

differently," I say. "Like those men who had taken me today? Well, several of them thought to have some sport with my poor self and made so bold as to run their rough hands over me. But then, suddenly, their attention was somehow distracted and they began to talk of purple clouds and purple birds flying about their heads, and other such things, and I was no longer bothered, as they seemed to have better things to do, like staring off into the distance with drool running down their chins, muttering about wonderful visions — visions far more wonderful than some skinny little gypsy girl."

"*Hmmm,*" says Buba. "Strange things you tell to me, Ja-elle."

"Well, you be careful with this stuff, Buba," I say. "You do not need to be known as more of a witch than you already are."

She snorts and gives me a level stare and again points her finger at my face.

"This old woman wonders" — she says with a slight smile and a shake of the head — "which of us is *really* the witch."

Well, I was once called a witch, back there in Puritan Boston that time, but it wasn't true.

Not really.

Chapter 51

James Long Boy Fletcher, Envoy
House of Chen
Onboard the Vessel Mary Bissell
In the South Atlantic
Headed West

Jacky Faber
Location?

Dearest Jacky,
  Actually, I get the feeling that you are somewhere close — like perhaps in the same hemisphere. I am probably wrong in that, but still . . .
  It is dawn on our first day out of Cape Town, and I stand on the deck and look out over the calm and rolling sea.
  No, I did not have to face the obnoxious Mr. Skelton on the field, or, rather, the deck of honor. No, I did not, as that gentleman departed rather hurriedly in Cape Town and has not been seen since.

Upon seeing the intent of Mr. Skelton and me to face each other on his deck, the Captain decreed that we meet after Cape Town, which was certainly agreeable to me and, hearing me say that I was unfamiliar with pistols, lent me two of his own with which to practice. I have the feeling that he did not like Mr. Skelton very much and, being a Yankee, wished to see a somewhat fair fight.

Assisted by young Master Jeremiah Lowe, I took up a position on the fantail, behind the quarterdeck, upon which Captain van Pelt habitually stood, and in plain sight of Mr. Skelton.

I bade Jeremiah scare up some empty bottles from the mess deck and line them up on the fantail's rail.

After making a show of listening carefully on how to load the pistols, I called up to Captain van Pelt, "What will be the procedure for this . . . duel . . . as it is called?"

"You and Mr. Skelton will stand right there, back to back, with pistol in hand. At my call, you will each step off ten paces, turn, and fire. Is that clear, Mr. Cheung?"

"Yes, Captain. Most clear. Like this?"

I stand with my back to the bottles and begin walking forward, while counting, one, two, three, four . . .

At ten, I turn, raise the pistol, and blast the first bottle to the right. It disappears in a shower of glass.

"Very much like that, Mr. Cheung," says Captain van Pelt, chuckling and looking back at a suddenly very concerned Mr. Skelton. "But perhaps it was a lucky shot."

"This humble person is sure it was that," I say, as I strip off my fine Chinese jacket and stand forth in loose white shirt. I roll up my sleeves to show my Shaolin dragon — Jeremiah gasps in admiration — and take up another pistol.

I go through the procedure once more, and again a bottle meets its fate.

"I see that it is a thing my Zen masters would appreciate," I say, nodding thoughtfully. "Mind, body, eyesight . . . and bullet winging to target. Very much of a spiritual thing."

Jeremiah has reloaded both pistols and I take them up. I do not bother stepping off the paces but merely send the last two bottles shattering into space.

When I turn, Mr. Skelton is nowhere to be seen.

I thought then of Master Kwai Chang . . . "It is better, Long Boy, to plant the Worm of Doubt into an enemy's brain, for then you may not have to put an ax into it."

So, Jacky . . . to America.

Jaimy

Chapter 52

We have left Cartagena and all of its charms behind us and we now camp in the pleasant little riverside town of Almería. We will spend a few days here and then the Roma will head west for Granada, and I will go south to Gibraltar.

I spend a lot of time with Medca, who seems accepting of her fate as future bride of Milosh. *Hey, sometimes a girl's gotta do what a girl's gotta do,* I say to myself, but not to her. I offer Jan what money I have toward the bride price, but he will not take it. *Stupid male honor — same the whole world over, I swear . . .*

Today, I seek out Marko, for he always brings me cheer, with his wide-open guileless grin and happy playful puppy ways. We join hands and walk along through the circled wagons. As we stroll, I see Medca and Tsura walking down to the river, water jugs on their hips.

Marko is trying, as he always does, to get me to slip under the nearby bushes with him for a bit of the old slap-and-tickle, but I fend off his advances and he takes it in good grace, and —

Then there is a great outcry in the camp. Tsura has burst in crying, "The *gadzsos!* Many of them! They have taken Medca! Down by the river! They are hurting her!"

God, no!

Jan, his face a mask of shock and outrage, rushes by me as I run to our wagon and pull open the door. Marko, too, is gone from my side. I leap upon my seabag and rip it open. I thrust my hands in and find my pistols and yank them out. *Damn! I must put in the caps! Hurry!*

I have kept the percussion caps in my pocket and I fumble for them. *Stupid, clumsy fingers! Yes! There they are!* I jam them on the pistols, pull the hammers back to full cock, and charge out of the camp, pounding down the path to the river. *Lord, I hope we are not too late!*

Cresting a small hill, I see Medca down below. She is on her knees on the riverbank, wailing, the front of her dress ripped open. Six *gadzsos* are upon her, dragging her to a waiting rowboat. She kicks and struggles, but to no avail. If they get her into it, she will be lost!

I am too far away for a good shot, so I close the distance as fast as I can run, the breath tearing into my chest, pistols held to my sides. But Jan gets to them before I do. He is on them like a demon. He takes his stand in front of Medca, swinging his fists and smashing them into any *gadzso's* face they can find.

"Let her go, bastard *gadzsos!*" he shouts, flailing his arms about him like a man possessed, as indeed he is. "Get gone or I will kill each one of you pigs with my bare hands!"

But bare hands ain't gonna do it, I can see that. One of the pigs has drawn a knife and brought it down on Jan's shoulder. It tears through shirt and flesh, and blood begins to pour down his arm. More knives are drawn as I burst upon them.

"Back, scum!" I shout, leveling my pistols at them. "Get back in your boat and go back to your pigsty!"

They all turn to look at me.

The one with the knife sneers at me. "She is bluffing. If a gypsy hurts a Spaniard, that gypsy will die in the *garrote*." He spits on the ground. "Dirty gypsies, they all should die."

"That is probably true, *bastardo*," I say between clenched teeth. "But, you see, I am not a gypsy."

I pull the trigger and *crraack!* The pistol bucks and I put a bullet into his upper chest. He staggers and falls back, no longer sneering.

"I have another bullet," I say, pointing the barrel from one to another. "Who wants it?"

It is plain, no one does. From behind me I hear the sound of the Roma men and women coming to our aid, no doubt with knives flashing.

The *gadzsos* see them pouring down the bank and think better of their ill-planned adventure.

"*Vamos!*" says one, and heads for the water. Two of his comrades pick up the wounded one and toss him howling into the boat. Then all climb in and push off.

The Romani are on us, shouting curses at the would-be ravisher of one of their own. Gentle hands are put on Medca, to lead her off, but she will have none of it and instead wraps her arms around Jan, crying, "Jan, Jan! They have hurt you! Oh, my dear sweet Jan!"

Jan is not hurt so badly that he cannot walk. He puts his good arm around Medca's shaking shoulders and they begin to stagger off, back to the wagons.

Zoltan is there, looking grim. "We must prepare to move. There might be trouble," he says. He looks to his daughter and her young man. "And Jan . . . you have paid the Bride Price."

We get Jan back to the camp and patch him up in one of the tents. I have seen much worse wounds than his — the *gadz-so*'s blade hit mainly hard shoulder bone, not deep flesh. He is brave during the sewing up, and well he should be, for his bride-to-be stands by his side, holding his hand tightly and looking at him with big, brimming, loving eyes. I wish I had some of my faithful Tincture of Opium handy, but I don't. And I don't think he really needs it, anyway.

When I step back out into the light, I am surprised to see the Romani in a bit of an uproar.

What's going on? I wonder. We have just survived a vicious attack, so why is everybody laughing and smiling?

I slowly realize that they are smiling at *me* in particular. Girls look at me and blush and giggle. Boys and men wink and laugh and shake their fingers at me.

What?

I find out just what is going on when I go to put my pistols back in my seabag and . . . *uh-oh* . . . the bag is lying open, its contents in disarray.

Nuri, I am going to kill you!

Steam is coming out of my ears as Fifika comes to the doorway of our wagon and says, "Buba Nadya wants to see you, Ja-elle. Now." Then she is overcome with a fit of barely stifled snickers and can say no more.

I go to Buba's wagon and knock.

"Come in, Ja-elle," she says. She does not sound pleased.

I climb in, and sure enough, lying on the bed is *The Virgin Maja,* glowing in the soft light. Buba sits in a small chair to the right and is gazing at the painting.

"Everybody has seen it, Buba?" I ask.

"Yes. Nuri took it all around the camp, showing it off."

Grrrrrr . . .

I see she has her cane next to her.

"Will I be beaten?"

She shakes her head, eyes still on the painting. "No, but it is perhaps best that you are leaving us. Not so much for this, but you did just put a bullet in a *gadzo*. There might be trouble. If they come, we will tell them that we threw you out and you were headed north."

"May I stay for Medca's wedding?"

"Yes, it will be tomorrow. You may stay till then."

"Very well, Buba. Will that be all?"

She says nothing for a while. Then she smiles and again looks to the picture and sighs . . .

"Oh, to be so young and so foolish . . . and so full of life. Goodbye, Ja-elle."

Goodbye, Buba Nadya Vadoma . . . and thank you.

Chapter 53

The Romani are gathered for the wedding.

Zoltan and Marta lead their daughter Medca to the center, the space between the wagons, where we usually entertain the townspeople. Medca is a lovely bride, of course, radiant under her crown of flowers, her hair braided with bright ribbons.

Jan, dressed in his best, is led to his bride's side by his parents. At Zoltan's signal, both bride and groom sit on chairs set side by side. Words are said and a piece of bread is placed on the bride's knee, and a similar piece is laid on the knee of the groom. A dish of salt is placed on the ground between them.

Medca reaches down and takes a pinch of salt and sprinkles it on her bread. Jan does the same to his. Then she gives her bread to him and he takes it and eats it, and passes his to her. She eats it.

A cup of wine is given to Medca and she drinks from it and passes it to Jan. He takes a drink and that is it. They are now man and wife, and the celebration begins.

The bridesmaids surround Medca to unravel the braids

from her hair and to place the headscarf, the *diklo,* on her head to show that she is now a married woman. She will wear that, when in public, for the rest of her life.

The Romani now turn to some serious feasting — kegs of wine are set out and meat is put on spits to roast over open fires. Guitars are brought out, fiddles, too, and songs are sung.

The wedding gifts consist mostly of money — some in packets and some in coins that have been made into necklaces that are then placed around the neck of the bride.

Me? I give them money, too, in my own way.

At the height of the festivities, I go up to Medca and Jan and ask them to follow me to Zoltan's wagon, to which I have tied Gabriella's reins. She is saddled and ready to go.

"You will need a horse to pull your wagon, and she is a good horse. Please treat her well. May you roam the hills and valleys of your beautiful country to the end of your days."

I untie the reins and place them in Jan's hands.

"Goodbye, Jan. Goodbye, Medca," I say, embracing them both. "May you prosper."

With that, I turn, sling my seabag over my shoulder, and leave the world of the Roma.

Chapter 54

It did not take me all that long to get from Almería to Gibraltar, it being only a couple hundred miles.

Yes, I could have used my good mare Gabriella, but I feel she is better off with Jan and Medca and, true, I did not have much money. I left a good deal of what I had earned while with the Roma in Gabriella's saddlebag—a leather purse with gold coins and a small watercolor of what I thought one of the Roma dwellings in Granada would look like, in hopes that the two of them would someday have one of their own. I drew it with flowers all about, and some chickens . . . and kids . . . in the yard. I'm sure they'll get the idea.

I had left in the midst of the festivities, not being very good at goodbyes, and hit the road. I didn't have much money left, but, hey, I had my fiddle and my wits. What more did I need?

I did, however, say a private goodbye to Marko. He, of course, professed undying love, and he offered me half of what he owned for *The Virgin Maja*. But I said no, I would keep that, and sent him off with a good and lusty kiss.

And there was one other who watched me go — a solitary figure clad all in black, who stood at the edge of the camp. I raised my hand to her, and she did the same to me. I turned and headed down the dusty road, and I have the feeling she watched me till I went out of sight.

The way down was pleasant. I traveled as a boy, of course, and hitched many a ride on wagons, and some in coastal boats, so, by and large it was good. Yes, the ground was hard at night, but the sun was warm in the day, and all was right with my world.

When I slipped into Gibraltar, I went right to the harbormaster's shack. The harbor was bristling with the masts of ships, but most of them bore the Union Jack, and I wasn't quite sure I wanted to get back into that life, not just yet.

"What's shippin' out, guv'nor?" I asked of him. "Who's taking on crew?" I have absolutely no money left after my journey here.

He checked his ledger. "Most all to England, but not hiring. *Hmmm* . . . There's one, lad, that's taking on men — the *Margaret Todd*. She's going to America . . . Charleston . . . New York . . . then Boston. You might try her. She's right down there, in that slip — the four-masted schooner."

Hmmm . . .

What I wanted was a berth on a ship bound for Rangoon, to see Jaimy, but that was not likely to happen, not here in this inconvenient corner of the world.

So I sat on the pier and considered . . .

Lord Allen is back in England under the care of Dr. Sebastian, and there's nothing I can do for him should I arrive there. And Jaimy's in Rangoon. Hey, it's easier to get from Bos-

ton to Burma than from Gibraltar to there, the Spice Trade and all. Plus, I should be checking on Faber Shipping Worldwide . . .

So, Jacky . . . to America.

I stride down the pier and walk up the gangplank of the *Margaret Todd.* There is a man standing on the deck, and I suspect he is either the Captain or one of the mates.

"What do you want?" he asks of me.

"I am told you are taking on sailors."

"Maybe. Who are you?"

I drop my seabag to the deck and say . . .

Jacky Faber . . . Seaman . . . Rated Able.